D0866770

cobwebs

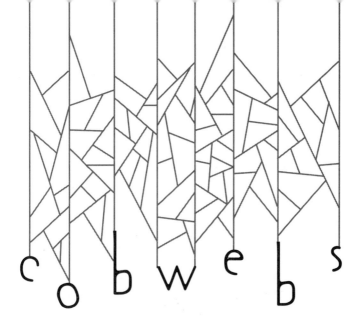

cobwebs

KAREN ROMANO YOUNG

GREENWILLOW BOOKS
An Imprint of HarperCollins*Publishers*

In the folklore traditions of cultures all over the world, there are spider stories of heroic transformations, romance among outcasts, weaving derring-do, extraordinary sensory abilities, and intriguing traps. *Cobwebs* is the creative outcome of years of fascination with the lore, art, and science of spiders, as well as weaving, jump rope, and other stringy arts.

—K.R.Y.

The quote on p. 142 is from *The Lives of Spiders*, Dorothy Hinshaw Patent (New York: Holiday House, 1980). Used by permission.

The text of this book is set in Adobe Caslon.
Book design by Chad W. Beckerman.

Library of Congress Cataloging-in-Publication Data

Young, Karen Romano.
Cobwebs / by Karen Romano Young.
p. cm.
"Greenwillow Books."
Summary: Sixteen-year-old Nancy enjoys the colorful ethnic mix of her heritage in several different Brooklyn households, not suspecting how very strange that heritage is.
ISBN 0-06-029761-1 (trade).
ISBN 0-06-029762-X (lib.bdg.)
[1. Parent and child—Fiction. 2. Brooklyn (New York, N.Y.)—Fiction. 3. Racially mixed people—Fiction. 4. Spiders—Fiction.] I. Title.
PZ7.Y8665Co 2004 [Fic]—dc21 2001045133

First Edition 10 9 8 7 6 5 4 3 2 1

GREENWILLOW BOOKS

IN GRANNY'S MEMORY

There was an old woman tossed up in a basket
Seventeen times as high as the moon.
Where she was going, I couldn't quite ask it
But in her hand she carried a broom.
"Old woman, old woman, old woman," quoth I.
"Where are you going to, up so high?"
"To sweep the cobwebs from the sky."
"May I go with you?"
"Aye, by and by."

—Mother Goose

cobwebs

1. The Thread

O God! I could be bounded in a nutshell,
and count myself a king of infinite space,
were it not that I have bad dreams.

—William Shakespeare, *Hamlet*

The first time Nancy saw Dion he was balancing on the rail of the Brooklyn Heights Promenade. Manhattan shimmered across the river. Annette was telling Nancy again how much she wanted a boyfriend, and Nancy was pretending to listen.

Nancy saw him first. He looked like he wanted to scale the skyscrapers. But the rail was only as wide as—

"Hello, *excuse me,* just what do you think you're doing?" yelled Annette.

Nancy grabbed her arm to make her stop. She thought Annette would startle the boy with her great big mouth, make him fall.

"I'm standing on the rail," he answered. He wore a

flopping, flapping coat of no particular color and had sticking-out ears attached to a bald head. Circles under his eyes made him look like he hadn't slept. He stood steadily on the rail, the cars whizzing by below on the Brooklyn-Queens Expressway. They didn't even honk. New Yorkers. They'd seen it all.

"Are you deaf?" screamed Annette. "Get down off there!" Annette's hands reached as if she were going to catch him or push him.

He didn't waver. "Are you blind?" he asked. "Can't you see I don't need your opinion?"

"I can see that you need your head examined!"

"Annette, you'll distract him," Nancy said quietly. Years of watching her dad, Ned, do this stuff (though not over an expressway—"You never should endanger others with your dangerous activities," Ned would say) made her still and calm on the outside. But she couldn't help thinking how scary things would look from up there. She walked smoothly closer and rested her hand on the boy's foot. His shoes were black boots of a softer leather than her shiny hard Doc Martens.

He looked down. "I won't fall," he said. He focused on Nancy's thin brown face, wild dark hair, solemn green eyes, and he didn't move his foot away. He might have kicked at Annette if she'd come near him. She was so freaked out, she freaked *him* out.

"Why don't you get down?" Nancy asked, wondering more than questioning.

His eyes were blue, with the whites so white they looked blue, too. Or maybe it was the sky, all blue with clouds, that made them look so blue. He said, "What do you care?" to Nancy, not Annette.

Annette snapped, "You could kill someone else with your stupid behavior."

He said, "They'd never even know what hit them."

"Retard!" she said furiously.

"Reject!" he spat back.

Fair's fair, Nancy thought. Both seemed right *and* wrong, being stupid and insulting each other that way. She had never felt torn between Annette and anyone else before.

Annette made a snarling exasperated sound. The boy made claw-fingers at her, like a cat would. Nancy hooked her arm through Annette's and dragged her away. "Forget him!" she said, knowing that she herself could not.

"What's *your* name?" the boy called behind them.

"Don't tell him!" said Annette.

Nancy looked back. The boy was still watching her. She would never forget his face as it softened, as he smiled and jumped down onto the Promenade. *Don't follow us,* Nancy said in her head. They kept walking away, Annette hugging Nancy's arm. "Did you see how he looked when he flapped his arms?" Annette asked.

"So?" *Don't do it again,* Nancy said to the boy in her head.

I never fall, she imagined he said back. Or maybe she could tell that he never fell.

Annette said, "His sleeves were like wings. Like he thought he could fly."

"What wings? Just too-big clothes."

"You know how people see things, hallucinating. Like those people who say they've seen that Angel of Brooklyn they've got in the paper."

"There's no such thing," Nancy told Annette.

"It's in the paper," Annette said, wishing it to be true.

"You ought to be in the paper. GIRL BELIEVES ANYTHING."

The real headlines were almost as silly: MUGGER GETS NAILED was a story about a mugger hit on the head with a falling box of nails. SCUMBAG OUT TO LUNCH told how a woman breaking a window to rob an apartment had been beaned by a lunchbox lobbed from the roof. The reporters hardly seemed to notice that potentially violent crimes had been averted. They were more excited by the violence that had done the averting. They were even *more* excited by the idea that someone on the roofs was acting like some sort of guardian angel for the unholy citizens of Brooklyn.

"You believe it, too, Nancy," Annette protested.

The trouble was, Annette was right. Nancy had seen a picture on the library wall that some little kid had drawn, a drawing of an actual angel stopping a bad guy on the Brooklyn Bridge. No doubt, if the believes-anything reporters from the papers saw the drawing, they'd want to interview the dreamy kid. Ridiculous.

There was a reporter in Nancy and Dion's story, too, a hard-nosed, deep-digging one, not a dizzy dreamer like the ones who wrote about the Angel.

It wasn't until the spring Nancy met Dion that the

reporter began to zero in on the truth. It was Dion and Nancy who would lead him to the Angel of Brooklyn, if they didn't watch out, if they weren't careful. But only Nancy was a careful person.

2

Annette recited one of her corny poems:

> "I need love
> Like a hand needs a glove
> Like push needs shove
> Like below needs above."

"Woe is me," said Nancy.

"I want a boyfriend," cried Annette from the balcony of her apartment, where she and Nancy sat. Annette didn't like being home without her mother; Nancy would stay until Mrs. Li came whistling up

Pierrepont Street from the subway.

"Oh, woe," said Nancy again. "Shut up, Annette."

Annette used to be a Tolkien freak who wrote Nancy notes in Elvish and wore glitter on her ears where the teachers couldn't see (it was against dress code), who collaged her notebooks with one word cut out from a hundred different magazine ads (the word was *word*), who wore plastic hobbit feet for Halloween. "A short, squat, Korean hobbit girl lived in a hobbit house under a hill. One room was all she needed," Annette said. "And a weeny refrigerator with room enough for *pie*."

Annette was still all those things, Nancy knew. But they weren't what Annette talked about anymore; she tuned them out and toned them down and pretended she didn't care (or maybe she didn't).

There were several different boyfriend candidates, all nicknamed little names that had to do with what they liked or did, such as Joe Vespa, the guy with the motor scooter, or Vinnie Video, the one with the Game Boy surgically attached to his hand.

It was as if, instead of picking a real person, Annette was choosing someone out of a catalog. Nancy herself, conscious that not just anyone off the street would fit into her peculiar family, had yet to notice anyone who interested her in any way, before the Promenade boy. She was a one-person person, and so far Annette had felt like plenty for her. But Nancy was not enough for Annette anymore. Annette wanted a boyfriend so she wouldn't be alone. Since she didn't know her father, and therefore didn't understand how marriage worked, she wanted to know all about Nancy's parents.

This created a problem. Nancy could talk about the *theory* of marriage, getting along and helping each other and not criticizing and all that, but in practice she wasn't sure her parents' marriage worked on any level but one. It was easy to see why Ned's moving out this spring—and every spring in memory—could be interpreted as a bad sign.

"Is he going to move back again in the fall?" Annette asked.

Nancy shrugged. She never knew. He always had before. "It's different this year," she said. This year Ned had moved out in March, before the clocks changed forward. "He said he needed to get up on the roofs," Nancy explained.

"It's been such an uncold winter," Annette said. "I guess that helps."

Nancy wondered. "He's happy, though," she told Annette. "You should see how happy he is. He doesn't need Mama in the spring."

"You know what you need?" said Annette. "Your own place."

"I need ice cream," said Nancy, fed up with choosing between two places, two people, and dragged Annette to the Kustard King truck playing its silly music on the corner.

Ned tangoed Nancy across his roof, his new roof, which gave out over Brooklyn and clear across to Manhattan. He had put the new roof there himself, to stop the rain leaking into the apartments below, just last week and the week before. He'd found out the little house on the roof was available, which meant nobody else wanted it. Instead of just renting or subletting, he'd bought the place. Nancy didn't like the permanence of the arrangement.

"Look at it, Nancy," he said. "House!" He threw one hand toward the little poky rooftop penthouse, its dirty glass panes that let in only faint checkers of light. "And garden!" He threw his other hand toward the broken, crumbling cement border of a hard, cracked rectangle of dirt. Then he leaped onto the wall at the edge of the roof on his skinny legs in the black jeans, and threw both arms wide to New York City and the sky. "I'm in love!"

"Dad, don't!"

He jumped down, bouncing a little in his springy way. "Sweetheart," he said. "Little egg. It's going to be beautiful." He stroked his strong fingers over the zillion black ringlets that floated around Nancy's head—the way his would if he didn't wind it up in dreadlocks. He walked her toward the odd little penthouse, to the open door. The house was one big metal frame, white bricks from the floor to hip level, then glass to the ceiling. "We'll scrub every window," he said, making it sound like that would be good entertainment.

When Nancy squinted at him, rainbows appeared around his head. She made herself lighten up and tease him. "We?" she said.

Her dad grinned in relief.

"There's plenty of sun up here," Nancy said.

"Yes! A garden!" He whirled from the edge of the

roof to the house. "We can fix it all," he said. "We'll need some furniture, but it's springtime, roof time. There'll be work from now to November. I'll make you a loft bed, Nance." His voice changed, rose. He wanted her there. "Or a hammock. What about a hammock? You can swing in the summer breezes and never even know you're not in Jamaica."

A hammock? So temporary. "I love it at Mama's," Nancy said, sticking up for her mama, Rachel, for Rachel and her basement apartment, with its three sets of stairs, one leading down from the street, one from Granny's apartment upstairs, and one from the court-yard with the greenhouse studio. Rachel had a cozy trundle that pulled out from under her bed for Nancy. Of course, a trundle bed was temporary, too, a just-in-case-Nancy's-here bed.

Nancy's parents loved each other but lived apart. She was strung between them like clothes on a pulley clothesline, going back and forth. Only Mama's end of the clothesline never moved, and Dad's always did. That had always seemed like a bad thing until now, when Dad's end seemed like it might be settling down, too.

"Nance," Ned said. She kept her eyes down. *He's not*

coming back this time, she thought. *He's moving to this rooftop, which he's in love with. He said so himself.* He lifted her chin and saw the tears. "Nancy Greene-Kara," he said. "You are a Greene and a Kara. This is your home, not just mine."

"This rotten roof?" she said. "This dusty, cobwebby old wreck full of—"

"*Our* rotten roof," Ned said. He grabbed her hands and danced her across the roof again, kicking out his feet in the pointy cowboy boots he wore when he wasn't roofing. Water tanks, chimneys, and TV antennas spun around them. Nancy couldn't help laughing along, and stomped her feet.

When they stopped, puffing, Ned raised one finger and said, "The first thing we have to do is learn how to get down."

She should have known. To most people that would mean the stairs or the elevator. But her father was very big on emergency procedures, precautions, just-in-cases. He led her to the edge of the roof. She took one look. "Oh, Dad, no."

"Oh yes, little egg. You're more than a ground dweller."

"Listen, you old Arach-Ned," she said. "You can't turn me into a drop-and-dragger just because you make me dwell on the roof."

"It's in your genes, Nancy."

She held up her palms so close to his face that he lost focus. "It's not in my hands!"

He pulled his head back to see her clearly. "Better late than never," he said. He turned her toward the edge of the roof. "Go on, Nance."

3

It wasn't enough to stand atop the wall. Next Nancy had to cross her ankles and turn around on her toes, turn her back to the air and climb down backward over the precipice. She turned, and froze.

Ned's father's father had built the Empire State Building, riveting steel bolts to steel beams high in the atmosphere. *His* father's father strung the cables of the Brooklyn Bridge, straddling the brown brick tower, with nothing but the East River to catch him. And Ned's daughter? A little bug afraid of heights.

Ned laid his large hands on top of Nancy's. They were always slightly sticky, and now he turned her hands over and rubbed his palms against them, to give her traction.

She tried to stand firm the way the boy on the rail had, though her hair threatened to act like a sail and pull her off the wall, though her stomach quavered and quaked.

"Don't look down," said Ned. But *he* looked down casually, as if he were reading a subway map, so Nancy did, too. Her instinct kicked in, the bad instinct that said, *Go no farther. Hold on tight. Don't step out. Do it and you'll be nothing but a squashed blob on the sidewalk.* "Let go, Nancy," he said.

"Why?" she asked.

"It's safest this way," he said. "If your body's going to learn to take care of you, you have to put it in these situations. Now go."

Nancy wondered how strongly the fire escape was struck on the brown wall of the house. She felt her way down the ladder to the first landing, the one that stretched above the windows of the apartment under Dad's new penthouse.

"What are you afraid might happen?" asked Ned.

"I'm afraid of splattering!"

He nodded. "I thought you were small but wiry."

Nancy grinned. It was what she always said. But now: "If only I had spinnerets . . . "

Spinnerets made lines like bungee cords. They saved you from falling. But Nancy didn't have them. Yet. Would she ever? She had grown lately, it was true. Her hair was longer and her legs were longer and Granny said her face was bony now, not soft. Her chest wasn't bony anymore. Still, there were no spinnerets inside her, no silk.

"What you folks doing out there on that fire escape?" a white-faced blond woman scolded from the nearest window.

Ned leaned out from the roof to see. He would have tipped his hat if he were wearing one. "We're your new neighbors on the fifth floor," he said.

The woman leaned out and stared up, her mouth like a fish's. "This building got no fifth floor."

"The roof, I mean. Or should I say roofhouse? Penthouse?"

Nancy didn't dare laugh. Here was her dad, already making the neighbors think they had a freak on their roof. If only they knew . . .

"This how you going downstairs every time?"

"This? Oh no. Emergency measures, that's all," said Ned. The window slammed shut, and Nancy saw the woman walk away inside it, shaking her head. "Emergency measures," Ned said again. "Go on, Nance."

Emergency measures were what Dion felt were needed just then. He felt it from the other side of Brooklyn, the very boundary of it, on the railing of the walkway of the Brooklyn Bridge where he sat staring toward the Promenade a mile away and thinking about the girl he'd seen there. Not the crabby Asian one. The other girl, the one with the hair and the eyes and the thin legs in Doc Martens with painted-on polka dots, nutty shoes that his little sister, Mina, would like.

Dion whipped off his Mets cap and wiped the palm of his hand across his bald head. A hollow feeling grew in the pit of his stomach, a feeling of being scared, not hungry. His palms turned sticky and sweaty. He wondered if this was an anxiety attack, something he'd heard of from his mother. His mother . . . Was he going to be like this from now on, because of what his father had caught his mother doing? Anyone who would jump off a roof, on purpose to fall . . . How could he go home and have dinner with such a person? Or with the person who would let her get into such a risky position?

"Stop chasing that Angel of Brooklyn," his mother, Rose, had said. "Leave well enough alone." She thought Dad was selling out, and selling the Angel out, and maybe selling the city out in the bargain. Dad said she was a bleeding heart, so worried about desperate people's problems that she didn't worry enough about her own family.

Rose had gotten angry enough with Niko that she threatened to hurt herself, then tried to. Did she think by hurting herself she'd hurt him?

Dion made himself think about the girl on the Promenade instead. Maybe he'd find her in that neighborhood or somewhere close by, if he hung around a lot. He pulled himself into a more comfortable position on the railing and suddenly felt a whoosh of nausea that came out of nowhere. He slammed his feet down onto the walkway and leaned there, gripping the rail, steadying himself.

• • •

There was nothing under Nancy. The fire escape ended a story above the street. Nothing but strips of rusty fire escape held her up. "Crawl over the edge," Ned advised. "Hang on by your fingertips."

With her hands above her head, she was six and a half feet high. (Ned had measured, so that she'd know.) It wasn't so far to the ground. Far enough, though. Her knees crackled when she landed. Relief for Nancy.

Down came Ned.

"Chicken," she said. Because there was no crackle landing for him. He landed softly on those slick cowboy boots that clacked when he touched the pavement. A strand of soft gray silk slowed his fall, glimmering just enough to be visible.

"Hey," he said, as they set off for the grocery store. "Which came first, the chicken or the egg?"

"*I* did," said Nancy. He let her get away with it, because, while she was still sweating, he was perfectly cool.

4

Ned was a son of Anansi. His mother Aso's side of the family were the African-Jamaican magical tricksters, able to leap and fall and disappear into shadows. Rachel's were the Scottish orb weavers (Granny's forebears, descendants of the unstoppable spider that had inspired Robert the Bruce) that hid among the thistles and the heather. Then there was Grandpa Joke's side—just plain old Italians. Nancy had her father's black hair—only a little softer, more Italian. She had her father's brown skin—only a little lighter. Her mother was pale white. Nancy's eyes were all Rachel, though. And inside?

"Anything new?" Mama Rachel and Granny Tina had been asking Nancy too often lately (for the last three years or so). Rachel said she had begun to become what she was at around thirteen. Ned began a little later, as boys do. Nancy was older than both.

"Same old beautiful me," she told them, though it made a sharp hurt inside her to say it.

Her mother and grandmother turned away to hide their faces. It was Grandpa Joke who stroked the hair back from her forehead and said, "That's fine." But lately she thought he was the one who looked most worried of them all. There was no special spiderness coming from anywhere inside her, no matter how hard Nancy listened for it, watched for it, waited for it. It seemed that so far Rachel and Ned's genes had canceled each other out in Nancy.

Canceled out meant no heights and no depths. When Nancy grew dizzy on one of Dad's rooftops, she'd leave. Down to Mama's basement, her pied-à-terre. Foot on the ground. Where, if you stood in the kitchen looking out toward the greenhouse, your nose was on a level with the grass. The truth was, Nancy wasn't really comfortable anywhere.

But she tried. It was the old nature/nurture question, which Nancy had studied in freshman biology. The question was what made you who you were: The nature you got from your parents' genes? Or your experiences? Her parents couldn't change her nature, but they were determined not to skimp on experiences, whether or not they drove Nancy nuts in the process. Rachel taught her weaving, that was her way, and asked for nothing more. But Ned was always pushing her, leading her, guiding her to the edges of things. And then telling her not to look down!

Clorox and Ajax and Windex. Sponges and mops and ammonia. A ball-peen hammer and brass nails. *The New York Times* and the *New York Post* and the *Daily News*. General Tso's chicken and moo shu pancakes and plum sauce. Red wine, and tomato juice and vodka so Ned could make his Bloody Mary in the morning. A box of Rice Krispies for Nancy.

Outside the cleaned-up windows, hours later, the lights of the city twinkled on and the moon rose up. Furniture would come later. For tonight, Nancy and Ned would sleep in sleeping bags, cocooned in their own warmth. Reflected light dappled the ceiling.

"Thirty thousand nights," Ned said.

"What?" Nancy was trying to go directly to sleep without thinking of the drop outside.

"That's what we're given on this planet."

"Thirty thousand?"

"Yeah."

"That's a long time."

"Long enough to get sick of them, take them for granted."

"So?" she asked slowly.

"So, we don't even look up to see if the stars are there or the moon is out."

"I do."

Ned rolled onto his stomach, leaned on his elbows. "What if you only got one night, Nancy egg? It'd be magic! You couldn't stop looking. You'd never go to sleep, all night long." He sat up so that he could see out the windows. He sat there so long that at last Nancy sat up, too, and put a hand on his shoulder.

"Dad, you live here now," she said. "It'll be here tomorrow."

"*We* live here now." He put his finger on her nose,

smiled a little, lay down, and went to sleep pretty fast.

How could Nancy sleep with that empty space waiting for her to fall through it, just beyond the low wall? She slid from her sleeping bag and pushed open the metal door. She padded silently to the edge, grasped the curved railing of the ladder.

You're going to have to, Nancy, said the voice in her head. She had been working on a theory, based on an article she'd read in the *Times*. Paralyzed people were learning to walk again by having their legs mechanically put through the motions of walking. Supposedly this electrified some part of their brains, the walking part made dead by paralysis, and brought it back to life. Maybe, Nancy reasoned, if she placed herself in spidery situations, she could electrify some inactive spidery part of her brain.

She stepped onto the ladder.

On a rooftop in Vinegar Hill where he was spending the night, Dion turned over in his sleep, pulled his overcoat up to his chin, and began to have one of his climbing dreams.

The rail curved slippery-slick beneath Nancy's hands, the metal so cold it felt buttered. Nancy forced her bare feet to climb the rusty-edged steps. She instructed her toes to hold on tight. At the top of the wall she crouched, scared to stand and raise her center of gravity into the wind. *Make it quick, Nancy; get it over with; don't think about how you'll get back up.*

With a nauseating twist she forced herself to turn, wrenching her body through dark space. Sweat sprang out in shudders across her neck and between her shoulders. City lights swirled above her. Her toe caught the step and her feet scrambled to save her. Somehow she landed her sorry self on the first landing of the fire escape. She collapsed, her hands cold and gritty with flaked-off rust. She'd made it one whole flight down.

She straightened her soft blue pajamas under her behind, wiped her streaming eyes on her sleeves, and wondered at the image of the boy on the Promenade that appeared suddenly in her mind. What must she herself look like?

She leaned back against the brick. She could breathe now. The breeze blew silver-lined clouds across the moon. The city lights trembled but stayed pretty much in place.

She thought, *I'll never make it to the bottom alone.*

5

"I want a boyfriend!" Annette moaned out over the balcony of her apartment.

I don't, Nancy thought. If she were to fall in love with somebody, if she were to want to marry someday, there would be all these *considerations.* It wouldn't just be a matter of pretty blue eyes. She poked her toes through the balcony railing and studied them. "You just keep doing what you're doing," she told Annette. Annette was going to every dance and church thing and strutting the streets lately looking like—well, looking like the other girls in their homeroom, with their curled eyelashes and fingernail polish and shaved legs. Those legs bothered Nancy. She wasn't allowed to shave hers. Instead she made her fashion statement with crazy tights and bright shoes that didn't go against the school dress code of black skirt and white shirt, even if they didn't exactly go *with* it.

"That's what Shamiqua says, too," Annette said. Shamiqua! Nancy peered at the little kids running around the Promenade playground across Pierrepont Place, and tried not to feel bad. Shamiqua was queen of homeroom, and queen of the dances. It was Shamiqua who had told Annette today that some boy named Jimmy might ask her out.

Annette flapped the *Daily News* at Nancy, changing the subject. "Look. He saw him again."

"Who saw who?"

"Well, nobody *saw* anything. Just the results."

"Who saw what results?"

"Nestor Paprika, that reporter. ROBBER IMPOUNDED. He says it was the Angel. Do you think it was that ghost boy from the Promenade?"

Nancy's mouth fell open at the stream of loose connections Annette had just made. She said, "If he were the Angel, he'd be trying to be inconspicuous. Walking on the railing of the Promenade isn't very inconspicuous."

"Spoilsport," said Annette. "He dropped a hammer on the robber's head."

"Ouch. Is he dead?"

"The Angel? I hope not. Shamiqua told me this fantasy she had about him. They were up on the roof and he was fluttering his black wings over his head . . ."

"Did you read the English yet?" Nancy said, to change the subject again. She had heard enough about Shamiqua. What kind of fantasy? Fluttering black wings on a rooftop. Yes, Shamiqua definitely sounded more interesting than *she* was. Nancy consoled herself: she was still the one Annette asked over after school to keep her company.

Annette made an annoyed sound, but took out the book. "Want me to read it to you?" she asked, as usual. Nancy nodded, as usual. They were reading Hemingway, which bored them, and Walt Whitman, which made them cry, the best thing so far in high school English since Greek myths freshman year.

> And you O my soul where you stand,
> Surrounded, detached, in measureless oceans of space,

Ceaselessly musing, venturing, throwing, seeking
the spheres to connect them,
Till the bridge you will need be form'd, till the
ductile anchor hold,
Till the gossamer thread you fling catch
somewhere, O my soul.

From the balcony over Pierrepont Place they peeked through the leaves of the Promenade trees at slivers of silver downtown Manhattan. Annette laid the book in her lap, and wailed out to New York, "I want a boyfriend."

"I know it, Annette," said Nancy wearily. "Half of Brooklyn surely knows it by now."

"Surely," mimicked Annette. "What about you? Don't *you*?"

Nancy wondered what made her ask now, when she hadn't ever asked before. She shrugged one shoulder.

"You *do*?" Annette peered into her eyes. "Who?" She knew enough about Nancy to know it wouldn't be just any generic boyfriend, but someone in particular.

Nancy shrugged her shoulder again, looked away. But *away* was toward the Promenade.

"Oh, *stop*," Annette said. "That freak?"

"Why is he a freak?" Nancy demanded. "Because he's got good balance?"

"Most girls wouldn't have good balance on their list."

"Since when do you care about most girls?" Nancy couldn't help herself.

Annette rolled her eyes, moaned. "He's got no hair, for one. Like a ghost. You like Ghost Boy?"

Nancy shrugged again.

"You don't know a thing about him," Annette said dismissively.

"But I do," said Nancy.

"What?"

"I don't know. Just—"

"What?"

"His eyes," said Nancy. "That's enough."

"You might never see him again!"

"Something might bring us together. It did once. I'm keeping my eyes open, that's all."

"Good plan," said Annette.

Nancy shrugged again. Annette picked up the book and started reading.

• • •

At school, in homeroom, the girls sat and complained:

"My mother? That witch! You know what she did/said/wants now?"

It made Nancy curl within herself. And, curling, she bent an ear forward to listen.

"If I don't clean my room/get home soon/change my tune, she's gonna—"

Nancy's mother made no demands. She showed Nancy weaving and told her information about the best yarn to use to warp a loom with, the sort of tea to brew depending on the weather, or the best kohl to put around your eyes. She didn't mind if Nancy slept at Dad's when it was his night. She didn't make Nancy call either one *home*. She made Nancy's bed when she wasn't there, rolled her comforter, tucked in the sheets, put away the trundle, kept her pillow fluffed on the dresser top, handy.

Nobody else's mother made their bed; Nancy had listened enough to gather that fact. It was a downright bone of contention, the idea that anyone had to make a bed at all.

"I've gotta/I hafta/I'd betta or I'll get pounded/punished/grounded."

Grounded? Nancy's father would never do such a thing. "That's no place for me," he'd say, "so how could I do it to you? What terrible things are you plotting, anyway, that you're considering consequences like grounding?"

Nancy just smiled, wanting him to think she was as brave a roof dweller as he was. And listened to what was going on in homeroom.

6

Rachel and Nancy's door stood behind a cobweb iron gate set under Granny and Grandpa's stoop. This afternoon Rachel was sound asleep when Nancy turned her key in the lock and stepped in. The apartment was dark and the air felt soft like down. The drawn shades let streams of dusty sunshine into the tiny underground kitchen. Like Thumbelina's house, Nancy had always thought. Her mama was the mole.

Nancy stood in the doorway that led from the kitchen up cement steps to the yard. She listened to Rachel snoring. Later in the day her mama would emerge, like someone with a star-shaped nose, to cook beautiful soup and bake bread or brownies to contribute to the big dinner Granny was making upstairs. She'd be happy, ready to nourish and nurture Nancy. Nancy knew this because from here she could see into Mama's greenhouse studio; she could see that Mama's loom was warped. New smooth shining threads like a river flowing over a dam waited there practically vibrating, so ready were they. Ready for what? For weft threads to swim through them, crisscrossing into a pattern that was visible now only to Mama, who was probably seeing it in her mind as she slept.

But here Mama came now, shuffling into the kitchen toward the kettle, saying guilty things, making a plea.

"You poor little caterpillar, Nancy, you ought to have a better mother. I can't even go for groceries without the screaming heebie-jeebies! And now we're out of tea."

"Mama, the tulips are blooming in Prospect Park," Nancy said.

"I know," Rachel said tersely. "I've seen them before. Why do I need to see them again?" She gripped Nancy's arm suddenly. "What's that?"

"It's just a car alarm, Ma. Out on the street."

Rachel could never get used to that. "Oh," she said.

How had Ned ever found Rachel? Grandpa had brought him home. Grandpa Joke had met Grandma Aso long ago, before she'd gone back to Jamaica. Her son Ned was an inside carpenter then, just getting started out of high school. Grandpa needed book-shelves, so when he heard about Ned, he asked Grandma Aso to send him over to look at the job.

Rachel was living at home, doing giant weavings hung on the wall. She and Ned fell in love. They rented the basement apartment. They fixed the greenhouse together. And Ned built the floor loom.

He thought it was all temporary, that he would soon make enough as a carpenter, and she'd sell enough weaving, for them to find a place of their own, some-place where they (and soon, Nancy) could be closer to the sky. He was a typical guy, Rachel said, who thought she'd just go with him wherever he went.

But she didn't want to. "I want my feet on solid ground," she said. She didn't need the whole world. Her loom—her web—was large enough.

Now, every spring, Rachel cried. "He thinks I don't want to be with him," she had sobbed to Nancy this March. "I *can't* be with him up there on that roof."

And he couldn't be with her, down on the ground. Now Nancy told her mama all about the new apartment, up high like the one in Mama's favorite TV version of *La Bohème*, the Australian Opera one, where everyone was young and beautiful and there was a big neon sign saying *L'amour* outside their apartment on the roof. She knew how Mama would feel, and now she'd made her cry, telling her about it.

"I wish I was different," Mama said.

"You're yourself," Nancy told her, grasping for soothing words. "My Greene Mamba." It was a favorite nickname, usually guaranteed to bring a smile.

"She thinks I don't love her," Ned had said. "She says if I loved her I wouldn't live on some empty roof."

"She's afraid of everything," Nancy had said sadly.

Nancy crawled under the loom, looked out at the nose-level grass and dreamed herself back at Dad's apartment. Open those glass doors and breathe, listen to the city breathing. The whole world was up there. She loved it, or she wanted to love it, but her body seemed to rebel against it, breaking out in shivers and shakes every time she approached the edge.

"I'm still afraid of heights," Nancy confessed to Rachel. It needed facing, this fear of hers that was so natural for a human, so unnatural for the kind of spider she wished she were.

"Needn't be," said Rachel. She laughed, and threw the shuttle that carried the weft thread through the shed of the loom. The shuttle sailed over Nancy's head, letting out rose yarn behind it like exhaust smoke.

"Well, I am," Nancy said, her voice heavy. She watched the weaving from her favorite angle, lying on her back, nestled at her mother's feet. She had her own yarn with her, and was knitting, the yarn unrolling from its ball inside her school backpack.

"Your father likes to be above it all," said Rachel. She stopped weaving and rolled her long brown hair into a knot, jabbed two pencils into it to hold it. It was a beautiful finish to what Shamiqua would call Mama's "look" (if she had ever seen her)—long teal skirt with giant roses, a T-shirt with a Buddha on it, red socks. Kicked into a corner were her shiny green clogs; Mama wove in her stocking feet, the better to feel the treadles.

"Very glamorous," Nancy said. About her father she whined, "Why does he always have to be up so high?"

Mama inhaled deeply. "Here's what they used to tell me about being afraid of heights," she said. Before she stopped trying to follow Ned to high places, she meant. Before she stopped leaving the house. "That what you're afraid of is yourself. Not that you'll fall, but that you'll throw yourself off."

"That's bizarre!" So bizarre it was almost true. When Nancy was someplace high, she had a sense of holding herself close, clenching her muscles to stay still. Why? Because the wind might blow her off? No. Because she could imagine herself jumping. Rising. Falling. *Would I?*

"I'm going to the store," she said, leaping up and making a fast exit. She careened down the courtyard steps, slammed through the apartment, and hit the sidewalk feeling all shaken up. She felt like Jell-O, not shaped yet. It was perfectly possible that she could slip off the top of something whether or not she intended to fall or jump. She wanted to solidify, to become, to choose her own shape or, at least, the bowl that shaped her.

Nancy bought her mother's springtime almond tea on Court Street at the Korean grocery, then on a whim ducked into the Everything store. Yes, they had the thing she needed. (They had Everything.) It was as if it were all planned; suddenly she was passionate about doing what she wanted *right now*. She took the tea back to Mama, dashed in and put it on the table, saying, "I'm going to Dad's."

"Tonight?" It was not Dad's night.

"I'll be back tomorrow."

"Why?"

"I've *got* to," Nancy said in a forceful, no-explanation voice she'd never used before.

"You haven't *got* to," Rachel retorted, fixing Nancy with her green Greene eyes.

"Okay, I *want* to," Nancy said in a lighter tone. "Okay?" This softening made it seem as if she were asking Rachel's permission; it did the trick. Rachel nodded.

Ten minutes later Nancy walked along Court Street to the subway with a cocoon of white cotton fishing net wrapped around her shoulders. And saw the Promenade boy for the second time ever.

Blue eyes, dusty shoes. He was up high again, perched atop the geodesic dome in the playground in Carroll Park. She had to walk right by to get to the subway. He watched her with steady eyes.

Now she saw his shirt, with a message she'd juggle in her head and on her tongue for the next few days: Alta, Utah. What did it mean? Nothing. Try saying it three times fast. It was as tricky a tongue twister as "Unique New York." Just then neither of them said anything.

Now she noticed his hat, a Mets hat, thank God, for who but Grandpa Joke could bear the Yankees? Skin brown, though not half black like hers. Eyes blue. *Yes, that's been noted.* So blue, those eyes following her.

"Staying safe?" she asked.

He said, "No."

The hairs rose up on the back of her neck. He studied her.

Nancy walked on. She carried the mass of white netting into the subway, and succeeded in not looking back. She rushed, because a train came into the station right as she was going down the steps. She leaped onto it, but there weren't any seats because it was rush hour, so she had to stand. The train zipped out of the tunnel and up onto the bridge above the Gowanus Canal. The city blossomed behind it, and Nancy found herself looking down into Brooklyn. She felt divided in two between being reasonable and hoping for crazy changes, between wanting to see him again and thinking he was weird and scary. She still didn't know his name.

At Seventh Avenue she climbed out of the station into her dad's new neighborhood, clutching the net around her shoulders like a silk shawl. A bouncing wave of energy hit her, and she ran all the way to the apartment, up all the stairs, and tossed the whole pile into Ned's arms with a yell.

It was a hammock. When Ned saw she'd really gone and bought it the way he said, he jumped in the air and clacked his cowboy heels together.

Metal girders held up the roof of the little penthouse. Ned started rigging up cable and hooks around them to hold Nancy's hammock.

"Hoo-rah!" he said, making a little salute toward the first hook on the first pole. "Soon you'll have a place to hang your—" He studied the second pole, eyeballing the distance from the first.

"My hammock?"

"No, your—" He got distracted, unfocused. He hooked the ring at the head of the hammock to the first pole and walked over to the second, a length of steel cable in one hand, a cotton cord in the other. "What's your mother doing tonight?" he asked.

"Why don't you call her up and ask her?" she asked. What was the purpose of the two of them being married, anyway? she might have asked, but already knew what the answer would be: "You," they'd say, both of them. She thought it was a cockeyed reason.

She went outside and sat down in a little café chair Ned had put there. It was a corner building, taller than the rest of the block, so she could see down onto rooftops and gardens, from a higher vantage point. Also, being in Park Slope, it was on a hill, which made it higher than lots of areas of the city. The line of skyscrapers stood out in the distance, a miracle made by people who apparently weren't worried by the sucking space between themselves and the ground.

She caught herself thinking that maybe that boy was a roof dweller, too, then did her best to erase the thought. What remained, though, were warm rubber crumbs that would not disappear: he had good balance, and she couldn't help wondering—hoping, really—that he had a secret hidden.

7

Dion did have a secret, several, in fact. The one that pressed hardest on his mind was the one he could do the least about. He and Mina had come home from school that day and found their apartment empty. Dion went to the roof to bring in the laundry left drying up there. But he was the third one on the roof. Mom had tried to fall over the edge, and Dad had made a massive leap across the roof to stop her. He had the scratches on his face to prove how she'd tried to fight him off.

Dion's oldest secret was that his mother, a counselor, needed help herself. It had started long before the day of jumping. Far from helping herself, it was as though she hated herself, hated her skin, anyway, enough to scratch at herself, make herself bleed. Dion's father had promised, *before*, to get his mother help. *After*, Dion had bawled at his father, raged at him: "You said you were getting that doctor in!"

His father still hadn't kept his promise—not that one or the promise to stop writing so many Angel stories—and Dion couldn't live in the same house with him. That meant not sleeping there. It meant getting by on his own. It meant eating less. It meant sleeping and washing, hanging his laundry on whatever quiet roof he could find. It meant cutting school. And he had shaved his hair; he would keep it shaved until things seemed different, better. What difference that made, he wasn't sure, only that he *felt* different without his hair, less recognizable, more invisible. He sneaked home when Dad wasn't there, to see Mina and check on Mom.

Dion's saddest secret was that his mother was worse now, not better.

At least his father had jumped. For jumping, Dad could be relied on. Dion's father was the best jumper around, the fastest, strongest jumper. *You should see him on a basketball court.* That was what Dion had thought about his father, back when he was proud. His father had a jump shot you wouldn't believe. It was just about the only way he used to be able to get around his mother, who was a formidable guard, though tiny and stocky.

Rose hadn't been on the basketball court in a while. Neither had Dion. He'd practically grown up hanging off the fence around the cages to watch Niko and Rose play one-on-one, or pickup games, when they weren't teaching him. Well, basketball was done now.

Another secret was that Niko and Rose didn't worry much about Dion, and Dion knew it. He guessed his mother was just too wound up in her own problems. Niko thought—or let himself think—that his son was close to home, maybe staying with a friend, and what with the needs of his wife and daughter, he couldn't do much more. "Let the little idiot take care of himself, if he wants to make so much trouble," Dion had heard his father say through the fire escape window. "There's a limit to what any human being can do. He's sixteen. If he wants to drop out of school, it's legal."

Niko's lifeblood was stories. He wrote under pen names: Nestor Paprika (for the *News*), Nobody in Particular (for the *Post*), and his favorite, Nick Pappas (for the *Times*). He went over the police blotters for signs of the Angel's involvement. He was good at filling the gaps to make the stories hang together. After all, there had always been stories about people on the roofs of New York, from the time when the roofs had first grown tall enough to look down from—from the spectators of the blimp races, to the people with tuberculosis who slept by the thousands under the stars, to the tar beaches on top of tenements. People flew, or rose, or fell. Girls and gorillas. Angelic and bad. Visible and invisible. The stories had kept on coming, growing taller and taller with the buildings. No one had come along so far to challenge what Niko said the Angel did. Why should they? New Yorkers liked a yarn, and Niko never made anything up. The interpretation alone was his; he said it was what made him an artist. Where real and fake divided, Niko was no longer sure.

Now Niko was searching for something more scarce than the Angel, more elusive than his son, more urgent than anything he'd sought before: a cure for Rose. He had bent his ear to an urban legend, a groundless rumor, an old wives' tale for his young wife. A family crisis, he told his bosses. They didn't want to hear about it; they wanted Angel stories.

But Niko put his considerable energy into tracing a surgeon who healed wounds faster than average. The surgeon had frequently switched from hospital to hospital around the city and was now practically retired from a very private practice—Green Medicine—which most people (correctly) assumed was holistic in nature. Niko hadn't written any stories about this person, whom he called the Wound Healer. He didn't want anyone making a connection between the Wound Healer and the Angel. While he looked for the Wound Healer, he kept on writing about the Angel.

Though Dion was grateful to his father for catching his mother, he couldn't go home. He couldn't face seeing his mother; he knew he'd have to ask her why. He got up onto high things to ask himself instead. It was just as well to live on the rooftops, to master climbing up and down and getting around, because he knew he wouldn't fall off anything he attempted to balance upon. He alone knew—until that girl on the Promenade held his foot and looked up at him with those clear green eyes.

Now he searched for her, too. The geodesic dome dug into his behind, got him moving. He jumped off and

walked in the direction his feet led him. He wanted to—
he *would*—be where she was from now on. Which way
had she gone? Toward Manhattan? Or toward Coney
Island? Uncertain why, he headed toward the water of
the Gowanus Canal, crossed it, and once on the other
side, scoped out a roof where he could spend the night.

8

The Greenes and Karas did things with their hands. Ned roofed, Rachel wove, Grandpa Joke was a doctor. Granny Tina was a potter and a knitter. Nancy had done nothing but draw, until Granny Tina started making her knit over Christmas vacation this winter.

Age was changing things for Granny. She had developed awful arthritis, a terrible condition for someone who lived through her hands. Granny used to have long, straight hair like Rachel's, although hers was silver and white. She could have gotten Rachel to braid it, but instead she cut it short, and got Grandpa Joke to keep it in trim. Nancy thought she looked punk. Like

Grandpa Joke, she had brown eyes, but his were slow and warm (and sometimes hot when his anger sparked up). Granny's were bright and quick, making a liar of her slowing, hunching body.

Granny used to dart around, up and down the stairs between the apartments, helping Rachel with the loom, throwing pots on her wheel in the garden shed, always simmering tasty recipes on the stove for dinner. Grandpa Joke took Nancy to the playground, but Granny taught her to climb the ladders of the big tall slides. Grandpa Joke walked Nancy back and forth to school, and Granny made sure he took her into stores and introduced her to people.

Now it was Nancy who darted around the house, Nancy who helped Mama with her loom, Nancy who went to the grocery store with Grandpa Joke and lugged home all the stuff. It was not a pretty sight, Granny Tina stuck inside her body, inside her house, not knowing until she woke in the morning whether it would be a wheelchair day or a walking day. Unlike Rachel, she had not chosen her prison.

As arthritis had taken the knitting out of her hands, Granny had done her best to put it into

Nancy's, pressing her to knit samples and mittens and boring long scarves until she could do it without thinking. Granny Tina didn't always approve of the results. For example, the black sweater Nancy was wearing had made Granny almost frantic. She hated the color with every shred of her being, and had told Nancy so the moment she came home with the yarn.

"We should never have sent you alone!"

"I *wanted* to go alone."

"And look what it's come to: *black*."

"What's wrong with black, Tina?" Ned had asked, sticking up for Nancy.

"It'll hide the mistakes," Nancy said.

Rachel began shaking her head.

"Mistakes!" sputtered Granny. "There aren't going to be any mistakes. I'm not teaching you how to make mistakes."

"Well, you'll have to teach her how to take them out, Mother."

"If that isn't a Rachelish thing to say! If you pay attention to what you're doing, you won't make mistakes."

"If that isn't a Tinaish thing to say," Rachel replied. "Nobody's perfect."

"No, but their weaving should be," barked Granny. It was unusually harsh for her.

"You mean *knitting*," corrected Grandpa Joke, making his first contribution to the conversation.

"Of course, knitting!" said Granny. "What did you think I was talking about?"

Nancy didn't want to learn how to undo mistakes. She would have thrown the whole thing aside. And she knew what else would go on while the knitting lesson did: more tiresome stories about Granny's childhood on that West Virginia farm. What was the point of hearing the same tired yarns over and over?

"You haven't got the point, if you don't know yet," said Granny, as if she'd heard Nancy's thoughts.

Nancy, turning her key to unlock Mama's gate, noticed a stray thread on the cuff of her sweater. When she tugged at it, a hole appeared. Drat. She looked up at Granny's windows, almost expecting to see Granny there.

The phone rang. Rachel picked it up. "Mother!" she said. It was Granny, calling from her apartment upstairs. "No, nobody called here for Pop." She looked at Nancy, and Nancy shook her head, confirming it. Dad had called, to give them the number for his new phone in the penthouse, but no one had called for Grandpa Giacomo—Grandpa Joke.

"Who do you think it was?" Rachel said into the phone, sounding anxious. "If he's gotten himself tangled up with some . . . "

Knowing Grandpa Joke, Nancy thought, chances were good that he had. She pointed her knitting needles into her work, jammed it into her backpack, and crawled out from under her mother's loom. Granny's voice crackled on the other end of the phone.

"All right." Rachel glanced at Nancy, and hung up the phone.

"What?" asked Nancy flatly. As if she didn't know.

"Please," her mother said. She sounded weary and embarrassed. "Go find Grandpa Joke, Nancy. We have to make sure he eats, at least."

"I was going to show Granny my knitting, Mamba," said Nancy. This thing they were asking her to do was her least favorite chore. Chore! It felt downright dangerous.

· · ·

"Hey, girl!"

Nancy's head snapped back down. Again! It was the strange boy from the Promenade, hanging out at the geodesic dome.

He worried her, but he wasn't her only worry now. She kept walking. From the corner of her eyes she watched him. His coat billowed in the wind. Was he plumpish? Or just strong? It looked as though he just took everything and chucked it into the same load of wash. All his clothes were so gray they were almost blue. Where did he get it all, from somebody's laundry line? She didn't think he'd ever been anywhere near Alta, Utah.

"Hey, girl!"

Don't speak to me. It was what Annette would say, or one of the homeroom girls: Shamiqua, the queen. He was blue now in the sunshine, but how gray did he get at night? Nancy thought he didn't go anywhere warm and good. No nest high or low. Railings. Playgrounds. And where else? She could just hear Annette. "Boy, you can pick 'em!"

But. But. But. "It's wrong not to say hello," Granny Tina told Nancy all the time. Granny had tried to teach Nancy what she had taught Rachel: "Say hi to people on the street, in stores. Let them get to know your face."

"Why? Why, when nobody knows Mama's face?"

"They used to."

"They don't now."

"Some still do."

"You hope."

"I hope! Then if you're in trouble you have someplace to go, someone to call to for help. Then you're not among strangers. It's country advice for the city."

Advice! Sometimes it seemed that what Granny wanted to do was open up the top of her head and pour everything in there right into Nancy. And maybe she already had, because Nancy looked up and said, "Hi."

That blue-gray boy with his no-hair head and his rainy-day eyes spoke to Nancy on this sunny day.

"Oh, girl," he said. "You *so* skinny."

Was he going to insult her now, the way he had Annette, after she'd tried to be friendly? "What do you think *you* look like?" she called back. She scuttled into the subway, caught the train to Flatbush. *Skinny!* He made her stand outside herself, looking back at a skinny bug in purple tights. Horrific!

9

Grandpa Joke leaned against a counter by the window in the Flatbush Avenue Off-Track Betting, his *Racing Form* in his hand. "Looky there," Nancy told him, imitating Granny's West Virginia accent. "Dancing Nancy, third race." She handed him a dollar from her skirt pocket.

"Only a dollar?" he asked.

"All I can spare, Grandpa Joke."

He crunched it back up in his fist, dropped it into her palm. "I'm flush today, Miss Nancy. I'll put down five, in your name."

Granny wouldn't like it. He never used to bet so

much that five seemed like nothing to him. Flush today meant broke tomorrow, and where was the money going? Even when he won, he never seemed to have enough anymore. "Who's *your* money on?"

"Far Rockaway in the second." The odds were good: 5 to 2. Grandpa Joke never did bet on the first race, a superstition of his. "Grasshopper in the fourth."

Hmm. Maybe he *wasn't* going for broke today. Grasshopper's odds were 9 to 1. A nice return, if he won.

"Two races only," Nancy said. "Then we'll eat."

He shook his head. "Winged Victory in the seventh . . ." The odds, 26 to 1, made Nancy raise her eyebrows.

"Okay, stop," she snapped. "Don't tell me any more." She pointed to the big sign hanging over the betting windows: BET WITH YOUR HEAD, NOT OVER IT.

He turned away from the sign. He did a little pantomime of putting an ax over his shoulder and marching in place. He sang, "I owe, I owe, so off to work I go," like the seven dwarfs in the old movie.

"*Who* do you owe?" she demanded.

"Huh?" He looked startled for a second, then waved her off. "It's just a song."

"Give me the five dollars," Nancy ordered him. "I'll place my own bet."

"You're not of age," he protested, pulling out the five.

She snatched it, stashed it deep in her pocket. But what good would one five do? "You're going to get in trouble."

"Who says?"

"I do! And Mama!"

He looked startled. "Rachel knows I'm here?"

"Of course! Why do you think I'm here? Let's go to Curley's, Grandpa. I'm hungry for lunch."

"Now? Baby, I can't leave."

"I need you to, Grandpa."

She'd always been able to get him out of there, before. The fact that they knew her name at Curley's diner on the corner showed just how often she'd been sent here. More lately.

Maybe she wasn't as cute as she used to be (*skinny!*) or as persuasive. She couldn't get him to leave. Or maybe he was just more obsessed than he used to be.

"Take your money home, Nancy," he said. "Take it to Granny Tina and put it in that big piggy she's got in the kitchen. For your future. And maybe this evening

I'll come home with Dancing Nancy's jackpot."

She didn't recognize the stubborn look in his cinnamon eyes. "Fine," she said shortly. "Bye."

She found a stoop down a side street that gave her a good view of the OTB door. She climbed the steps and watched out over Flatbush Avenue, her knitting in her lap. She got through the ribbing of the back of the sweater she was making, and started on the flat stitch. When Grandpa Joke came out of OTB she sneaked down the street behind him, following him to a curving street in Cobble Hill, an old, old street from Brooklyn's farm country days. The trees all grew toward the middle of the street from both sides, reaching into the sun. The angle of the trees made the houses seem to lean back, as if they were considering action.

Grandpa Joke climbed a stoop under a sycamore tree and pressed the buzzer. He put his hands in his pockets and waited. Nancy scooted into the shelter of a stoop across the narrow street, not twenty feet from the front door. Grandpa buzzed again. A voice came out of the intercom, a polite man's piped-in deep voice: "Yes?"

Grandpa Joke took his hands out of his pockets and

rubbed them on his thighs, as if they were wet, sticky with sweat. "It's me," he said.

"Have you got the money?"

"No," Grandpa said.

There was a pause. Grandpa Joke waited. He buzzed again, and got no answer. Then he turned and walked away, toward the subway. Nancy watched him go. How slack his pants hung from his rear (he was thinner). How slumped he walked (more than before). Older. Tireder.

Nancy gave him time to get to the station, catch a train. Then she bundled up her knitting with clammy hands and went back home to tell her mother that her mission had failed.

10

Nancy was still in the shadowed kitchen when the voices reached her from the sunny courtyard. "She weaves," Rachel said. "But that shawl she did the fringe on last week . . . I'm still shaking my head over that."

"Well, she's been knitting like mad," Ned said in his upbeat way.

"Mad," Rachel agreed. "But not like my mother. And that fringe! So many Granny knots, but not the Tina kind."

"She slipped, that's all," said Ned. He sounded hopeful.

"But were you this un . . . this unclear, at this age?"

They both said nothing for a few moments.

"How's the climbing going?" Rachel asked.

Ned made a humming sound, not so optimistic now. "Well?"

"I watched her the other night."

That night she'd gone outside alone, sound-asleep Ned had *watched*?

"And?" asked Rachel.

"She tries, Rache, she tries. She made it to the first landing down, but only by crashing into it."

Nancy's stomach rolled into a little ball.

Rachel said, "She slipped, that's all."

Nancy knew she ought to be glad that her parents came together over her. If only it wasn't to despair. *I'm going to be grounded,* she thought. *Me and Grandpa Joke.*

"Nancy?" her mother called. "Are you back?"

Nancy ascended the courtyard stairs, stood in the doorway, and looked at her parents. The way they sat together moved her. It was chilly, but they seemed warm. They sat on the same side of the picnic table, but turned toward each other, facing, eyes into eyes. Their hands were entwined on top of the table, their different-colored fingers crisscrossing.

"You guys?" she said. "Don't push me."

Rachel put up a finger to stop Ned from saying anything. "Nance? Go on up," she said. "Granny wants to see what you've been knitting. She's on her own up there, right?"

"Grandpa wouldn't leave, Mama. I don't know where he is. He should have been home by now. But he lost."

"How do you know?"

"Because I stayed."

Ned leaned in. "You watched?"

"Sort of. I'll tell Granny." Nancy, never in one place long, hoisted her backpack to her shoulder, and set off up the stairs.

Once, when Nancy was seven, she had stumbled close to the edge of the subway platform and dropped her stuffed poodle, Poochie, onto the tracks. Her scream must have reverberated through the entire tunnel.

Ned fell into a deep squat beside her. "What is it?"

She pointed. A glimmer of light lit the tracks from far off. The train was coming. Nancy froze in horror, but Ned dropped from the platform, snatched Poochie, and sprang back up again.

The train roared in; the conductor hadn't even tried to brake. Suddenly Ned was back beside her on the platform. Nancy grabbed Poochie, Ned grabbed Nancy, and he jumped into the train. Had anyone noticed? Nancy never knew. She only had eyes for Poochie. "Poochie's dirty!" she said, pulling a long gray sticky strand from the black fur. Ned gathered the stringy thing into a ball, tossed it aside. But when he wiped the tears from her cheeks he left another sticky strand there. "What *is* that junk?" she asked.

He told her what it was. Mostly protein, like hair or fingernails, but something more, too. Something to help him jump back up from the tracks.

"Are we spiders?" she'd asked.

"Well, I have spider silk," Dad said. He hadn't said no.

"I'm telling Annette," she exclaimed.

He told her she couldn't, because of the normal people and the other ones, the ones with spiderness.

"Who? Where are they?" She looked around the subway car at the polyglot melting–pot people.

"They could be anywhere."

Ned had wiped his hand across his eyes before he

answered. "Lots of families have things they like to keep quiet, Nance," he'd said. "You can't tell."

"Why not? Is it something bad?"

"Not bad." He seemed stunned by the idea. "But it could be dangerous, and you have to trust me on that."

Dangerous!

Nancy considered the heights of this city, where falling onto the third rail of the subway was the least of the falls you could take. She wasn't the only one who boasted of a great-grandfather who built the top of the Empire State Building and a great-great-great-grandfather who had worked on the Brooklyn Bridge. Even today, when it seemed beside the point to go any higher, the horizon was still spiky with cranes and the steel skeletons of buildings-to-be. All along the webbing, people bustled up and down and side to side. Though they were certainly graceful, though they were possibly fearless, Nancy had seen them spit on their hands to gain traction, seen them buy gloves with rubber grippers on the palms.

Were there any who had silk in their hands and dwelled on the rooftops at night? This was the thought that pulled Nancy out from under her bedcovers to drag her reluctant self up and down the side of Ned's new building: *Will I be the first completely silkless generation?*

Grandpa Joke entered the front door, a box from the bakery in his hand, just as Nancy reached the first floor. Rachel and Ned, picking up the uncomfortable vibration from the elder quarters, soon followed up to Granny and Grandpa's apartment to make coffee and share the cannoli. Nancy hadn't had the chance to tell Granny about Grandpa's losses; she didn't need to.

"So black a sweater. Makes you look like a rat in the subway." Was Granny scolding her instead of Grandpa? Nancy knew he'd get it later.

"It helps me blend in," she said. It had been a long afternoon, and it was getting longer.

"Too true," Granny said. "But well knit, Nancy."

Nancy's face went hot with surprise and pleasure. She had carefully knotted a strand of yarn through the hole she'd found. Did it matter, since she'd fixed it? Granny didn't let her feel proud for two minutes before starting in on the color again. "A pretty face like yours . . . You've got a face like a flower, but you keep it all boxed in. You ought to get that black hair off your face and wear some color."

"I've got color!" Nancy flipped up her skirt to show off the purple tights.

"On your backside! Who needs color there, besides a baboon?"

"Show her, Nance," said Rachel. "See what she's putting together now, Mother." She closed the cannoli box and pushed the little plates away. Ned turned his back on the room and stirred the big pot of sauce on the stove, but Nancy knew he was listening as closely as the others. Grandpa Joke nibbled at his cannoli, not close to finishing it, and watched Nancy.

She dumped her new project out of her backpack onto the table: balls of Mama's scrap yarn in every jewel tone. Red and purple, pale blue, turquoise, all the dark blues, emerald green, and one black. All she would need to buy was gold.

Granny grabbed. She had to touch such colors, couldn't resist. She rolled the balls into a row with her gnarled hands. "What pattern are you knitting?" she asked.

A stand-out sweater, Nancy said to herself.

"No particular pattern," she told Granny.

"Why, yes it is," said Mama. "The stripes are all exactly two rows wide."

Grandpa Joke raised his eyebrows. "Ah, a nonesuch sweater."

Precisely. "Each time I start a new stripe I reach into the bag and pick whatever comes out."

"Every time? Whatever comes out?" Grandpa's eyebrows bent down.

"Yeah, unless it's too much like the last color or it's too ugly a combination."

"Oh, so your taste *does* come into play?" Ned asked.

Triumphantly Nancy said, "No. Sometimes I use them anyway, because they're so different from what I would normally choose."

"Uh-huh," said Granny. Except in her West Virginia accent it sounded like "aha." Maybe that was what she really was saying. She leaned back in her wheelchair, looked out the window at the courtyard where Mama's greenhouse hovered over her loom. Everyone waited to hear what else she would say. "In the country," Granny said, "it is very dark at night."

They all looked at her for a beat. Only Grandpa

didn't look away. Rachel, Ned, and Nancy caught one another's eyes.

"Yes, Tina?" Grandpa Joke said.

Granny Tina laughed. She didn't finish her thought. She didn't have to. What she meant was that Nancy's nonesuch sweater could be knitted in the dark, if it was as random as all that.

Nancy was the only one who got it. "You think the pattern is choosing me," she said quietly.

Then the others understood, too. They all nodded. Then they burst out in hoots and hollers of laughter. *What a family.*

The phone rang. Ned scooped it up. "Hello?" A tremor came into his voice. "Giacomo Greene? That's what you said? Yes, this *is* his number, but Green Medicine—" Pause. "No, that's not our listing. You'll have to try the operator." He hung up.

Then three people said, "Nancy—" Her mother, her father, her grandmother. Not Grandpa Joke, but maybe he would have, too, if the others hadn't been so quick.

"What?" she said, staring. Why were they all trying to cover up the fact that Ned had been lying on the phone?

Rachel pushed the sauce to the back of the stove and

said, "We're not going to have time to wait for macaroni tonight. I've got that big thing of minestrone in the fridge downstairs. Go get it, will you?"

Nancy made a lot of noise jogging fast down the stairs, and then, just as quickly, she ran back up without making any. When the phone rang again, Grandpa Joke picked it up. Ned must have hit *Speaker*, which they had so Granny wouldn't have to cross the room in her wheelchair to have a telephone conversation. On the landing, Nancy held her breath.

"Tell me you'll see my wife," said a man's quiet, forceful voice. "Or I'll put it all over the papers what you do."

"What do you know about what I do?" There wasn't any tremor in Grandpa Joke's voice.

"What I've heard," said the man. He made it sound like he'd heard plenty; he knew how to do that with his voice.

Nancy slipped into the kitchen with the pot of soup. They all stared at her in horror.

"I'll see you tonight," Grandpa Joke said abruptly, and hung up the phone.

"Who?" asked Nancy. Everyone was silent.

"A patient," said Grandpa Joke.

"Some old guy, right, Joke?" Ned said.

Rachel set the pot on the stove, turned on the gas, lit it with a match. Then she set about cutting the bread into thick slices, her back to her family.

"I'll go with you," Nancy said. "As usual?"

Nobody said anything. They weren't about to tell her this visit wasn't usual. They hadn't ever admitted there was anything unusual about a doctor who still did house calls in these times, about his wife who went along with him. There wasn't anything unusual, was there, about Granny Tina going in to say hello to the folks? She didn't get out of the house much anymore, after all, and if Grandpa Joke was willing—with Nancy's help, of course—to help Granny Tina up some steps, then why shouldn't she go for a visit?

The minestrone heated up, and Rachel served it, with bread on the side. But Nancy knew the voice on the phone was the same voice that had come out of the doorbell speaker at the house on the sycamore street where Grandpa Joke had gone after he lost big at OTB. Granny Tina put down her soup spoon and crossed her arms. "Giacomo," she said. "We have to talk."

At this Grandpa Joke looked more defeated than the loss of any amount of money could have made him. "There is nothing to say, Celestine," he said.

"She's not going," Rachel said. "You can go, but why should Mama? It's asking too much."

"Granny wants to go," said Nancy, wondering where it was all leading.

"Nancy!" Rachel began to scold her daughter, then turned to her father instead. "I've had it with these house calls," she complained. "It takes you an hour by the time you've driven down there, found the house, seen the patient, had a cup of coffee to be polite."

"What would you have us do?" Granny thundered. "Ignore the call? Send her to the emergency room?"

"Well, what would happen if—"

Grandpa Joke let out a big sad sigh, almost like crying. "Fact is, it's taking too much out of her, Rachel."

"What is?" asked Nancy.

Everyone shook their heads at her.

"It is not," said Granny.

"I know," Rachel answered Grandpa Joke.

"If you could—" Grandpa leaned on the table, his eyes hard on Rachel.

Rachel was pleading. "Papa—"

"See, she won't," said Granny shortly.

"She's just not going to yet." Ned's hand pressed Rachel's shoulder. Was he comforting her? Or holding her back?

Nancy went and stood between her grandparents. She laid a hand on Grandpa Joke's arm. "I'm coming," she said. "I'm helping with Granny as usual. And if you want to tell me what's going on, it's up to you."

Silence. Nobody looked at anybody else. Nancy felt they were all avoiding looking at *her*.

"Well, I'm going," Granny announced.

"Just this one more time," said Grandpa darkly.

Granny Tina took a deep breath. "Rachel," she said, "get me my canes, will you, dear?"

Rachel unhooked the canes from the kitchen towel rack. She and Nancy helped Granny descend the curving stairs to the stoop, one on each side of her.

Saint Christopher, the patron saint of travelers, with the baby Jesus on his shoulder, smiled from his niche beside the front door. He belonged to the land-lady, who lived on the parlor floor. They were not Catholics, although Grandpa Joke used to be, the same way Granny Tina used to be Scots Presbyterian, back in West Virginia. Now they were none of them anything, really, unless you counted Arachnids, which was more of an ethnic thing. Nonetheless they each had their ritual sayings upon leaving the house.

"Saints preserve us," said Grandpa.

"Amen," said Nancy.

Granny said a West Virginia "Forevermore."

Rachel, who wasn't leaving, said nothing. She stood in her red socks, rubbing Saint Christopher's toe with one finger as she saw them off.

In the car Grandpa Joke broke the silence to say, "Let's get ice cream when this is over. Häagen-Dazs."

Nancy knew it was a peace offering.

"I second the motion," said Granny.

"Chocolate chocolate chip," Nancy said.

"Make it two of 'em," Grandpa Joke said.

"Rum raisin for me," said Granny.

"You're not telling me everything," said Nancy. "Why not?"

"Not now, Nancy," said Grandpa Joke. The tilt of Granny's head revealed nothing. Well, Nancy would soon get her alone.

the thread

Grandpa Joke parked in front of the house on the curved street, slammed the car door, climbed the steps, and buzzed. A small light flickered on above the front door. He disappeared inside.

Nancy knew that her role was to wait for a sign from him to bring Granny up to the door, but she didn't want to. Impulsively she leaned forward from the back seat and hugged her grandmother, her cheek against Granny's leathery-soft one.

"Too bad I can't drive yet," she said. "Then I could drive us to Häagen-Dazs while we wait for Grandpa."

Had Granny been asleep up there in the front seat? She startled as though she had been, and her eyes darted wildly, taking in the trees and the house, dark except for one inside light. Nancy sensed Granny's nervousness, so bright around her it almost glittered.

"But he needs me inside, don't you realize that, girl?"

"Why?"

Granny sat straight up, staring into Nancy's eyes. "Nothing!" she snapped.

It wasn't even the right word, Nancy thought. Granny had definitely lost the thread. "Don't worry," she told her grandmother. She sat back, not wanting

Granny to notice how her heart was thumping, glad for the dark that hid her face. Glad for her knitting, too, and for her nonesuch pattern that didn't depend on light, because it didn't matter which color she chose, or because whatever color she chose was right. At the moment she didn't care which of those ideas was true; she was just glad to have work to do with her hands.

She hoped Granny wouldn't start telling her when-I-was-young experiences; lately whenever that happened Nancy felt like running, itchy and antsy and dark. It disturbed her to feel so cranky and closed in; she used to like hearing that stuff. *Tell me what I need to know!* she thought at her grandmother.

"Where's Giacomo, Nancy love?" Was she awake, or sleep talking, or what?

"He only just went in, Granny. He'll be a little while."

Once this winter when Nancy had spent the night, Annette had sleep talked about the lunch table at school. "He only likes Twinkies!" she said. "Yodels taste stale." Nancy had made fun of her for the next week, asking her who the Twinkie liker was. This, now, Granny saying strange things, reminded her of Annette's sleep talking.

Granny said, "You want driving lessons?" *What next?* But then came Granny's story-telling voice, all calm and warm. "Honey bear, we'll sit here and rest and I'll tell you about driving lessons."

Grrr. Nancy tucked one foot under her, to hold herself still, and tried to settle back, knitting her knots, her eyes on the dark face of the house where Grandpa was doctoring.

I was sitting at the dinner table waiting for George to pass the potatoes, but he wouldn't. Ever since Pa had let him drive home from church that morning, George had hardly spoken to me.

"There is more than one way of being a spider, Nancy," Granny interrupted herself to say.

"Huh?"

"Wake up back there. I'm trying to tell you something."

"I'm awake," said Nancy tolerantly. "Tell me."

But Granny just went on with her story.

I could see George meant to hog the mashed potatoes. I leaned my elbows on the edge of the table, and said, "Pass the potatoes, George."

Well, George was being rude, too, ignoring me!

But it was me who got the cold stony stare from

Mama, who had frozen in the doorway, the basket of biscuits in her hand.

Pa, at the head of the table, stuck his tongue in his cheek and looked me over. "Pass the potatoes, George, *what?*"

"*Please,*" I said, but it was too late.

Pa slammed his fist on the table so hard the dishes hopped. "You can eat your potatoes and the rest of your supper in the barn, Celestine. Come back to this table when you learn some manners."

My sister Josie made a noise, but shut her mouth fast when Pa looked her way. I bolted from the room with my plate in two hands, the fork tucked underneath. I never did get any potatoes.

I crossed the yard in the hot sun, kicked off my shoes. (Mama wouldn't like that, but I didn't care.) I climbed the loft ladder with my plate and ate my dinner. I sat staring out the high window at the blue mountains, eating food that tasted like watery clay. I pictured my brothers and sisters eating inside, more polite than usual, with little halos, and my tears got all mixed up with my ham and carrots.

It's the way she tells it, thought Nancy. *It's almost as if she handed me down this memory along with high cheekbones and the knitting gene. Yeah, well, what if I don't want it?*

Why shouldn't she want it? It was just a picture, just words. She made herself breathe. She could see the West Virginia evening, see Granny's green-and-white-checked dress. "And then Josie came with the pie," she said.

"That dear love Josie," Granny said, sighing. Nancy was just a hair away from being in that loft herself. "But, oh, it was a day of reckoning in more ways than one."

The front door light of the house where Grandpa was doctoring switched on, and then abruptly off. Granny's face was turned back toward Nancy, and she didn't notice the light.

"I spied on Papa when he was teaching George to drive," said Josie. That was Josie, always so dramatic.

"So what?" I said. "Anybody can drive a horse."

"But they were hiding up in the woods," Josie said.

"You can't learn to drive in the woods," I said through a mouthful of pie.

Oy, thought Nancy, and sat on both her feet.

The little fibber went right on with her crazy yarn. "George did, with no wagon. He ran along holding the reins."

George was a fast runner. For a second I almost believed in this cuckoo picture I had of him running along behind a horse, towed by the reins. "Which horse? Bunny or Bounce?"

"Papa was the horse," said Josie.

"Now I know you're lying," I said.

"Papa had the reins around him like this—" Josie used a hand to circle her chest and shoulders, the reins running back over the shoulders to George's hands. "And he tied his hanky around his eyes and ran in and out of the trees. George had to run behind him with the reins. Papa made him use them to tell him which way to go."

"What, gee and haw?" I asked.

"No. George wasn't allowed to talk," said Josie. "Papa said if George yanked his neck, he'd make him chop every tree he hit."

What a family, thought Nancy. *How could he not hit trees?*

"How many did he hit?" I asked drily.

Josie put up her thumb and finger and made an O.

"Josephine. What actually did Papa tell George to do?"

Josie's eyes were big and dark. "To tell Papa what to do just by using his hands."

"Did he?"

"That's how it looked to me," said Josie.

That's how it had looked to me, too, watching George drive Bump that morning. He was a natural.

Granny stopped talking. Nancy thought, *The End.*

"What about you?" Nancy asked Granny. "Didn't you drive?"

"Papa'd have let me drive earlier than sixteen if I could talk with my hands like George," Granny said.

"And did he?"

She looked down at her hands, and closed them into soft fists. "I was gone by sixteen, came here to New York."

The sky behind the house had faded, and the front of the house stayed shadowed.

"Granny?" Nancy asked. "Why'd you tell me that?"

"To get you thinking, girl," said Granny.

"Thinking about what?"

"Anything!" Granny sounded bleary again, as if she'd already forgotten the story, as if it had gone right out of her mind.

Well, it has, thought Nancy. *Now it's in my mind, whether I like it or not: people running around blindfolded in the woods behind horses!* She asked, "You don't think I think?"

"Don't talk nonsense!" Granny sputtered.

This was the night when Nancy started to feel as if Granny's stories were unraveling and then raveling again, knitting themselves into a new shape, and that she, Nancy, was getting knitted right in. It was unsatisfying: she wanted to know why that man wanted the doctor, and instead she got driving lessons in the woods. *Don't talk nonsense.*

"What's keeping Giacomo?" Granny asked indignantly. "I've been sitting too long. Go on up and tell him I'm ready."

Nancy and Granny usually waited in the car until Grandpa Joke came, but Nancy's itchiness now increased so that she jumped out of her seat and through the car door, trailing knitting yarn. Why had the man turned the light off? Or had Grandpa done it? She wanted to get everything moving. She felt furious with Grandpa Joke for owing anyone enough money to get into this mess, but she was curious about him, too. What had Granny come to New York for? Just to marry Grandpa Joke? Nancy didn't even think Granny had known Grandpa when she came to New York.

She rolled her knitting around itself like a meatball and threw it through the open door onto the car seat. As if she were the grandmother and Granny were the grandchild, she said, "When you're finished visiting, we'll go get ice cream." Granny didn't say a word when Nancy slammed the door and walked to the house.

Dion hid on the roof of his own house. His father, Niko, didn't know he was up there, and his sister, Mina, didn't know, and his mother, Rose, didn't know, so they didn't try to make him come inside. He slipped down the fire escape, though, got as near as he could to Rose's window. There were people around his mother's bed: his father's back, broad shoulders in a blue shirt; the doctor's back, his suit jacket over the chair nearby; and Mina's eyes, at the window.

He snapped back against the wall. Had Mina seen him? Someone was buzzing at the apartment door.

Nancy hit the buzzer again. She stood in the dark and waited. When no one came, she tried knocking.

After about twenty-five knocks the door opened a crack. No light came on.

"Yes?" asked a polite voice, a man's voice. Nancy saw no one in the darkness, but she recognized the voice—or the hair on the back of her neck did.

She made her own voice strong and sure. "I need to talk to the doctor. Please tell him it's Nancy."

The door banged shut. There were voices inside, whispering. She thumped the door with her fist. Furious. Curious. It opened. Grandpa Joke was there, nobody else. Nancy reached for his hand and he stepped out. The door shut behind him. "What's taking so long?" she demanded. "Granny wants to come up."

"Hush, Nancy." He gripped her shoulder. "I'm trying to guess if he saw your face. It's bad enough he'll know your voice."

Nancy didn't ask who. She didn't ask why. She said, "I'm bringing her." Her voice shook now.

"Stay hidden," he said.

She whirled and dashed down the steps to pull open Granny's car door. Grandpa Joke came to walk on the other side of Granny and help her up the steps. The front door swung open onto a hallway with a dim light.

Now there was another face in the doorway: a girl with long black hair. *Josie,* thought Nancy irrationally.

"You come, too." The girl took Nancy's hand.

Nancy stopped in the doorway and bent down. "What's your name?"

"Wilhemina," the child said.

"You have wings." Red ones, made out of a clothes hanger or some other piece of wire, covered with sheer red material (maybe from a sexy nightie or ballet costume) and, on one wing, a sleek layer of red feathers. "How did you—"

"Hot glue." Wilhemina pulled Nancy into the hall and said, "You've got angels on your tights."

They were cupids, left over from Valentine's Day. Rachel had sent Ned to buy them at Ricky's. There was a commotion down the hall. "Where's Mina?" called a woman's voice. "I found the other bag of feathers—"

"That's my mom!" The girl seemed surprised. She turned and ran toward a door at the end of the hall.

Just then a man came out. Nancy dropped back onto the stoop, eased the door almost shut. "Mina," the man said, "Mama's too sick to do more feathers now."

"It's already taken a week to do that one," Mina said.

Nancy thought she sounded sympathetic, not snotty.

"Where's your brother?"

"How am I supposed to know? Nobody tells me anything."

Nancy could still feel Mina's hand pulling her in. A warm hand. Good she wasn't the sick one. Then who was? Her mother?

Nancy stayed outside, hidden like a spider under a tree. There was not a soul on the sidewalk to see her. *This is why we waited until dark. This is why they don't tell me anything. So I won't know.*

12

The stories said it was hard to watch for the Angel if you didn't know what you were looking for. It was easy to miss the Angel if you were looking somewhere else.

Dion stood at the front edge of the roof of his house, watching Nancy go down the steps and disappear under the trees. Whether or not his father knew Nancy's voice, Dion already knew it, recognized the girl from the Promenade in his bones and veins the instant he heard her on the front stoop.

He sped down from the roof. From the shelter of an alley near the corner, he watched the doctor's car drive away under the trees and around the curve, the old man and woman and the girl inside it. It was definitely the girl from the Promenade.

Not that he hadn't known she might be there. Hadn't he seen her from this very roof, watching the doctor this afternoon? They had both heard the same intercom-to-stoop conversation. Dion wondered what it meant that the doctor hadn't gone inside right then to see his mother. Money, that was it. The doctor hadn't had enough money. Wasn't that what his father had asked for on the intercom?

Dion rubbed his sore hands together. Shouldn't *Dad* be paying the doctor? Maybe there was some special medicine the doctor needed to buy; maybe he had come back this evening to bring it. But it had sounded like the doctor owed Niko money.

Dion shivered, and it wasn't from the cold wind on his hairless head. Why should there be a girl involved with the Wound Healer—and why should it be the girl he'd seen on the Promenade, the girl he'd been goofing on and flirting with from the playground dome? He had associated nothing so messy and scary with her. He'd thought she was more like the Angel of Brooklyn might be.

Dion slipped through the dark back alley and up the

fire escape to the window of the room he shared with Mina. He scratched his fingernails along the glass until she appeared and pushed up the window. "Meens," he whispered. "Is she better?"

Mina shrugged, a one-shouldered shrug that clearly meant *not much better*. "We've got Oreos," she said, and disappeared. Dion leaned on the wall and listened to himself breathe.

And then his father grabbed him by the arm. "Get yourself in here," Niko said. But the angle was wrong from the window, and Dion sprang back. For once he was the faster jumper.

"What are you doing?" his father demanded. Dion pulled his baseball cap low over his eyes and his coat collar around his neck. He didn't want Dad to notice his hair was gone.

Niko didn't reach for him again. He leaned out the window and said, "You're surviving, then?"

Just about, thought Dion. "Where'd you find that doctor?"

Niko shrugged. "Connect the knots," he said. It was what he always said about reporting, how it was just a matter of making connections from one person who'd heard some information to another person who'd heard something else.

"Where?" Dion asked again patiently.

"In the OTB on Flatbush."

"Come on, Green Medicine is not in the phone book." Niko Papadopolis knew how to trace a story. Dion used to listen to him putting connections together, before, back when he admired his father and was proud of him and thought maybe he himself would like to be some kind of writer or investigator. *Green Medicine is not in the phone book.* How many times had Dion heard his father say that? Niko had muttered it to himself as he dialed the phone or walked the bars and betting parlors and bocce courts and coffee shops and Curley's diner and the other places where the kind of people who interested him congregated, swapping tall tales about themselves, spreading rumors.

"You won't come in?" It wasn't like Niko to ask for anything; he usually just ordered Dion to do things. But Dion thought his father seemed nervous, jumpy in a new way. He didn't mind the feeling it gave him, as if he, Dion, might have the upper hand. He shook his head and said, "That old man?"

"Joke is what they call him," said his father. He lit a cigarette, and leaned on the windowsill. " 'That your real name?' I asked him. We were at the OTB window that day.

" 'Giacomo,' the guy says.

" 'An Italian? What's your last name?'

"He says, 'Verdi, up to the moment we came through immigration. Then we made a translation.' " Dion waited.

"Greene. With a silent *e*.

"So I go with him into Curley's and sit beside him at the counter. He gives his order: grilled mozzarella sandwiches and curly fries with extra paprika."

Dion started to chuckle, turned it into a cough. "Enough with the journalistic detail."

"Yeah? Well, it's detail that saves the day, my friend."

It was almost like a nice conversation, except for the fact that Dion was outside freezing, while his Dad stood in the bedroom, which was warm and had Dion's bed in it. Dion stood up.

"Listen here," his father said. He reached a hand toward his son. Dion stood still. "Details. Good shoes, Italian shoes, worn down at the heels. Baggy pants, as though he'd lost some weight. And his wallet seemed baggy, too."

"So what?"

"So I thought maybe he was low on funds, that's so what. And I knew he didn't know what I knew about him." This kind of convoluted sentence was typical of Niko Papadopolis in speech, if not in writing. "I asked him if he was retired. He was still a doctor, he said. I already knew it. So I say—you know what I said?"

Dion was silent. A doctor without a hospital? A doctor with a failing practice? How did that happen?

"I say, 'Once a healer, always a healer.' He says he doesn't treat insured people. He's a hero. He's here to help the poor. He thinks I'm too smooth. But I tell him, 'I recognize you.' He doesn't ask what I recognize about him."

Dion didn't ask either.

" 'We both love our wives,' I say. 'Our wives are both special people, with great natural gifts.' He gets my meaning."

"He needed the money," Dion said, testing. He was more than curious about the money. What did Dad care about the doctor's wife, anyway?

Niko took a quick puff from his cigarette and gazed at his son, though his hand on the cigarette shook a tiny bit. "A cynic at sixteen," he said. "Yes, smart guy, he did. And he's going to need more, if you see what I mean."

"I'm leaving," Dion said acidly. He saw, all right. First the research was for his mother, but next it would be for the papers. And what would that mean to the girl? To his father, it was all just different kinds of business. He stepped lightly up the steps above his father's head, going roofward.

"Stay dry," Niko said.

That's it? "What does that matter?"

"Eh, you're like me. You'll be all right."

Like him how? As a finder of things? As a jumper? Or as a tough guy who was willing to overpower some old man who might have helped him for free if he was nice about it? What could Dad have to hold over an old doctor like this? If the doctor knew where the Wound Healer was, why wasn't Dad paying *the doctor* to tell him?

No, Dad always had to have a sense of winning. He might not be the biggest guy, but he was the strongest. He might not be the best basketball player, but he had the best jump shot. And he might not be the smartest reporter, but he was the most persistent. If his bosses at the papers still wanted stories on the Angel of Brooklyn, Niko would find them—and maybe some Wound Healer stories, too. But did he *have* Wound Healer stories? Dion wished he knew.

"What do you care if I stay dry?" he asked his father.

Niko bowed his head, and for a moment Dion felt remorse, and longing. "You won't come back?" his father asked, then answered his own question. "No. Tough, like your old man. Well, I thought I could conquer the world, once."

"Dad, when did you ever stop thinking you could conquer the world?"

Niko laughed a short, sour laugh. "Yeah, well . . . "

Dion wished he had not asked the question. Knowing the answer was not going to make him feel any better about his mother. But once he'd started asking, he couldn't stop. "Is she any better?"

His father swore, then stopped himself. "It's too soon to tell. The doctor only just left."

Dion could have gone to see his mother.

He could have asked what the doctor said.

He could have tried to pry more out of his father, maybe an invitation to come home.

Instead he turned and kept going, up the steps.

"You've got somewhere to keep the rain off?"

The dryness question again. Dion didn't answer.

Below, Niko stubbed out his cigarette on the windowsill and called up softly, "It'll be the making of you."

"Daddy!" From inside, Mina called. Dion stopped climbing. He watched the window for a moment. His father did not reappear.

Dion slipped back down the steps, pocketed the Oreos Mina had left on the sill as he stepped over it. On tiptoe he sneaked into the hall where the phone was. Hit *Redial* and—*yes!*—read the numbers on the screen. The phone beeps drew his father to the hall, but by the time he got there, Dion had run away again.

Dion could pounce on an idea as quickly as his father. Now he hit the Internet café on Atlantic Avenue, found the address that went with the phone number. It was in Carroll Gardens. So he went traveling. He found the doctor's car parked on a street full of brown brick apartment houses, the kind of street that had crazy lights at Christmas and Virgin Marys in the front yards all year round, not a tasteful street like his parents'. Was this where the Wound Healer lived? It didn't matter to Dion that most people thought the Angel of Brooklyn and the Wound Healer were as made up as other funky fantastic urban legends.

Dion wasn't sure the roof he settled on for the night was Nancy's. That didn't stop him from hunkering down there, his back against a chimney, trying to stay out of the wind. He missed his mother. Dion had always looked out for Rose, in the ways a good boy did for his mother in the city. He held the doors, he wheeled the heavy shopping basket all the way home from the grocery store, he walked next to the street and let her have the inside of the sidewalk, the way his father had taught him. He had walked her home from work every day all last winter. He said it was because it was dark so early, but really it was because her office was so full of people with scared eyes, people who had seen too much trouble, people who had lost their place and didn't know how to find it. He didn't know which day Mom had begun to lose her place herself. Did her bleeding heart bleed for him, too? He made himself think of the girl instead. In the courtyard in the back of the apartment houses, there was a greenhouse with a light inside. Someone was down there, but it wasn't Nancy. He played with her name in his mouth a little. Nancy.

Sleep crept up on him.

Dion hunched his shoulder against the chimney and pulled up his hood to cushion his head. Down in that greenhouse he noted the rhythmic motion of some machine working. It nearly put him to sleep.

And then the sound of a door opening below brought him to his feet. A glance over the roof edge sent him dashing toward the fire escape. He found the alley he'd scoped out on the way in. Let the girl think he could appear and disappear. He liked to think that she'd think about him at all.

13

When Nancy awoke on Granny's couch, a crick in her neck and the stitches slipping off her knitting needles, the bedroom door was shut and the light was out, and Ned stood at the kitchen window. She knew what he saw: Rachel, weaving down there in her bubble of light.

From above, the warp threads looked as lacy as those white cobwebs that shone in patches on the grass in the courtyard on spring mornings. "Look!" Granny had told Nancy once. "The fairies are doing their laundry." That's what the webs had looked like: white fairy dresses, drying on the grass.

Mama had knelt in the grass and peeked under a little white piece of laundry. "Who's there?" she called. Nobody answered.

In her faded sweatshirt and flowered pajama bottoms, Rachel hunched cross-legged on the floor, her arms reaching to her many threads, arranging them among the heddles as calmly and sedately as an old eight-leg in the corner of an attic. "She Who Cannot Be Disturbed," Nancy said, slipping under Ned's arm. He wrapped her in his long arms and stood with his chin on her head, watching Rachel. "Did you just come in?" Nancy asked.

"Yeah, I went out for a while. Some work to do." Nights, Ned often went to visit people who wanted their roofs done, in order to give them estimates of what their jobs would cost. "Ready?" He fished in his pocket for his Metrocard.

"The house call tonight was strange," Nancy said as Ned opened the door to the stoop. The street glowed dark green this late at night, the leaves of the bushes lit up by people's stoop lights.

"Holy Saint Chris," said Ned to the doorway saint, a hand on the statue's foot.

"Amen," answered Nancy, as always.

"Strange how?" Ned picked up the thread again.

"It took a really long time," she said.

"How long?" The wind was cold. They hurried up President Street.

"Dad, it was like they weren't going to let Granny leave."

"They did," Ned said matter-of-factly. But his eyes darted around more than they normally would, checking the traffic on Court Street before crossing.

"Yeah, but . . . Why wouldn't they?"

"Oh, the healing process," Ned said vaguely. "Whatever works, I guess."

"What kind of work *is* it?" Nancy asked.

"Just medicine," he answered.

"What kind of medicine? Voodoo?"

He stared. "Voodoo it certainly is *not*."

"Then—"

"Then stop it."

But she couldn't. "Dad, those people scared Grandpa."

"Why do you think so?"

She was careful in her response. "Well, I don't think it's just the money he owes." She thought her father was more surprised than he showed. "Dad," she said. "Granny said tonight that there was more than one way of being a spider. What do you think she meant?"

"They're not all our kind," said Dad tensely.

"What all?" she asked. "Who?" The Greene kind? The Kara kind? And what kind was Grandpa Joke? What kind was *she*?

He said, "You must know it's hard to identify them."

"Why?"

Dad waved his hands at the low Brooklyn buildings around them. "It's the way this city is. People come here from all different places, and they all turn into New Yorkers." That meant: Fast walkers. Subway riders. Multicolored crowds. "Some groups don't fit in so well. They hang together more than others. Most are underground, trying to stay unnoticed until they get their chance."

"Get their chance to what?"

"To—" He stopped. "Nothing."

"Dad, come on!"

He shook his head, a tense movement that hardly moved his dreads. "It could cost us too much," he said.

"Is that why Grandpa Joke needs money?"

He looked confused. "Not that kind of cost."

"Then *what*?"

"Nancy, we're not the only roof dwellers, and not the only ground dwellers. But this other thing—"

"Medicine?" She stood still on the sidewalk to say it.

He had to stop, too. He cocked his chin sharply, not wanting to answer.

"Why won't you—"

"I *won't*," he said. He cut dead the conversation. He walked on, and she followed. She felt hot behind her eyes, but if he was going to hold back because she was too young, the last thing she was going to do was cry. *Whatever this is,* she thought, *it's something else they're waiting to see if I have. It's something else I don't have.*

Ned's long legs stretched out. Nancy hustled to keep pace. But they didn't move so fast that she missed the eyes of the boy on the dome as he turned to watch them pass. Ned didn't seem to notice him as he hustled toward the station, hurrying in part to get away from her questions, Nancy figured.

"Dad, I think there's a train coming into the station." The slightest jiggle in the sidewalk clued her in. She began to run.

"How'd you know?" Ned ran along, keeping pace.

"The ground shakes." Everyone in New York knew that. People five stories up—or even more—took it for granted that they could feel the subway passing in certain areas.

"I didn't feel anything," he told her.

"Guess I'm just lucky," Nancy said, thinking nothing of it.

"It's a gift," Ned agreed.

Nancy felt irritated. Some gift, compared to what he wanted her to have. She fell silent, and let her knees bounce along with the bumping of the train, more than was necessary. She walked her hands up and down the steel pole, not wanting to be in one place, seeking the cold places in the metal. Seeing that boy again had made Nancy all jangly. She didn't know what it meant that he had seen her dad. It felt like another step closer to . . . what? In her head, she asked him, *What's your name?* He didn't reply.

Their subway car had a lot of empty orange seats and a dirty floor. Ned loved the subway this time of night. He hated it at rush hour, couldn't stand touching strangers as a rule. "Do this, Nancy," he said. He reached for two metal straps, one for each hand. Hauled himself up and flipped over backward, feet in the air, skinned the cat with his feet on the silver-gray ceiling of the subway car. "What a feeling," he said. As the subway came aboveground to cross the canal, the city rose up huge and sparkling, making the train seem tiny.

Nancy glanced at the platform of the station they pulled into, saw just one old man Grandpa Joke's age waiting for their car. She dropped her backpack onto the seat. Leaped to catch the straps in her hands. Walked up the wall and window and flipped (good thing she was wearing tights, not just kneesocks) and landed, "Ta da!" on her Docs.

The old guy, entering, let out a *tsk* of irritation.

Ned caught his eye. "You ought to try it," he said. The man snorted, smiled. Ned and Nancy spun and flipped, shooting along through the dazzling New York night.

Ned's station had no playground outside, no playground inhabitants, just the Uprising Bakery on the corner, darkened for the night, leftover rolls in the window. "I'm hungry," Nancy said, throwing her pack onto her shoulder, running up all the stairs.

"Rice Krispies and raisins," Ned said. "Then sleep."

Nancy jolted awake in the middle of the night.

It was never really dark in the penthouse, not with all those city lights out there. Ned was out cold—she was absolutely certain this time—in his bed in the corner, snoring most convincingly under his mosquito netting. "Lends a romantic air," he'd said, and lent privacy for Nancy.

She pulled her black sweater over her pajamas, opened the door without the least creak, and hesitated, breathing in the night. *Here's what I'm going to do,* she directed herself: *Walk straight and slow across the roof to the ladder, and up and over it and down to the first landing.* There would be no pause in the rhythm, no pause in the pace. She'd been there already, she'd lived through it twice. *Let three times be the charm.*

Some charm. She was wet with sweat before she was halfway across the roof, nauseous and dizzy before she mounted the edge of the wall, and her knees were so jelly-useless by the time she reached the final landing that they collapsed beneath her.

Holy Saint Christopher! Would she ever get over this fear?

Her toes sank between the metal slats as if they were monkey toes, trying instinctively to reach around and hang on.

"You okay?" A whispered call came from above.

Oy. What woke Dad up?

"Come on, girl!" His voice was echoey, encouraging, hoarse (with sleep?). She didn't let herself think how high up he was, how far she had to climb back up to reach him. She forced herself to think as a spider might, focusing on what was precisely in front of her: Wall. Steps. Railing. The dark damp spring night air. *So what if I'm not a natural. So what if I've got no spinnerets and no talent, either. I can still find some ability to work with. Focus.* One stitch at a time. One step at a time. She couldn't have been any less steady if she were climbing a steel knitting needle.

She made it.

She squinted around in the dark: nobody. She found Ned inside, lying in bed. She lifted the edge of the netting, found his eyes closed. *Faker.*

"Dad?"

"Hmm?" he murmured. And then, "It's a lovely evening for some fresh air."

"Go to sleep," she told him. She climbed into her hammock and passed out from exhaustion.

Nancy woke early the next morning, steadied the hammock by lying still and reorienting herself to the idea that no part of her—nothing she was directly connected to—was connected to the floor. Revelation! The hammock was the ideal place to knit a sweater of many colored stripes. She dropped each ball of yarn on the floor and threaded its end up through a loop in the hammock's netting. Each time she started a new stripe, she simply picked up a new end. Beneath her, the balls rolled around the floor freely and didn't get tangled.

Dad came through the roof door. "It's a lovely morning for some fresh air," Nancy said, and watched him. He didn't seem to react to her words. Had he really been awake when she came in last night, or just sleep talking? *And if it wasn't Dad talking to me last night, who was it?*

"What are you doing?" Ned asked, his voice still sleepy.

Nancy held up the sweater.

"What's wrong with the black one?"

"It's finished, remember? I was wearing it last night."

"Oh." Ned leaned closer and kissed her on the cheek. "You'll be so bright in that," he said.

"Don't start with me. Granny thinks I'm too dark in the black one."

"Even a spider makes use of camouflage, little egg."

Some spiders do. Not me. Nancy felt cranky. She wanted to be bold, get noticed, be one of those garish bright spiders that stood out fiercely on their webs, even if the purpose was only to make themselves unappetizing to birds. "I want to look big and colorful and scare people," she said.

Ned laughed. "Scare who?"

"People." The man whose house she'd been to last night. That boy on the dome. Whoever was outside last night.

Ned tossed the hair out of his eyes and looked at her inquisitively, but she kept her thoughts to herself. "What are you doing today?" he asked. He was pulling on his hobnailed boots, ready for a roofing job. It was Saturday. Nancy had that gold yarn to buy. She'd promised to see Annette. And she had some questions she wanted to try asking her grandparents.

"Home," she said. "Mama."

"Is she sleeping?" Ned asked, tying a boot. His hair dangled, hiding his face. Nancy knew the trick.

"Yes." She couldn't lie. Rachel *snored* when she wasn't with Ned, lay on her stomach spread-eagle on the bed, heavy blankets kicked to the floor, pillow over her head, out like a light, deeply secure.

"Ah." Ned looked into Nancy's eyes, his face pure calm, except for one cheek twitch. Only one. Nancy knew that in fall Rachel had insomnia, walked the floor, plucked at the strings on her loom, ached for Ned. In spring it seemed to Nancy that fall would never come. But this year she sensed some different ache in Rachel, for something else, not Ned.

14

Boy on the Promenade railing. Blue eyes. No hair.

"Hey girl, where's your daddy?"

Nancy pulled her sweater sleeves down over her hands, clutched them there, felt her palms sweat.

"Girl, know what you got?"

Annette shuddered. Her gleaming hair shook. But he wasn't talking to her. "Keep walking!" she said in Nancy's ear.

"Wait," said Nancy.

"Got hair like a nest!"

Nancy whirled at the corner of Pierrepont. "I do not!" she screeched.

Another surprisingly beautiful smile came out of that gray-blue uglyish face. "I know about your father," he called teasingly.

"Oh, why did you answer?" moaned Annette softly, walking on. Nancy just stood there; she let Annette leave her behind.

"Up high a lot, isn't he?" the boy asked.

She wasn't sure what that meant. "He works on roofs."

He laughed. "I'm pretty good on a roof myself."

Nancy's heart thumped. Had it been him? *Are you the Angel?* "What's your name?" she asked.

"Dion," he said. "Remember that."

"Dion *what*?"

"My mother's going to wonder where I am," Annette said. She was back, Nancy was sorry to note. *Sorry? About Annette?* She pulled herself together. She turned away, went after Annette.

"Hey girl!"

Nancy kept going. *Can't catch me.*

"Didn't say what *kind* of nest, did I?"

"Nancy," hissed Annette. "How does he know 'your daddy'?"

Nancy glanced sidelong at Annette, who was just

being a good friend, just trying to protect her. "He was on the dome in the playground when Dad and I went by last night."

The boy sat on the rail behind them, swinging his feet. The space between them yawned. Annette pulled her to the corner and kept demanding in her ear, "Is he following you? *Stalking* you?"

Nancy pulled away. She would call the boy's bluff. "My girlfriend thinks you're the Angel of Brooklyn," she called across the space.

"Me?"

"Yeah." She took three steps toward him. Annette hugged her elbows, still back at the corner.

He said nothing. The girls waited. He didn't ask her name. He stared at his feet, which made her stare at hers. Her polka-dot Docs, his feet in soft gray boots.

With a thud of his boots, he dropped from the rail and in an instant stood before her. She froze. He reached toward her. She shrank back. But all he did was gently touch the back of her hand with one finger. "Just tell me one thing, Nancy," he said.

"*What?*" He *did* know her name.

"What does your grandfather do when he goes on

his house calls? How does he heal the wounds?"

She yanked her hand away, dashed to Annette, and hauled her away from the Promenade, enduring a barrage of Annette's street talk scolding of both of them until she reached some kind of personal limit and barked, "Shut *up*, Annette!"

Next time, she told herself, she wouldn't let him know she knew anything, would act like she didn't even remember his name. *What do you mean, next time, birdbrain?* she shouted at herself inside her head.

"Well, if he saw your father, I hope your father saw him," Annette said. Nancy could see that Annette thought it would be a good idea if her father had seen the ghost boy. "That boy is just nasty," said Annette, trying on a homeroom word.

Nancy started to imagine what touching Dion's head would feel like. He had stubble, but stubble—the way it sounded, rough and trouble and bumpy like pebbles—was not how it would feel. She didn't know why she so wanted to smooth his head. She could tell it would be silken, tiny fronds of hair woven into a soft carpet that would have been invisible if it weren't so dark.

"What sort of a person would cut off all his hair?" she

asked Annette. "Even his eyebrows. As some kind of disguise?"

Annette shook her head.

Nancy went on, "They could be looking for some kind of hair—dark hair—and wouldn't guess he'd be bald."

"Why would anyone be looking for *him*?" Annette said.

Nancy said, "If they were, would he be hanging out in all these public places?"

"He's creepy," Annette said.

No, he's not, thought Nancy. She didn't say it aloud. What Annette didn't know couldn't hurt her. But what the boy knew could hurt Nancy. *His name is Dion, and he knows my name. But what does he know about my grandfather?* And why had he asked her about him so that Annette wouldn't hear?

Again Nancy felt the touch of his finger on the back of her hand. Why was Annette so disgusted by him? She looked over at Annette, walking along, and linked her arm through her friend's. A distance of a different kind still gaped between them.

She asked Annette, "Do you hate being an only child?"

"Why?" asked Annette, confused.

Nancy said forcefully, "It's like I'm the only one."

"Only one where? There's plenty of people in your family."

"I'm the only kid. It's like I'm the only kid in the universe."

"I'm here," said Annette.

"I am the only one of *me*!" She knew she sounded insane.

"Thank God."

Nancy wanted Dion to be there in the empty space that yawned around her. She pulled Annette closer. "Come on, 'Nette. Let's go home and knit."

"Knit! Why would you, when you can just buy a sweater?"

"Why would you write a poem, when there's Walt Whitman?"

Annette said,

"There once was a Nancy who knitted.
But nothing she knitted ever fitted . . . "

"Woe is me!" said Nancy. "You know, I knit my hair into it sometimes by accident." It was fun to gross Annette out.

"Eeeesh!" Annette danced along on her toes, her arms bent, squeamish.

"Never mind," Nancy told her. "Is that it?"

"I didn't finish yet. Something about 'half-witted.' Promise me you won't knit me anything, especially with your hair in it."

Like a nest, thought Nancy. "Not till you have a baby, 'Nette. With, let's see . . . Twinkie Boy?"

Annette sighed. "He's so sweet. If only I knew who he was."

"How about that boy Jimmy in basketball who won't get out of your face?"

Annette warmed to the subject. "Like glue, stuck on me."

"Or Velcro," Nancy suggested.

"Jimmy Velcro!" they squawked. *Lord,* thought Nancy, *I helped come up with one of those dumb nicknames.* Jimmy hadn't asked Annette out, though Shamiqua still said he was going to.

In Nancy's head she heard the ghost boy's voice. *Hair like a nest.* What kind of nest? He was pushing her. For what? Echoing, hoarse, fading away. She thought of her dad, flat in his bed last night, and an idea came to her all of a sudden, a bolt from the blue. *Oh, come on, Nancy. Don't be a dumb bug. How would that boy get on Dad's roof?*

Annette's mother said it was too cold to sit out on the balcony, where Nancy might at least watch for another glimpse of the boy from the Promenade. Dion. She hung around near the living-room window.

"Nancy, how's your mother?" Mrs. Li asked from her desk. "I was disappointed not to see her at Sophomore Night last week."

"Dad went," Nancy said. *And thanks for bringing it up.*

"Yes, I know, but I'd just love to see your mother."

Mrs. Li and Rachel had gone to the same school as girls, but they hadn't been friends. It made Nancy uncomfortable, which was nothing compared to what it would have been if Mrs. Li found out that Rachel never went out anymore.

"Come here, Nancy," Annette called from the bathroom. "I'm all set up."

"Set up for what?"

"Your pedicure."

Annette had laid out a towel and set up scissors, a

file, some bottles of oddly tinted liquids, and a few thingers of nail polish in different colors. "Your choice," she said grandly.

My choice is to run out of here screaming. Nancy pointed to the green polish.

"Oh, to match your eyes?"

"How long will it take to dry?" She wanted to leave, leave, leave, be alone, keep her socks on, go back to the Promenade and look for the boy.

"You on a schedule?" asked Annette sarcastically.

Nancy sat on the edge of the toilet seat.

"Naked feet, please," Annette said.

Nancy was wearing jeans, and that was good, because on a school day she'd have had to take off her tights, and she was chilly enough already. But that didn't stop Annette taking a good look up her leg and letting out a yelp. "Listen," Annette said. "Is there anybody in this day and age who can truthfully get away with not shaving her legs?"

"I can. I do."

It wasn't that she hadn't heard the discussion and didn't know the tools. They'd been the subject of debate all week in school: Nair vs. Neet vs. Gillette Foamy vs.

Shamiqua whose mother took her to have her legs waxed (expensive!) vs. Khadija whose mother made a paste of sugar water to pull off the hair (barbaric!) vs. (silent, completely silent) Nancy whose mother had asked her not to shave her legs.

"Why won't you?" Annette must have realized that Nancy hadn't said a word in those homeroom conversations.

"Sheep shave," said Nancy. "That's what my mother says."

Annette's mother appeared in the doorway, and Nancy knew she must have heard. One more strike against Rachel. "That's a nice color for toenails," Mrs. Li said, and went away. Annette plopped Nancy's foot into a basin for soaking. "You have pretty legs, you know," said Annette.

"That's why I wear tights," said Nancy. "Sheep shave," she said again.

"Goats don't!" retorted Annette. "Why wouldn't you?"

"Baa," said Nancy. "Following along. Doing what everyone else does."

"So?" It was Annette's turn to be defensive.

"We don't shave in my family," Nancy said. "It's politics."

"What politics? The Hairy Leg Party?"

"It's against nature," Nancy quoted Rachel.

"If you wear tights, your mom'll never know."

"I don't want to talk about it," said Nancy tightly. She put in her other foot to soak, and Annette began trimming her toenails.

Annette whispered, "I would shave whether my mother liked it or not."

Nancy answered, "I can shave my pits if I want."

"That doesn't make any sense!"

"Well, it's what she said."

"She's lucky you're such a good girl," Annette said slyly.

15

Nearly noon, and Mama's house was only now waking up. Grandpa Joke was making waffles in the dining room, the only place where the plug was in the right place for the waffle iron. "Sustenance," he said.

"It's just food," Nancy said. She felt stubborn.

"Want some?"

"I guess so."

"First go and help your granny, baby."

Granny was sitting on the edge of her bed, looking like everything hurt, in the flannel pajamas that she'd bought because they had no buttons.

"You okay?" Nancy brought the wheelchair close to the bed.

Granny Tina made the big effort to stand up and get in the chair. "Another day," she said.

Nancy's heart ached. "Plenty more," she said.

"I don't know how many more there are going to be, Nancy love," Granny said slowly.

Nancy felt hurried. "Granny? What would you do if you wanted to know all about someone?"

"You don't need to know all about someone," Granny Tina said. The words sounded slurred and angry.

"But I do," Nancy protested. *There's this boy with no eyebrows from Alta, Utah . . .* She pushed the wheelchair, but Granny already had it moving herself, and fought her. The door wasn't open far enough to let the wheelchair through, so Nancy reached to open it, but Granny had already rolled up to it. Was there going to be a tug-of-war?

Then Granny backed up, Nancy opened the door, and Granny reached for her hands. Her brown-black eyes seemed flat, not sparkling like Coca-Cola the way they usually did. "If you want to know all about someone, learn what he *does*." Then she said to herself, "Not 'do.' *Does*." She fluttered her fingers toward her head a little.

Rachel came into the kitchen to start the coffee. Granny looked up at her and said, "I'm going a little crazy, Rachel."

Rachel smiled nervously, but said, buttery-smooth, "That makes two of us, Mother. How about you, Nancy?"

"Yeah, me three."

Grandpa Joke listened to Granny closely, and watched her face and Mama's. Rachel's eyes were tired, too. Sometimes after warping, she wove all night. The air felt zingy with tension. Nancy was grateful that no one asked where she'd been or what she'd been up to or whether there was anything new with her.

Later she holed up with Mama in the greenhouse, her Docs tossed in the corner with Mama's green clogs, doing her homework under the loom, knowing Rachel was too busy (too obsessed) to talk, knowing that she liked Nancy being there. "Mama," she asked, "what would you do if you wanted to know all about someone?"

Rachel ran her hand across her loom. "Find out what he loves," she said.

"Enough to fight for," said Grandpa's voice from the greenhouse doorway. The afternoon had warmed up enough that Rachel had the doors open, so they hadn't heard him coming on one of his rare trips out there. "Nancy, who are you trying to find out about?"

Oh, there's a direct question from someone who won't answer any. Nancy shook her head, wouldn't answer.

"Pop, is something wrong?" Rachel asked.

"Your mother," he said in a voice grown old. "Rachel, do you think you could give her a back rub?"

In an instant the slow-moving Mamba was moving quickly out the door and up the stairs.

"It's not an emergency, Nancy," Grandpa said, seeing her face. "She just needs Rachel's hands, that's all."

"Why, what's she got that you haven't got?"

Nancy might as well have slapped him, he looked so hurt. She could see that whatever was wrong with Granny, he felt responsible. Maybe a doctor always did, when someone hurt.

"She's a daughter," he said. "It's that blood connection."

"What about a granddaughter?"

"That's good, too," he said, and smiled.

"It might be." Nancy pushed the words out, though her throat felt glued together. Grandpa looked away from her, ran a stubby finger over the weaving on the loom.

"Grandpa, what—" *Careful, now.* "What's the matter with Granny?"

"You know, Nancy," he said wearily. "Arthritis. And that stroke last summer didn't do any good." It had been the beginning of Rachel's fight against the house calls.

"Why do the house visits take so much out of her?" *Careful.*

He studied the pattern in the weaving. "Moving around. Seeing new patients."

"What does *that* take out of her?" *Something I have? Something I could give her? Say yes!*

He leaned against the doorjamb, eyes closed, sunning, silent. Was this saying no? "Energy," he said. His eyes were still shut.

Nancy turned. *Energy I've got. I do! If it's just a matter* of that—But she knew there was something missing. She sat down on Mama's loom bench and studied the pattern to figure out what came next. She took off her shoes and pressed her feet down on the treadles to make the right frames rise for the next thread. She picked up the submarine-shaped shuttle full of weft yarn and shot it through the shed.

Wump. It did not sail through smoothly, as it did when Mama wove, but hung up in a stray thread from a treadle not pushed down firmly enough. *Rats.* Nancy pulled the shuttle out and disentangled the thread.

"Learning to fix your mistakes?" Grandpa asked, peeking through one eye.

"Maybe," Nancy said. It took effort not to throw the shuttle across the room, let it take the whole pattern with it. She laid the shuttle back on the beater bar. "Grandpa. What do you love enough to fight for?"

"This family," he said abruptly. "What about you?"

"Granny," Nancy said.

He opened his arms to her.

Rachel came down looking twice as worried as she had when she went up. Nancy was alone, on her back under the loom, thinking crabby, questioning thoughts, her feet resting backward on the treadles.

"Nancy Ariadne," her mother said. "Green toenail polish?"

"It matches my eyes," Nancy said. She fluttered her fingers at Mama; the polish on them shone silver. "What's up with Granny?"

"She's tired," Rachel said. "It matches my eyes, too. You'd better get me some."

"Tired from *what*?"

"Tired from life! Would you mind moving your feet?"

"Not tired to death?"

"Nancy," Rachel said in a warning voice.

Nancy lay there trying to whistle like Annette's mother.

"Could you stop that?" Rachel was barely patient.

"I want to shave my legs," said Nancy.

"Why?"

"The other girls at my school—"

"Followers," Rachel said. "Be a leader, Nancy."

"Right," Nancy said. "I'll lead a new fad of hairy legs."

Her Greene Mamba had the good grace to smile. "You'll be all right," she said. "Just keep the hair on your legs."

"Can't you explain? It's *not* politics, is it? It's spiderness."

"Yes."

"Something else that's either going to show up or not?"

Her mother was silent for a long moment. "If you're eighteen and you don't need it, you can shave it off."

"Because I won't be a minor anymore?"

"No. Because it'll be too late by then."

"Too late for what?"

"*Ack!* It's better if you find out yourself."

"Find out what? Nobody's telling me anything." She pulled herself up from the floor. "Look, Mama, I'm no roof dweller, but I can climb. I've been learning. I'm getting better. And I'm not even as scared." *So she was lying. Wasn't courage more courageous when you were scared?* "I'm no ground dweller, but I'm getting better at knitting. My new sweater is beautiful." She was shivering, wanting so badly to be clear, to be understood. "Here's what I want to know: One, what good is my leg hair? Two, what does Grandpa Joke need so much money for? And three, why does Granny look near death just because she went along with him on a doctor's house call?"

Rachel steadied herself, both hands on the strong wood of the beater. "Nancela," she said. "You went up to the door last night, and you weren't supposed to. What happened?"

Nancy swallowed. "There was a man—the man on the phone, I think. And a girl with wings."

"Excuse me?"

"You heard right." She held her mother's eyes with her own. "What else do you want to know?" Would Mama bargain? "Mama?"

"Don't shave," Rachel said. "That's all the information I'm giving you. It's better that way, and you've got to trust me."

"Because what I don't know can't hurt me?"

"Something like that."

"I'm going to Dad's tonight."

"Good," Rachel said. "He said that he wanted you tonight. But he's not going to tell you, either."

For a moment Nancy stayed there, studying her mother's green eyes. "Give, Mama," she said.

Rachel seemed to grow even more still and quiet than usual. "It's either there or it isn't, my darling. I can't just 'give' it, and you can't just take it."

"Give *what*? Take *what*?"

Nancy felt abandoned. She bolted upstairs, stood breathing on the landing until she was calm enough to enter Granny's kitchen. At the window upstairs she filled the birdfeeder and watched Rachel sitting at her loom, rubbing her forehead. Granny, in her wheelchair at the table, struggled to paint a pot, which was an interesting course of action, considering the sort of day she'd been having, or a testimony to Rachel's daughterly powers. She watched Nancy watching. "The trouble with you is, you don't know your own strengths."

Nancy turned from the window. "What strengths?" She felt that everyone was disappointed in her. And they wouldn't even tell her what was missing, so it wouldn't hurt her! Well, it *was* hurting her.

"Strengths. But you'd better start finding out. Time is getting short." Nancy banged the window shut, making the birds fly away.

"Everyone around here talks in riddles," she said.

"That's *your* problem," said Granny.

16

Nancy woke in her hammock at Ned's, and saw, on the window before her nose, a spider. She closed her eyes to shut it out, and opened them a few minutes later. It was gone.

What had awakened her was a door closing. Was Dad here? There was a note tucked into the webbing of the hammock beside her head: GONE TO MAMA'S.

Mama's? Without her? Had she seemed so sound asleep that he hadn't wanted to wake her? In that instant she spotted her father, crossing the rooftops. He was already a few buildings away and heading off at a steady trot, running the roofs as if they were an obstacle course, dodging chimneys and water tanks, antennas, and skylights.

She thought back on all the times Ned had come home over the rooftops. It had never occurred to her to go with him before. When he was with her, he traveled on the ground. Now she leaped out of the hammock, hitting the floor with a bang. She felt freaky, as Annette would say. *Breathe deep, Nancy,* she told herself. *Go after him!* Nancy knotted the laces of her shoes together and slung them around her neck as she crossed Ned's rooftop.

And then she was doing it. There was only one way to get from Ned's roof to the next: *Jump.* There was no gap to fall into, just the different roof levels to account for, and the walls to cross. *Jump.* So what if she'd never done such a thing before. So what if going *down* the walls scared the snot out of her. If only she had silk.

She didn't. She tried to put thoughts out of her head and just blast along.

I can do this. (Maybe.)

Climb the wall. (Just like the other time.)

Don't think twice. (Yeah, right.)

Leap for it. (Only as far as absolutely necessary.)

the thread

Land on all fours on the next roof. (Ow. No, actually it didn't hurt. Why doesn't it hurt?)

Jump up and run.

She kept Ned in sight, his tails of hair bobbing and springing. It wasn't that light out yet, but a gold edge to the sky showed her the way. How had it gotten to be morning so fast? She hated to lose him, but couldn't thud too heavily with her feet, tried to sound like nothing more than a squirrel or a pigeon on the roof. This would have been harder with her Docs on. Her feet were already sore and scraped.

Over the rim of a roof came the sun, shining on brave Nancy, leaping roof to roof. *It's easy, really, not the biggest jump I'll ever have to make, just across, not down. If it's so easy, why can't I catch him?*

Yes, Ned was faster, so much faster, inhumanly fast and as practiced at it as Anansi the shape-shifting spider himself. Through a network of rooftops, he led her, and the gap continually grew between them until he was nothing but a black dot with legs, scampering in and out of view. She leaped up onto a wall to glimpse him again and reeled backward, sick and spinning. There was no other roof to leap to, only the street far below and, across it, a tall white church, then the high train trestle that took the trains across Fourth Avenue and the bridge over the Gowanus Canal.

No time to sit gagging, her head whirling. *Stand up and find him.* But he was gone, her Arach-Ned. And she was there alone on the top of some strange yellow-colored building, with a lady coming out the door with her washing and looking aghast to see her there.

The lady probably believed she was about to be attacked. Behind her, Nancy saw Ned reappear atop the train trestle, across the gap, a small dark model of himself. How? How how how *how*?

"You get the hell off this roof!" the lady yelled.

Nancy skimmed over the wall to the fire escape. *Oh, horror!*

"Stupid kids! I'm going to call the cops if I catch you up here again!"

Don't think about it. Keep moving. She was going down down down now, and she couldn't help the way her feet felt stuck in tar, not fast enough, like in a dream.

Inch by inch, sweating, stuck, she forced herself. At last she dangled from her fingertips and dropped, landing hard, not light and airy like her dad. Nancy cleaned her palms on her hips and examined them closely. Nothing there but dirt. She still wasn't a drop-and-dragger and perhaps never would be. If Ned had taken her with him, she would only have dragged him down.

It was even slower going, down in the street. Nancy didn't much like the area around the canal. It wasn't so nice, although people said it was "up and coming." It was grayer, with not as many trees as other parts of Brooklyn, and it smelled of garbage and dirty water. Nancy was scared. She tried not to run, tried not to call attention to herself, to blend in. So much for the garish, bright spider.

Soon enough she climbed the hill up from the canal and was among houses again. She found herself walking under trees with the lower ten feet of their trunks covered in ivy; they made her think of poodles' legs (really large poodles) or satyrs, those half men–half goats from the Greek myths she'd read in freshman English. She laced her fingers in the ivy as she passed, skimming the papery, cool leaves with her fingertips and thinking she'd like to crawl inside them.

Nancy didn't blame Ned for keeping to the roofs. He

beat her easily to Rachel's. What did he need to go so fast for anyway?

She let herself quietly into the basement apartment. Mama was still sleeping and Dad wasn't there. She had had a quiet hope that sleeping with Mama was his reason for leaving Nancy in the penthouse so early in the morning. She stepped back out again. She could smell Dad's almondy smell in the old, gold-wallpapered hallway.

She climbed the stairs to Granny and Grandpa's apartment but stopped short of knocking. Nancy knew where to find her grandfather, this early on a Sunday morning. Some people were already in the community garden working, laying out sticks and strings for seed rows, weeding out what was already growing. Sure enough, Grandpa Joke was in his little plot, putting metal rings around the tomato plants to support them as they grew.

"What's going on, Grandpa?" she asked, hands on her hips.

"Child! What are you doing here so early in the morning?" He looked at his wristwatch, hung over a fence post.

Nancy snagged the watch on her finger. "You're going to lose this," she said. "Where's Dad?"

"Who? Here, Nancy, steady this plant for me." His large hands moved the dirt around like shovels. The tomato leaves were soft fronds of the warmest green color. They practically had bubbles of life coming off them, they were so healthy. Nancy squatted down in the dirt and lifted the leaves of a tomato plant, felt the gentle bristles of its thick stem.

"Another early riser!" Ned was at the fence, his dark eyes glinting at her in a mood she couldn't identify, an old wooden ladder in one hand and a saw in the other. The ladder was one that had been stored in Rachel's garden shed for years.

"What are you doing with that?" Nancy asked. "What is this, gardening day? Is Mama out gardening, too?"

Ned put up his hand like a shield, as though she were blowing wind on him.

"Mama's still asleep," he said. "What are you doing here at the crack of dawn tying tomatoes?"

"Getting a lesson, what else?" said Grandpa.

"In what, gardening?"

"Or how to get here safely at the crack of dawn?" Grandpa's voice sounded accusing.

"Looks like she got that figured out," Ned said.

"Not exactly," Nancy said, glaring.

"I'm going to saw this in half, Joke. That's what you want, isn't it?" Ned asked. "Nancy, come lend a hand." Nancy grabbed the ladder. Ned started to saw it in half. The ladder shook so that Nancy had to put all her weight on it to keep it from shuddering out from under Ned's saw. He paused, bent close to her ear. "Don't look now. There's a boy on the corner acting like he's got business being here staring at you. Here, don't look! Hold the ladder!"

Grandpa leaned over the fence. "We're going to stand this up at each end of the garden, Nancy," he said. "Then we're going to string from one ladder to the next, make a support for our peas and beans."

Nancy kept her eyes on the ladder. The saw bit into the worn old wood, Ned's dreadlocks hung down, sawdust drifted onto the sidewalk.

"Can you think what it's going to look like, Nancy?"

"Nope." *What do I care, Dad?*

"Wait and see!" Why was he trying to distract her?

Half the ladder dropped out of her hand and clattered to the sidewalk. She shot a look at the corner. Dion!

Ned heard her intake of breath. "It's not the first time, is it?" he asked, low.

She shook her head, glanced at Grandpa Joke, who was merrily planting his half of the ladder in the dirt, oblivious. With a spool of brown string, he connected the halves of the ladder. The string slumped between them. He tied another string to the fence, to the ladder top, let it drop with the other string, then brought it up to the other ladder and across to the other fence.

"Is it the bridge?" Nancy asked.

"What bridge?" Ned demanded.

"Our bridge. The Brooklyn Bridge."

"The spiderweb bridge," said Ned.

"Listen to this!" Grandpa Joke put a finger in the air, made a little speech with the ball of string in his other hand, in a position like the Statue of Liberty. Nancy prayed Dion was too far away to hear. "A quote. From a scientist. 'It is a rare person—' "

"What is, a spider?" Ned asked.

Nancy thought: *I have no spiderness. I am not a rare person.* She glanced toward the corner. In this golden light, Dion's clothes looked gray, almost pale brown. He was wearing his old Mets cap, sloppy on his head, and paced on the corner as though he were waiting for a bus. He moved like a marionette, his joints too loose, bouncing up off the balls of his feet as if gravity affected him only minimally.

"No. A person. 'Listen: It is a rare person who does not feel at least a bit uncomfortable in the presence of a large, dark, hairy spider darting across the floor.' " Nancy bent over, giggling, a bundle of jangling nerves. She felt as though she were connected by invisible wires to each of the people around her—her dad, her grandfather, Mama and Granny in the house, and Dion on the corner—and as though each of those wires were vibrating with some different and separate anticipation or warning. A change was coming, advancing toward her.

When Nancy looked up again at last, Dion wasn't there.

"No more fly on the wall," Ned said.

Grandpa Joke asked, "What fly?"

Ned answered, "Never mind."

Grandpa said, "Ask your granny about flies on the wall."

"Huh?"

"Ask."

"Dad," Nancy said, "what would you do if you wanted to know all about someone?"

The question flustered Ned. "Well, what would *you* do, Nancy?"

"Follow him," she said fiercely, yanking a knot.

"Follow whom?" asked Grandpa Joke.

"Me," said Ned, his hand on Grandpa Joke's shoulder. Nancy didn't bother correcting him. *Let them think what they want.* Besides, it was true that morning.

But this answer made Grandpa Joke afraid. "Oh, Nancy," he said, leaning heavily on the bridge, which, surprisingly, took his weight. "Go slow."

2. The Knot

Our souls sit close and silently within,
And their own webs from their own entrails spin;
And when eyes meet far off, our sense is such
That, spider-like, we feel the tenderest touch.

—John Dryden, *Marriage à la Mode*

Dion, it seemed, was everywhere now. Not just on top of the geodesic dome, but drawn down off it. By her? Not just outside the subway station, but inside on the platform. Far away at first, then nearer, then in the same subway car, then getting off at the same place Nancy did for school. Not just on the street corner, but following her down the street, loping along as if he were stepping on springs.

It felt a little scary. It felt a little pleasant.

Nancy would have walked the whole way to school if it hadn't been raining that Monday morning, and he might not have found her at all.

She noticed him as she stopped to put up her umbrella, then he disappeared among all of the umbrellas bobbing along the sidewalk of Atlantic Avenue. Nancy glanced back once, and saw his face getting wet under the too-narrow brim of his hat. Of course he didn't have an umbrella.

Last night, over a dessert of Ned's coconut pie, Grandpa Joke had said, "Tina? Tell Nancy about the fly on the wall."

"Fly on the wall? What fly?"

"You know." He smiled at her, encouraging.

"Ask me again later," Granny said, "When I'm not feeling so doo-lally."

"The poor little fly on the wall?" Rachel suggested, wanting to help her old mother.

Then Granny Tina said in her slow-motion way,

> "Poor little fly on the wall.
> Ain't got no clothes on at all.
> Ain't got no petti-skirt,
> Ain't got no shimmy-shirt.
> Poor little fly on the wall."

Nancy thought it was cute, but now, walking along with Dion getting wet behind her, she felt differently. *Poor Dion, in his blue-gray clothes, making me nervous back there. What does he want?* Calmly she folded her umbrella and dived ahead, ducking under and around people.

She skidded around the corner of Hicks Street to Joralemon, darted into the little grocery, stood there breathing deeply, looking into the drink case, and chose V8 juice, lured by its warm redness on this gray day. She stopped under the awning outside to poke a straw into the bottle, and Dion appeared beside her, pulling a big bottle of Welch's out of the crook of his arm. No bag. Had he stolen the juice, straw and all? Horrible thought: *Does he have any money? What's he living on? Rainwater?*

"Going to school?" he asked, blue eyes staring.

She sipped her V8, narrowed her eyes at him. Other kids were walking along toward the old brick building around the corner. She turned a shoulder to shut out her view of Shamiqua passing. She didn't answer Dion. *See what he does,* she told her chilly-calm self. *And stop thinking his name!*

He walked along beside her. *It's my hair,* she thought, *in its usual rat's-nest condition, that's got his attention.* But then Dion plucked the end of a strand of wool from the flap of Nancy's backpack and pulled it, so it looked like she was working a spinneret.

"Watch it, Dennis!" She stopped walking. "You'll unravel my work."

"It's not Dennis," he said. "It's Dion." He stared at the wool as if trying to identify the animal it came from.

"Oh yeah, right," she said carelessly, pretending.

"Dionysus," he said. "I'm Greek. And Navajo."

She thought, *I could love him.* She felt raw around the edges, unfinished and uneven. She liked the feeling. "Are you homeless?" she heard herself ask him.

"What if I was?" He straightened. His voice held warning, and patience.

"Then—"

Then, a shelter? Or city services? At school, the guidance office? Or, if he was hungry, should she bring him food? Maybe he *was* safer not going home. Who knew what his home was like? Who was she to say, home good, dome bad?

"It's just a word," she said.

Shamiqua tore past, going into the store with a homeroom buddy, making big eyes at Nancy. Nancy turned aside, blocking out the view of Shamiqua, who raised her pointed nose and went on.

Nancy blew out her breath at Dion. "Why are you always hanging around me so weird anyway?" She grabbed for the yarn, trying to get it away from him without pulling it. She pictured stitches sliding away from her wooden needles, the pretty ones Granny Tina had given her just last night, with strawberries painted on the knobs. She should have packed it more carefully. Now she'd have to fix it in homeroom, and the nosy girls would want to know what she was doing, or worse, they'd just stare. Nobody else knitted in high school. Worse, they'd want to know who that boy was who Shamiqua saw her with. Nobody. *Nobody!* she'd say.

Dion took Nancy's free hand and wound the yarn onto her pointer finger. *This looks idiotic,* Nancy thought, *a string coming out of my backpack and ending in a spiral around my finger.* Her school was around the corner. People walking by were mostly going there. It didn't take Dion two seconds to put the string on her finger, but it felt like a space opened around them. She felt the eyes looking. *"Who was that boy, Nancy?"*

When Dion saw her watching the faces, he made a little snorting sound. He said, "I don't go."

I don't go. Where? He turned the corner quickly and was gone, as she stood there calculating how long it was before school started and how many people had seen her.

She ran after him. *How could I act like my sweater was more important?* He was gone.

Dion didn't want anybody feeling sorry for him. He had a deep fear of feelings in these times. When a feeling got too close, too personal, he jumped. Off the dome? Off the rail? Off the deep end?

No, just away. Of all the people in New York that his father could have trailed, why had he chosen Nancy's grandfather? Dion knew why. What mattered to Niko was strength. It was what he had that his parents hadn't had—beaten-down immigrants who couldn't adjust to the need to blend in. Like many a social climber, he had married Rose Browning as much for her bloodlines as her beautiful Navajo eyes.

Now Niko wanted help for his Rose, and he didn't care what he had to do to get it. Help was help, and if Nancy's family had a way of helping—or two ways, or three—then Niko wasn't going to wait for them to reach a hand out. Time was much too pressing, and, like most reporters, Niko worked best under pressure.

That didn't mean it was best for Nancy.

Ned had been unpacking again. He concerned Nancy sometimes, the way he kept things, such as all of the newspapers and *The New Yorker* cover from when the World Trade towers came down, the towers in blackest black over a black-gray sky. Nancy touched the papers to see if they were those old ones. No. This one was much more recent. DOES BROOKLYN HAVE AN ANGEL?

She skimmed the article, the usual story about someone doing bad deeds who got clonked on the head by a something falling from above—in this case, a screwdriver. Right here on the bed Dad had plenty of articles about the Angel, a dozen of them, all covering events that happened last year, mainly in Brooklyn, but some also in Manhattan.

The stories were all by different reporters, all with the initials N.P.: Nick Pappas, Nestor Paprika, even a byline that had to be a pen name, Nobody in Particular. That was the *Post,* so goofy.

The hammock was still strung with yarn, the balls of wool motionless on the floor underneath. Nancy experimented with Ned's rigging, hoisted the hammock up as high as she could get it, and discovered how it felt to climb up there and slip into the sling.

Nancy settled into the lovely feeling of being alone when you know someone will be home soon. The rooftops were the colors that boy Dion was: a wash of pale blues and grays and Brooklyn brick, russet, rose, and brown. The sky looked blue and warm and made her sleepy and comfortable. From so high, she could see it all—Dad's tiny tomato and marigold plants in the garden patch, the peonies he was trying to start, some roses that were nothing but thorn sticks. For a vague moment just before she fell asleep, she imagined Dion crossing the roofs, his shirts and jacket flapping like wings.

Afterward she thought she should have known. On Tuesday Nancy called *The New York Times* from the pay phone in the front hall at school and asked for Nick Pappas. They gave her another phone number. She braced herself for a voice barking "Pappas," like in movies about newsrooms, but instead heard a quiet "Hello." This made three: the speaker phone, the dark doorway, and now the phone at her ear. It was him all right. Niko Papadopolis, and Nick Pappas, and probably the other N.P.s as well.

"Oh," she said, flustered, then said the words she'd rehearsed. "I'm doing a report on criminal investigation for school. I saw your byline on a crime article in the *Times*—"

"Your name?"

She said the first name of the first girl she spotted down the hall and the last name of the second. "Jessica. Hyde."

"And what is it you want to know, Miss Hyde?"

"How you get your stories."

He laughed, a huffing sort of sarcastic chuckle. She felt embarrassed, patronized. The way some people talked to kids . . .

"I mean, where does the information come from? The police records?"

"Yes," he said in a way that could have meant yes or could have meant not exactly. "And from other sources."

"What other sources?"

"Uh, Miss Hyde, I'm not sure this is—"

"Like people on the street?"

He paused. "At times."

Was that all he was going to say? "Well, how do the *police* find out a crime is happening?"

"Miss—"

"I mean, everyone can't dial nine-one-one, can they?"

His voice grew stern. "Surely you realize that a journalist reporting a crime is working after the fact."

"What I want to know is, who tells the police?"

"Whoever happens to be in the vicinity to witness a crime in progress," he said. "Now, if there's anything else you need to know, may I suggest you call—"

Before he could brush her off and never take a call from her again, she said, "Just one other thing."

"Yes?"

"As a reporter, say you want to know all about someone, what do you do?"

He cleared his throat. She guessed this was more

the kind of question he expected from a student. "Start with the basics," he said. "Who, what, where, when, and why. Who he is, what he's done, where he works . . . Just keep asking questions. It'll lead to the truth."

"Thank you," Nancy said, hung up the phone, and went to math class. She already knew the where, she realized. She even partly knew the why. But who . . . *Start with the basics.*

18

That afternoon Nancy made three cups of tea. She made the first cup, the sky blue one with the big brown cat on it, in the basement kitchen, then took it to Rachel where she sat weaving in the green-house.

"Hot tea," she announced. "Here's a sandwich, too. Mama—"

Rachel was at the loom, still in her nightgown, clogs in the corner, morning tea cold and congealed in a cup on the floor. She had that look on her face that Nancy hated, that I'm Creating So Don't Get in the Way look. "Angel," she said softly to her daughter.

157

It startled Nancy off-course. Instead of what she was going to say, she asked, "What does it mean, Mama, all your weaving?"

Rachel ran her hand over Nancy's curls, then the same hand coasted over the weaving held tight across the beater. "It's how I make sense of the world," Rachel said. "The pattern."

"It's not only weaving that makes patterns," Nancy said. "It's webs! They're everywhere at school. Longitude and latitude, trigonometry, music staffs. Even the notes look like spiders. The greenhouse,"— she pointed to the spines of metal that formed its frame, like the structure of Dad's penthouse—"the playground dome by the subway. And this kid on top of it who uses it for *his* web."

"Uses the dome?"

She dared to tell. "Yes. The one by the subway. The one made out of triangles."

"Is he trying to catch someone?" Rachel asked, trying to follow this curious line of thinking.

It was clear that what Rachel said was so.

Rachel thought Nancy's silence meant she didn't understand the question. "Trap you," she explained.

" 'Step into my parlor,' said the spider to the fly."

"No! *I'm* the spider." Dion was the fly, wasn't he?

Rachel curled up on the loom bench, rubbing her arms and looking up at Nancy. "It's catch or be caught, baby girl. Chase or be chased. It's what Granny would tell you to do."

"Granny!"

"Let him think he's caught you, but really—"

"Catch him," said Nancy.

Her mama nodded, her eyes clear as the greenhouse glass.

"Mama?"

Rachel's shoulders dropped a little. "What?" She may as well have said, *What now?*

"Why'd Granny come to New York?"

"She was drawn here," Rachel said quickly. "Life in West Virginia wasn't so much for an—" She hesitated. "A creative girl."

"Like New York was a magnet?" *A magnet for weirdos of any kind.* Spiders were just one kind.

Rachel smiled. "You mean it was a test of her mettle."

Nancy groaned. "Her metal?"

"Mettle. What's inside her."

Nancy got the pun, but pondered the meaning.

"Pay attention to what draws you, Nancy."

"Mama," Nancy asked after a long moment, "if I were in danger, would you be able to go out to help me?"

"Are you in danger?" Rachel asked sharply.

Nancy hunched one shoulder up to her ear and shook her head against it. "What if Dad was?" She didn't meet Rachel's eyes.

Rachel caught her breath. "Is he?" she asked.

Nancy didn't reassure her, only stood up and climbed the steps to the other apartment.

Nancy made the second cup of tea in the upstairs kitchen. She used the black cup and saucer, and put a little shot of amaretto in it, the way Grandpa Joke liked it. He hunched over the steaming, almond-fragrant cup, studying the tea and a swirl of cream the color of the grape vines at the edge of his garden.

"You okay, Grandpa?"

"Nancy." Grandpa Joke took her hand and pulled her to him, hugged her with his arm around her waist, his brown eyes on hers. "We've got another house call tonight."

"Same place?" she asked. Her stomach felt like little holes had been punched out of it.

He nodded. "I'll need you," he said.

There was almost a pattern to the way her family was letting her in on or leaving her out of information, each in his or her own way deciding whether or not it was time. Nancy thought it was. Maybe Grandpa Joke—the other not-very-spidery one among them—thought so, too.

"Honey, show Granny Tina your knitting. Take her mind off."

"Take her mind off *what*? Your patient? Or is it hers?"

He rubbed his face with his hands and waved her away.

Granny Tina had made the mug that Nancy brought her. She had thrown it round on her wheel, baked the clay, glazed it dark red, and fired the glaze to make it shine. It was beautiful, and, like all of her pottery, phenomenally strong.

Nancy flipped the tea bag into the sink, added honey. With one foot she pushed her backpack full of knitting along the polished floor ahead of her, into Granny's room.

As soon as Granny Tina saw Nancy, she snapped her reading light off, her deep dark eyes bright with expectation.

"Show me what you're doing, then," she said. "Still the pattern that isn't?" She took a sip of tea and leaned back against her pillows to watch Nancy knit. Two more inches of the front piece, and in came Grandpa Joke.

"Tina?" he said softly, his hand on her shoulder. Nancy looked up to see Granny asleep, her tea mug empty. She must have stayed awake long enough to drink it.

"Grandpa?" Nancy asked. "Granny is—" She leaned forward and caught Grandpa Joke's eye, made a shaky-hand gesture to show him she thought her granny was not quite all right. "How's the patient?" Nancy went on, hoping to catch Grandpa unaware.

He searched her eyes. He didn't say it was his patient, not Granny's. Well, that was something she knew that Dion didn't. "She's going to die," he said.

Nancy asked, "Of what?" She was shocked to have gotten a real answer.

"Failure to heal."

And another! She hadn't heard of this before. She

thought back to that first phone call. "But I thought she was a heart patient."

"Heart? Your granny doesn't treat heart patients."

"Because she is one herself?"

"No, because—"

"Anyway, why can't you make the patient better?" Nancy pressed on daringly. "What are you doing at that house?"

"The self-inflicted wounds are the most difficult to heal," said Grandpa Joke. "It's impossible if the patient herself doesn't want to get better."

He took the blood-red mug and went out. Nancy stuffed her yarn and needles into her bag. As she stood to leave, Granny opened one eye. "It's not impossible," she said.

"What?"

"Well, don't expect him to tell you *everything*."

"Grandpa?"

Granny nodded slowly, then said, "Do you know how I knew I was in love with him?"

Nancy shrugged one shoulder. She wanted to go out, and no, this was *not* the story she wanted to hear right now. Look what had happened after the last story—

how she'd lost her mind and gone up to that door, met the reporter's little girl, and met the man himself. Well, she'd met his voice at least, and now they were going again tonight. She hadn't changed anything last time. Granny had still come home older, weaker, sapped.

"I've got homework," Nancy said firmly. "*Hard* homework."

"Do you think this is going to be easy?" Granny asked.

"I don't have time for a story," Nancy said. "I have to—"

"You sit here," said Granny. "And take in what I have to say."

"I—"

"Nancy," said Granny. She rolled her fists together and trumpeted through them. "Now hear this!"

"Why?" Nancy gripped the arms of the chair. No, she didn't want to hear any story about anything or anybody! Granny didn't make it better by being funny.

"He was tall, so tall his legs poked out the gap between his socks and his trousers. Have you ever seen his legs?"

Nancy nodded. Well, of course she'd seen his legs. He was her grandfather, wasn't he? Then again, had she? Granny threw back her head and laughed. Nancy tucked her foot under her to keep it from getting going of its own accord.

"They're pale as ghosts, as if they're scared of daylight. And the longest, finest black hair. And he was so pigeon-toed, even then. Oh, you should have seen him!"

Nancy would have liked to see him now, would have liked to hear him tell her she was wearing out her grandmother, instead of the other way around. And yet she thought she could see him, the way Granny described him. Or had she seen some old picture somewhere? He was as vivid and young before her eyes, in all his pigeon-toed glory, as bristly as Dion on his dome.

"The first time I ever saw him, oh my. He was chasing the bus. His glasses were so heavy they banged on the bridge of his nose, and he ran so comically, his big feet flapping. Fast, though, honey. He caught that bus."

What if he hadn't? Then the pattern would have been broken.

"After that I saw him in the OR," Granny said.

"In surgery?" Nancy asked.

"We all had masks on then, of course. And his hands! Well, they were large and strong and graceful. His stitches were works of art. All his patients healed so quickly."

"Why did they heal so quickly?"

"He was a good doctor!" Granny retorted immediately. She stared for a moment, then chuckled. "Oh, you know. Especially once I noticed him." Her voice had gone woozy again.

Granny leaned back against the pillows and closed her eyes. "Thought you had some place to go."

Nancy stood up. Granny didn't stop her this time. It was fallen-Catholic Grandpa Joke who had told her what *amen* literally meant. She said it now as she fled: "So be it!" She banged the door behind her.

19

Shamiqua was at Annette's, and as soon as Nancy heard her voice, she wished she hadn't come. But, "Come in, lovey," Annette's mother was saying, pushing the door wide and calling for Annette, and in the next instant Annette and Shamiqua came barreling in, shoving each other against the doorway and welcoming Nancy way too enthusiastically.

Jealous! The evidence that Shamiqua was, in so many ways, what Annette had wanted Nancy to be lately, was all over Annette's room: essentially, the room looked like they'd bought stock in Cosmetics

Plus and were setting up shop right here. Nails, hair, eyes: all had been done.

The fact that Jimmy Velcro had really asked Annette to some dance, and of course Shamiqua was going with Buddy, had the two of them practically bouncing off the ceiling. Now they were looking at Nancy as though she were a blank canvas and they were inspired artists. Well, Nancy had wanted to get away from the house to someplace where she couldn't put anyone at risk, couldn't do anything to cause herself or family trouble. A makeover was innocent enough. Maybe.

"You've got such a pretty face," Shamiqua said generously. "Why don't you get your hair out of it?" Shamiqua's hair was done in perfect tiny braids, all pulled into a ponytail as if it were straight hair like Annette's.

"It's my trademark," said Nancy, who had read a few *Seventeen* magazines herself.

"Have you ever been in love?" Shamiqua asked Nancy, not expecting an answer, and she and Annette laughed hysterically at each other as though they'd been asking each other that question since school let out.

"No," said Nancy automatically.

"I saw you with that bald-headed boy."

"I can't stay long," Nancy said to Annette.

Shamiqua kept going. "I'm *so* glad to get a chance to talk to you without people around. I've been dying to ask you where—"

Where is your home planet?

Where you learned to knit?

"—you buy those gorgeous tights."

Annette went into a pretend coughing fit, since Nancy's tights were one of the big things they differed on.

Shamiqua looked intently at Nancy. "Well, a girl with thin legs . . . ," she began, then changed her tack. "You know, Annette, my grandma says we've all got something, and it's all about what you do with it."

Annette laughed a big "HA!" of a laugh and covered her mouth with her hand.

Nancy did have a few gorgeous pairs of tights—paisleys and florals and a rainbow pair—but these were just purple-and-black stripes, nothing miraculous. "Ricky's," she said.

"Oh, where's that?"

"There are a bunch of them. Mostly in Manhattan."

"Oh, *Manhattan*!" Shamiqua's face fell as though she never got across the East River.

"It's not that far," Nancy said.

"Yeah, but . . . Well, maybe . . . Do you think? Oh, this is so embarrassing!"

"What?" Annette seemed fascinated by how Nancy would respond.

Shamiqua put her hands on her slender hips and stuck out a leg. "You know how they don't let you try them in the stores? What if I spent the money and then they didn't fit?"

Nancy shrugged.

Shamiqua tried flattery. "You have such cute legs," she said. "Mine are . . . longer." That was true. Longer and perfect, and, Nancy saw, perfectly smooth. If she could tell that on Shamiqua's dark skin, how much more evident would the black hair be on her own medium-brown legs?

"Well, do you think I could try them on?"

Nancy saw no gracious way out of it. She took off her shoes—"My feet probably smell," she said—and shimmied out of her tights. Then she bounded into one of Annette's bedroom chairs feet first, curling her hairy legs beneath her. Did she look as alarmed as she felt?

"You know, cornstarch helps with foot odor," Annette said.

Nancy stuck her tongue out at Annette behind Shamiqua's back, and said, "It's all about what you *do* with it." Annette looked shocked and glanced at Shamiqua, who showed no sign that she'd heard, and was taking the tights from Nancy with a smug smile.

Nancy had an idea that Annette had possibly mentioned her unwillingness to shave to Shamiqua. *It's not that I'm unwilling,* she caught herself thinking. *But Mama would have my head.* She just knew Shamiqua would have a clever answer for that, too, but she kept it to herself. She could almost feel the hair on her legs sticking out. *That's ridiculous,* she scolded herself. But it was still true.

She watched Shamiqua to see if she was looking at her legs, but Shamiqua was trying on the tights, which of course stretched to fit.

"These are adorable. Do you think I could carry them off?"

Nancy wished she could just tell Shamiqua to keep the tights, to leave them on, to go home now, to get out! But Shamiqua had been invited to stay for dinner. Mrs.

Li said Nancy could stay, too, but all Nancy wanted was to yank her tights back onto her own furry-feeling legs and get on out of there.

In the street again in her tights and shoes, hot and embarrassed and fed up beyond her limits with her family and their weirdness, she conjured up Dion in her mind, imagining him around every corner. But he did not appear.

20

Grandpa wouldn't let Nancy help Granny Tina to the door. He didn't get the wheelchair out of the trunk. He had Granny walk with her canes across the street, over the sidewalk, up the steps to the door, slow and steady.

The door opened, letting out a beam of light as someone let Nancy's grandparents in. The door closed, then opened again a few inches. A boy came out, slipping a slouchy baseball cap over his head, and descended the steps. He skimmed the sidewalk, quick and quiet. Nancy would have sat upright if she'd dared. The pale blueness of the light on his shoulders reminded her of Dion. If it were any brighter she could have seen his face. If it were any brighter, he could have seen hers. He seemed to try, peering out toward the parked cars shaded by the trees, and bouncing as he walked.

She leaned forward to watch the dim figure of the boy walk along the street, look back once, then head for the corner. He walked directly under the streetlight, which shadowed his face even more under the brim of the hat. If it *were* Dion, and why should it have been, other than that it looked like him, what was he doing here?

Nancy kept her eyes and ears open. She got the car door open, too, stepped out, closed it enough to douse the car's dome light, but not enough to make a noise. The boy was at the corner now, and he didn't notice when Nancy got out of the car.

She dashed after him, but when she got to the corner he had disappeared. A little grocery store glowed like a jewelry box, the colors of the fruit and flowers gleaming out. *I'll make it look like I'm on some errand.* She stopped at the window, peered inside. She'd step in just long enough to buy a V8 juice—

There was an odd squeaking sound overhead. Nancy backed up quickly. It sounded as if maybe the store's security gate was dropping down in front of the entrance. But it wasn't. An alley ran between the grocery and the row of buildings where Grandpa and Granny were. Nancy peered in from the sidewalk, giving the dark alley a wide berth the way Granny Tina had taught her. It was nothing but a regular Brooklyn alley, the back gate to the courtyard, the garbage cans and clotheslines, clotheslines that stretched right up to the roof, and a fire escape that, because it went down the back of the building, not the front, reached near enough to the ground for her to jump up and grab it.

Nancy was drawn up the fire escape as though pulled by a magnet, the test of her mettle, or metal, with no time to think about fear. Fear! *If that had really been Dion coming out of the house . . .*

She made herself imagine she was just on the fire escape outside Dad's nest. At the top, she reminded herself, was the sky. She crept up slowly, moving precisely, until she was high enough to see over the curtains into the room. Inside she saw her grandmother's hands, smoothing a coverlet of soft gray silk around a small, dark woman. She saw pink roses near the bed, and a hand that held—what was it? Something orange.

A child-sized basketball? How odd.

The lights were dim, the woman's mouth was closed, Granny Tina was talking softly. Nancy could tell by the way her mouth was moving. Her heart went out to her grandmother, so old and sick, yet so tender and intense.

From above, there was the screech of metal on metal, and Nancy practically fell off the fire escape. It was hard to believe Granny didn't look up, that everyone inside the apartment didn't come running to the windows. And then Nancy wanted to kick herself for being so jumpy. The racket was only a clothesline pulley squeaking as someone brought in the washing. Just in time, too, because it was starting to rain.

"What do you see up there?"

Dion stood below her in the garden, staring up at the fire escape. There was no way to hide what she was doing. She didn't dare call down an answer.

"Come down here!" His voice was quiet as wind, and as light.

She pointed a finger toward the window, which lit her for Dion to see, and raised the other hand, as if to ask, "Who's that?"

He waved her down. She crept down the iron steps. He gave her his hand at the bottom. "Is that your grandmother?" he whispered.

She nodded. "Is that your mother?"

He looked away. It was.

Did he know what her grandmother was doing? Did he know—what Grandpa had said—that his mother might die? Into her mind came Granny's words: *Did you know how I knew I was in love with him?*

"What's the matter?" she asked, to find out what he knew.

No answer supplied. A drop of water hit her cheek. Another hit Dion's forehead. His eyes were shadowed, but the water glimmered just above where his eyebrow should have been.

"Were you in there?"

He shook his head. "On the roof."

"Why?"

Suddenly his face lit with alarm. "Don't let him see you!"

She flattened herself against the wall in the dark, and watched from the corner of her eye as a dark curly-haired man came to the window and lowered the blinds.

"Is that your father?" she whispered.

In answer he climbed, springing rapidly step over step to the roof, and she was cursed if she was going to let him see her fear. *It's easier going up,* she reminded herself, and followed.

The fire escape passed more windows, but the one that caught Nancy's imagination was a room with a loft bed surrounded by posters; in the darkness up there she could see faces, but could not tell whose they were. Beneath it, a child's bed stood, lit by a Lava lamp on the bedside table. In the glow of the Lava lamp, she saw a pair of red wings hung over the bedpost. Mina's room—and Dion's?

Rain was falling for real now, and thunder came on the wind. The metal steps felt wet and grimy. Her shoes slipped and slid. One flight up Nancy heard the heaviness of a street door closing. The visit must be finished. The hair on the back of her neck prickled and the insides of her knees broke out in a sweat. She tried tiptoeing and ended up skidding, skinning her knees and the outsides of her wrists, falling backward as fast as she could down the fire escape to the ground. She made a break for the street.

Then came that sound again, from above: the

clothesline squeaking. What was Dion doing up there, bringing his laundry in from the rain? Why was he hiding from his own father? She pulled open the car door she had left unlatched and climbed inside, sat panting, watching her grandparents advance toward her.

21

Granny returned home exhausted practically to the point of falling into a faint. Rachel came dashing to the door to help get her upstairs, then stayed to rub her back and make her tea and fuss over her.

Nancy had to get out. When she pulled Grandpa aside to tell him where she was going, he was too distracted to protest much. "At this hour?"

"It's only nine, Grandpa. I'll be fine," she said firmly. Oh, how his eyes were tired and sad.

"Nine? It seems like midnight."

She went, poking the saint and saying "So be it," wondering what that meant tonight.

She walked along quickly toward the Carroll Street station, knowing Dion would not be on the dome. Little by little the swift events on the fire escape came back to her, just as the scrapes on her elbows and shins began to lightly sting. She licked her palms and rubbed them on her arms, letting the wetness draw the cool air to these hot spots. She rubbed at her knees, too, although she couldn't wet them through her tights and almost tripped, trying, just before speeding up to run for the train she knew was coming into the station.

Dion was not on the dome.

Ned sat at his table in a worn black T-shirt, the desk lamp lighting up the shots of silver in his long hair. Nancy let herself quietly into her father's nest and scooped a clipping off the stack on the table before Ned even noticed she was there. The top one was by Nick Pappas; it was about a burglary that had happened in Canarsie two weeks ago. She knew this because Ned had neatly written in the date. He slid the clipping swiftly out of her hands and slipped it into a gray envelope.

"Why aren't you at Mama's?" he asked. "Isn't it her night?"

She studied his face. She thought he didn't like her reading that clipping. "I didn't feel like it," she answered starkly.

"Didn't feel like what?" He was his usual sweet self, not getting annoyed by anything. She knew she was acting annoying.

She shrugged, refusing to answer, or not knowing where to begin.

"How about a cup of tea?" he asked, stood up, and bustled over to the little stove.

She followed him, rubbing her hands, but when he had set the kettle on the burner and lit the gas, she finally said, "No, thank you, I don't want any."

"Oh! Okay! What, then?" He peered down at her, rattling his fingertips on the counter. It sounded the way she felt, as though her nerve endings were bumping into one another and fighting for space on the surface of her skin.

"Who do *you* think is the Angel of Brooklyn, Dad?" she asked, rubbing goosebumps from her arm.

He shrugged.

"You must have a theory, with all the stories you read."

He said nothing about the stories. "Let's go outside, little egg. It's such a beautiful night."

It was. No stars (there weren't ever many in New York anyway) but a soft mist was left over from the rain. Dewy droplets outlined the wall and penthouse and fire escape like those on the Brooklyn Bridge in the photograph over Dad's bed.

"Hey, Dad. Watch this!" She kicked off her shoes, peeled off her tights, climbed to the top of the wall and stood there, not holding on, her fingertips resting on the rim of the ladder. Her hair billowed up moist and bushy behind her, the only thing about her that moved.

This wall had nearly lost its power to terrify her. Nearly. With her feet bare and damp, she didn't feel worried about slipping. She could focus not on the distance to the ground behind her, but on the wall under her feet. She felt it all through her legs, so solid, reaching all the way down to the ground and into the earth. *I will not throw myself off, and I refuse to accidentally fall off, either.*

She stood there until Ned walked over steady and smooth and gave her his warm sticky hand to guide her down.

"What changed?" he asked. Nancy felt him check

the palms of her hands with his fingertips; she knew he would find they were dry. She stayed on the wall.

"Well, you know how I sort of feel where the subway is? It's like that."

"How so?"

She thought about it. "Well, when I'm coming into the house I think I can tell whether you're here or not."

"Really?"

She nodded. "Mama, too."

"How about Granny and Grandpa?"

"Maybe if I tried from Mama's house, I'd be able to figure out if they were there, too."

"How about now?"

"Now it's different, because I already know where they all are. You mean, could I tell from here?"

He nodded solemnly, his eyes alert.

"Maybe." And thought about Dion, and how often she'd run into him lately, and how he hadn't appeared that evening when she'd wished for him. "But the climbing is the big thing," she added. "I can go farther than ever. I've been practicing on my own."

"I know, I know," he said, hushing her. He looked up at the sky.

"You all don't need to think you have to teach me everything in the world. You could *tell* me things instead."

"What things?" Cautiously. Didn't he know? Didn't he know that she had followed him across the rooftops?

"What's up with Granny, for one thing. What you're clipping those papers for, for another. And—" Her knees were shuddering in the damp, betraying the fear she'd ignored all evening. A delayed reaction to the heights she'd scaled? Her real self coming seeping up from under the false bravery she'd been feeling? "Tell me about the clippings," she said.

"Nancy," Ned said. "You don't need to know."

Her knees, the wall, the drop . . . she was trembling. "I need *you* not to keep secrets."

She was throwing herself off-balance. Ned reached his hand toward hers, didn't touch.

"Did you ever think maybe I need help?" she asked, her feet wide apart on the wall, the wall cold beneath her.

"Help?" Ned's eyes were fearful.

"Information," she told him. "I don't know what I'm supposed to be—what I'm trying to—do." The strands came together inside her, and blanketed her once and for all in the knowledge that there *was* some sort of a task before her. A quest. A challenge. A struggle. "How hobbit-ish," Annette would say. But Nancy hardly felt heroic.

"I feel as doo-lally as Granny," she said. "And now every time Granny tells me one of her stories, things happen."

"What things?"

"I get—" Feelings. Janglings. "I find—"

"Trouble?"

Tears sprang to her eyes. "Yeah!"

He grasped her hand again then. "You'll figure it out," Ned said.

"I have to figure it out myself?"

He nodded, swallowed. "Like everybody else does."

"Not Annette. Not the kids in my school. Not—"

"It'll come," said Ned. "Or it won't. Maybe—"

Nancy waited. The city wavered behind her.

Ned shook his head.

"Maybe what?"

Another shake. "I'm afraid to go out on a limb here."

"Even for me?"

He nodded. She took her hand away.

" 'Cause either you *will* find out, or you *won't*. Does it help to know I have faith in you?"

She sat down abruptly on the wall to quiet the rising fear. Ned turned and backed up to her. She put her arms around his neck and let him carry her inside.

He let her in the bathroom first, then cozied her under her comforter in the hammock. She thought he was going off to take his turn in the bathroom, and she began to berate herself for not quizzing him harder. *I am just too tired*, she admitted to herself. What came to mind was *Gone with the Wind*, a book Annette's mother used to quote to the girls during a sleepover when they were up too late messing around and wouldn't knock it off, something about saving some trouble for tomorrow.

How to end this day? She wished she had *Gone with the Wind* to page through now, to help her settle down for the night. Ned came back from the bathroom and began rummaging through one of his boxes. More clippings? He came walking toward her, bringing a book held up on his fingers like a tray: *Charlotte's Web*.

"Oh, *brother*," she said. She knew it word for word and didn't even bother to open it, but rolled on her side and tucked it against her chest, and fell asleep.

22

Next morning Dion was on the roof—the roof outside Ned's nest, the way she'd pictured him that night—when Ned came loping along on his way to a job. What kind of job? Nancy wasn't sure anymore.

"Hey!" yodeled Dion.

His voice woke Nancy in her hammock. She leaped out so fast she almost killed herself, having raised the hammock so high. She caught herself from falling through the window, palms slapping on the windowsill so hard it hurt.

And then he was yelling her name. "Nancy! Nancy!"

Where's Dad, anyway? What's Dion doing here?

She staggered out onto the roof, and he landed on the wall before her. The Alta, Utah, shirt, purple in the early light, and his legs long and straight in those jeans. She pulled her cloud pajamas straight and wrapped her arms across her stomach. Had she drawn him to her?

"How long have you been here?" she asked.

"He's gone," said Dion. "He disappeared."

"Disappeared?" she said.

"Right," said Dion.

"He's just fast," she said, thinking about the morning she'd chased her father. "He's used to the rooftops. It's how he gets around. Do you have a problem with that?"

"He's just *gone*," Dion said, snapping his fingers.

"Is that what you've been trying to tell me?"

He nodded. "One of the things. Haven't you watched him? Haven't you seen him come and go?"

She was silent. Then, "You think he's the Angel of Brooklyn. Or is it your father who does?"

He nodded. He said, "No."

She gave him a funny look. "No? Or yes?"

"I think there ain't no angels in Brooklyn." He didn't respond to what she'd said about his father.

She said nothing, stared at the place her father had been.

"What do *you* think, Nancy?"

"My father doesn't know how to turn invisible, if that's what you think."

"*I've* seen him disappear before. Haven't you?"

Nancy felt the hair stand up on the back of her neck. *No.* Being somewhere else wasn't the same as disappearing. Other times he hadn't been where she expected him to be, had sort of twinkled away behind her, like that time she'd dropped Poochie in the subway. *I look one way for him, the way I think he went, but he's not there, so I look the other way, the way I don't think he went, and there he is.*

She couldn't let Dion know she was even considering this crazy disappearing theory. And *yet* . . .

"What do you do, follow him?"

"Yeah. Like I follow you."

"Why? I can't disappear."

He smiled at her, his eyes crinkling up around the blue. He said, "You know why I follow you. The same reason you keep finding me."

She couldn't help grinning, then sucked the grin

back in. She hadn't *just* realized that her Dad could disappear. She'd been pondering the phenomenon for some time now, more frequently since the morning she'd followed him to Mama's, and, face it, more since she'd become braver herself on the rooftops. And faster.

"You must be pretty fast on the roofs yourself," she said. She rubbed one foot over the other, to get the roof grit off.

"It runs in the family," he said.

"Oh? Greek? Navajo? Which part?"

"No part that disappears," he said. "And no part that heals."

"What are you saying, then? What part?"

"We jump," he said. "And I live on the roofs, like your kind of spider." He straightened, taking the stance he'd taken when she'd asked him if he was homeless that day.

She whispered, "Not my kind. I'm the African kind." *At least I hope I am.* She didn't mention Scottish. She didn't mention Italian. She figured everyone knew Anansi, and he was her most important ancestor anyway. By now, she knew there were a whole lot of different ways spiderness could show up in people. And there were ways it didn't show up. "Spiders don't *disappear*," she added.

"Your kind does," he said. "Don't you even know that?"

"Get off our roof," she told Dion in a quiet, dark voice. "Leave us some privacy."

He backed up fast against the wall, as if she'd pushed him.

"I'm right," he said.

She stared at him, seeing stubble where his eyebrows should have been. Were. "Didn't you hear me? Go!"

"Nancy," he said.

"Stalking around. Sneaking up on me. Stealing juice. Acting like you're—"

His chin went up, blue eyes on hers. "Acting like what?"

"Acting like the Angel of Brooklyn yourself, like I said before! Spying on everybody. I thought you ran away from your father, but it looks like you're helping him."

"You don't know one thing about it."

"*What* don't I know?" Plenty, but she wasn't going to show him that.

"How much they want those stories in the papers. The more my father finds, the better."

"For whom?"

"That's just the point, girl. They don't care if it's for real, if *he's* for real." He pointed a finger in the direction Ned had gone.

"Why?" she asked. She was genuinely curious.

He leaned on the precipice and studied the view. "Because it's cool," he said. "It's unreal, except it seems real. And the more real my dad makes it, the more it's a piece of journalism, the more they like it."

"What if it's *not* real?" asked Nancy. "What if he's lying?"

"What if he's not lying?" Was he warning her about his father or informing her about her father, or informing her about his father and warning her about her own?

"People can't disappear," she said.

"Some kinds of people can."

Nancy covered her face in a confusion that seemed like a whirlpool in the East River, silent and sucking. It could bring them all down. And then here was this beautiful-ugly boy at the heart of it all, and in spite of all her anger and whirlpooling conflict she wanted to chase him back to his rooftop lair—wherever that was—grab him by the ears and, well, who knew, after that.

"You have to go now," she said to him. She turned, went inside and locked the door. If only there were curtains—but there weren't. The daylight made it shadowy inside, though. She grabbed her clothes, locked herself into the bathroom, and when she was dressed for school she snatched up her backpack full of knitting and headed for the door. She did not look back, she did not scan the windows, she closed her ears and her eyes and the hair on the back of her neck to the possibility of Dion's presence. She closed the door and went down.

On the stairs, the tears released and streamed down her face. *No!* In the little lobby she dropped her backpack on the floor, dug out Kleenex, and blew.

She hoped she would never see him again. If his mother died, she hoped he'd go home and look after Mina. She didn't know anything about his father. What she could see, all she could see, was that the only reason Dion had been following her around was in hope of getting closer to the family he thought could help his mother. It wasn't her, after all, that had drawn him.

"Pay attention to what draws you," Rachel had said. *Nothing draws me,* thought Nancy. *Watch me pull away.*

23

"Pretty good," said Ned that evening. He was examining the sketch she'd left beside her hammock on the floor, her notebook open to the page. It was a sketch she'd drawn of Dion, from memory. *Catch him*, her mother had said. "Nancy, could you get ready to go out, please?"

"Listen, Dad. That guy who writes about the Angel of Brooklyn—"

"Who?" said Ned.

"I think he's got lots of names. Nestor Paprika, Nick Pappas . . ."

"What about him?" Quietly, almost to himself, he said, "That's all the same guy?"

"All the same. And Niko Papadopolis."

"Who's *he*?" Louder.

It made her tired and teary to think of telling him. She pointed her finger at the drawing of Dion. "His father."

"What?" Quieter.

"He thinks you're the Angel of Brooklyn."

Ned laughed, a big explosion. "It doesn't matter what anybody thinks." He rolled his eyes, chuckling, broke eye contact, turned away, big hands in the air, fingers splayed. "Come on, Nancy," he said breathlessly.

"Come on what?"

"Angels have wings," he said.

"So?"

He threw her black sweater at her. "Let's go."

"Where?" She didn't want to go anywhere. He was already at the door. He hadn't denied what she'd said. Did he realize the boy in the picture was the one who'd spied on her from the garden, who'd been on the dome that night?

"Granny is expecting us for dinner."

"I don't want any dinner," she said, all snarly. "I'm the complete opposite of hungry."

"You're coming, Nancy," said Ned, sounding tired and angry himself. It was an unusual attitude. What was this all about? Why did it matter so much to Ned to go over there? What if they went and Granny told her another story—and she got another crazy inspiration? What would happen *this* time?

She jumped out of the hammock so suddenly he almost fell over in surprise. "How are we getting there?" she asked. She would find out what her family wanted, and get what she wanted, too.

Ned cocked his head at her and swung the door. "I thought we'd take the subway," he said.

"Now? At rush hour?"

"Unless you have a better idea," he said, challenging her.

"How about the roofs?"

"You want to go all the way to Mama's on the roofs?"

"I never have before," she said.

"You're not going to now, either," he said. He held the door for her, and they went down the stairs the normal way, to the street.

Dion wasn't on the dome. Maybe he was home.

• • •

Grandpa Joke was acting all ceremonial, with a white towel around his waist and a white cloth on the table. There was a beautiful smell of garlic coming from the kitchen, and he ran back in there as soon as he greeted Ned and Nancy at the door. He wouldn't let them help with anything, just made them go sit down. Granny and Mama were in the kitchen as well.

"What's up?" asked Nancy.

Ned just shrugged. All the way over on the subway, he had hardly said anything. Now he seemed to come to some decision. Waiting at the table, he said quietly to Nancy, "You know, I've seen him."

"Dion?"

"Is that his name?"

Nancy nodded. Where before Dad had had a warning tone when he spoke of Dion, now he seemed suspiciously light and airy. "At first I didn't recognize him, down on the ground."

"Yeah, he's always on the dome by Carroll Street."

"That's not where I meant."

"Then where *have* you seen him?"

"I'm sure it's him. He has a distinctive way of moving."

"*Where?*"

"Across a few blocks of roofs."

Up high. She leaned closer. "What do you think about him?"

"He's light," Ned said. "Everything about him. He's quiet. He's smooth. He knows how to blend in. He's a good—"

"Wow, you *do* know him," Nancy interrupted.

Ned glanced at the kitchen door, nodded. "As much as you can know about anyone by just watching him."

Grandpa Joke entered bearing a bottle of wine and five glasses, all in his two big hands.

"Who's coming?" Nancy asked, counting the glasses.

"You are," Grandpa said. "Coming along. Ladies!" Rachel and Granny Tina came in from the kitchen. Everyone was looking at Nancy expectantly.

Grandpa Joke poured a little wine in each glass. "On your feet," he said. He raised his glass to Nancy, to Ned.

Ned, with his arm around Nancy's waist, clinked her glass with his. "Here's to you, little egg," he said.

"*Salut!*" said Grandpa Joke in Italian.

"*Salut!*" agreed Rachel and Tina, raising their glasses and kissing Nancy's cheeks.

"Thanks," Nancy said stiffly. She had never been toasted before, and she didn't know why they were doing this now. The family ate beautiful eggplant parmigiana and drank the wine that tasted cool and hard when Nancy sipped it, but went down her throat warm and soft. The talk was nothing but chitchat. Nancy kept waiting for serious words, some explanation or question or challenge. They seemed to have gotten her here for a reason they all clearly agreed upon. But nobody said anything much. They discussed crops, of all things—stuff people were growing in the community garden.

Nancy couldn't sit at the table anymore. She got up and carried the plates into the kitchen and washed them. Grandpa came in with the parmigiana dish and patted her shoulder. She turned and said, "Grandpa Joke, why'd you give me wine?"

"Didn't I ever do it before?"

But he knew he hadn't.

"Does there need to be a reason, Nancy? I enjoy you."

Such a formal thing to say.

"You ought to drink wine with the people you love."

What came to her mind was the winged girl who had

opened the door at the Papadopolis house during the first visit. "There's something I want to know, Grandpa Joke."

"Don't find out too much!" he interrupted in a jolly voice, as if he knew exactly what she was going to ask.

"You'd be surprised what I know," she told him. "You're going to have to tell me more sometime, Grandpa."

Grandpa Joke inhaled through his nose, as if he were getting extra oxygen that way. He looked over his shoulder at Ned as he passed behind him on his way to spray water into the sink, filling it with big white suds. "You were asking me a question the other day," he said quietly. "I've been thinking about the answer."

"Which question?"

"That question about *knowing* someone."

"Yeah?"

"Kindness, Nancy. Show him some kindness." He glanced at Ned again.

"Kindness!" she whispered. "To Dad?"

He shrugged. "To anyone. Kindness brings a person out."

"Out of what?"

He didn't exactly answer. "Kindness," he said, tasting the

word. "To everybody. Show everybody some kindness."

It should have been a poster on the subway.

"Do you want me to stay tonight?" Nancy asked Rachel, less because she wanted to than because she wanted an excuse not to do what she was about to do.

But Rachel didn't save her. She said, "Baby girl, I'm deep into work on my masterpiece." Nancy thought she probably meant it, about the weaving being a masterpiece.

"How's it going, Rache?" Ned asked.

"What do you care, dear?" She may as well have said, "Now *go*."

It was still full light out, a long lovely spring evening, when Ned and Nancy left the house. "Holy Saint Chris," Ned said with a sigh.

"Amen," Nancy began, and then changed to "So be it." She jammed her foot into the house door. "There's something I want to show you," she said.

"Now?"

She pulled him back in and slammed the door so that those inside would think they'd gone out. "It's on the roof," she told him. "This roof. You've been asking for it, so don't blame me."

24

Nancy closed the roof hatch carefully behind them. "That's how *I* get here," she said, fighting the quaver in her voice. "From the street, up the stairs. I want you to tell me how you get here, Dad."

Ned's breath caught, then he let out a ragged sigh.

"Dad?"

It was as though his chest had gone hollow. Sharp-shouldered, he walked over to the parapet, the edge of the roof, and looked down. "Joke was right," he said.

"About what?"

"The wine." He closed his eyes. "You."

"Dad, listen. I followed you the last time you came here."

He nodded. He knew.

"But I couldn't follow you for real, Dad. You're too fast."

Eyes still closed, Ned raised his eyebrows.

"How can you be that fast, Dad?"

"Practice."

"And—?"

"And what?"

"Dad. That boy, he said—And I didn't believe him, but then I realized he was right. I couldn't figure out where you went. I have really good eyes, Dad, but you were *gone*."

"Nancy—"

"It's not just practice," she insisted.

He opened his eyes, turned and held his hands out to her. "No, it's not. You're right. But that's all I can—"

She wasn't having it. "Dad, I want to know about you. I think I already do. So you have to tell me now."

"Little egg!"

Ned's hands were on her shoulders, his face against her hair. She could feel him trembling. He stood back and gave her a long look, his eyes looking blacker than black with the sunset sky behind him. He let the breath go out of his chest, blowing gently. Then he dropped his hands and walked away to the edge of the wall, climbed over it.

He was gone. He just suddenly was not there. No Ned.

"Dad?"

Nancy hung over the parapet. The street below reflected the evening light, so far away it looked like a river. The back of her neck and palms had gone hot and cold with fear, and now not just the hair on the back of her neck, but also the hair on her head, felt like it was standing on end. She felt electrified, scared rigid. Scared stiff. She whirled, looked every which way on the roof, but Ned was gone.

"Nancy!" Ned's musical way of saying her name floated on the air, came through low and level.

She turned back to the street, searching, searching. There he was! She spied her dad on top of the building on the other side of the street, on the roof opposite this one. He leaned both hands on the parapet of that building, smiling nervously at her, his eyes still so serious, the sunset purple on his hair.

She didn't ask how or why. She said nothing. She didn't dare speak or call out. There were people walking on the sidewalk below. Dion! Dion and a little girl, that sister of his, walking down the block along the community garden. Spying.

Nancy backed away from the edge and waved Ned toward her with both hands, as if pulling water toward her in a bathtub. *Come back.*

From this distance she watched him bend below the wall. She waited seconds, a minute, standing back from the edge out of view of Dion, should he chance to look up, waiting, wondering where Dion was, wondering what was happening to Ned—for something most assuredly was happening to Ned. She was caught fast and tight as a warp thread in a web of unbelievable strands: her father, invisible; her grandparents, healing people; and Dion, at the center of it all, somehow magically but completely expectedly and continually finding it all out through her, through Nancy herself. *This is why Mama stays on the ground, in her web,* Nancy thought, *because of times like this.*

Ned climbed over the edge of her wall, walked over to her.

"Did you see me?"

"I saw you disappear," she said.

He grinned, ducked his head, looked up and laughed, hair in his eyes.

Nancy pushed the dreadlocks out of the way. "That's

how you did it right? You disappeared. Did you go somewhere else, like the guys in *Star Trek*?" *Beam me up. That'd be a good strategy for the Angel of Brooklyn.*

He shook his head. "Neither," he said. He blew out his breath again, bent down lower, and in a kind of swooping motion, quickly wrapped his arms around his knees. He was like a woolly bear caterpillar, the fuzzy kind with the orange stripe that curls into a ball in the hand of a child who picks it up. As he curled, he shrank, quick as a gasp, there on the rooftop with Nancy. His hands hung down, his hair hung down, and everything about him—grew smaller and smaller. And smaller. She felt a sort of frozen panic: *This will probably freak me out later.* Right then she simply kept her eyes open.

Ned was a spider. A spider! A black spider, a little bit hairy, with nice long legs. His dark clothes had shrunk so small they faded into his skin, and his dark spider color was all of a tone. A perfectly regular spider like the one in the corner of a doorway.

It was appalling. Could everyone in the family do it? *Am I going to do it?* Nancy felt her knees go weak with shock, collapsed, and flopped to the roof on her bottom.

Ned skedaddled, eight legs moving fast up the wall,

then over the parapet and gone. She bounded up again to see where. He'd disappeared again, and the evening grew darker. The last light of day picked out the sheen of window glass and light posts, street signs and the crisscross webbing of the fence around the community garden. Yes, Ned was gone.

But no. This time she spied the faint silken thread dropping him down ever so gently, past windows and doors and stoops, to the bushes beside the sidewalk.

She lost sight of him. The roof she stood on was too high. He was too small.

A car made its way down the street, and people clomped along the sidewalk in shoes that seemed suddenly heavier and more potentially lethal than Nancy's Doc Martens ever could. He was the most vulnerable thing in the city, a practically invisible spider. Had he dropped onto the sidewalk or let the breeze take him across—

On the other side of the street there was nothing to see, but Nancy focused on the rooftop and waited.

And then her father's dear old head popped up from behind the parapet and his eyes—his laughing Dad eyes—were looking at her out of his human face again.

He thinks this is funny!

Another minute and he was back at her side, crouched against the wall, Ned again, Arach-Ned no more. For the moment.

He grabbed her hand, sticky with silk, and pulled her down with him, side by side below the parapet.

They sat hidden on the roof on the sticky tar paper, their backs against the wall. Nancy knew she should have needed a thousand explanations, but she only really wanted one.

"Does it hurt?"

She realized her face was covered in streams of tears, and she pressed her palms to her cheeks, making her hands even hotter and sweatier and stickier than they already were.

"Oh, Nance," Ned said, holding her tighter. "Oh, egg. It's just—it's just *me*."

You'd think I'd have known that.

You'd think I'd have realized.

You'd think I'd have noticed just once that my father wasn't just spiderlike, he was a spider.

"Only you?"

"In my generation. My father was, too."

"None of your cousins?" Her father had lots of cousins.

He shook his head.

"Only you?" she asked again.

"In my family." He studied her. "So far," he said.

Surprised wasn't the word . . .

"It is the other part of what I am."

Of course, she thought, Anansi, who changes himself into a man, and into other things, too. "But a spider is Anansi's main thing," she said. "Isn't your main thing—"`

"A man," said Ned.

She swallowed. "And Grandpa Lester?" He had died before she was born, before Ned had married or even met Rachel.

Her father said, "Lester was more of a spider. Less of a man."

"And you're less of a spider?"

"And you?" Ned asked.

It was a long time before Nancy managed to say anything else at all. "And *I'm* afraid of heights," she finally said.

He said, "I'm afraid of being squished."

She didn't know why she laughed, then thought of all the times he had avoided the subway, especially at rush hour, or how he never ever rode the bus. "Yeah," she said.

"Yeah? Your old dad just turned into a spider, Nancy. Is that all you're thinking?"

"No."

He studied her and waited. "I couldn't always do it," he said. "Only since I was fourteen."

"Fourteen!" *I am less than I could be,* Nancy thought. She thought about the way her father had talked about Dion earlier, as if he were special, wonderful, light, a good—

A good what?

"What about the other spider people?"

He shrugged.

She shrugged back. "Don't you know?"

"How would I know? It's not something you advertise."

She said, "You know I said I knew when you were home? I can tell when you're coming, too." And Dion. She didn't tell him it happened with Dion, too.

"On the roofs? In the subway?"

"Yeah."

"I don't come in the subway that often."

"Well, you know. When it's not rush hour." They

smiled at each other. "Squish hour." It was such an oddly vague feeling that she wondered if she was exaggerating. And yet she wasn't lying; she *could* tell.

"How?" He hadn't asked, before.

"I'm not sure. I think it's my feet or my ankles or knees."

"You're picking up vibrations from the trains," said Dad.

"And yours," she said.

"Even my tiny little spider vibrations?" He watched her eyes intently, wanting to know what she knew.

"Maybe," she said. "I hope so." She thought she understood why they hadn't told her before: maybe suggesting it would have changed the way she felt it. She wasn't sure whether she was just making an educated guess. But she wanted him to think she showed some promise.

"Well, that's encouraging." He said it so lightly.

"What use is it anyway?" she asked. "What good does it do? It's not like I'm about to turn into a spider and run around being practically invisible. What good is knowing someone's coming?"

Ned pulled her up by one hand. "Think about it," he said.

They headed home in the regular way, walking on their own two feet, or four feet, or however many feet they had between them, Nancy and her spider Dad.

25

Angels have wings, Nancy said to herself, thinking back on what Ned had told her. That didn't mean he wasn't the Angel. It didn't mean Dion wasn't, either.

Nancy lay in her bed at Mama's, snuggled down like a bug in a rug, keeping her thoughts to herself. They were keeping her awake.

Why did the newspapers want more Angel stories? What did it mean to the newspaper people—the *Times*, the *Post*, all of them—that some winged spirit was in New York with nothing better to do than help people?

This much was clear: Dion's father was hot on the

trail of the Angel of Brooklyn. And Dion was trying to make Nancy think that Ned was the Angel. How long would it be before he clued his father in?

It was like falling off solid ground into a dark hole and whirling downward, to think that all her life—and long before—her same old father might have been doing this amazing thing. Because, she thought, if anyone was the Angel, *he* was.

Nancy tossed the covers off and kicked them.

Dion didn't need to know that in the last year she'd been with her father when he had replaced two "missing" screwdrivers and a hammer, tools that the Angel had been reported to drop from a rooftop heaven to break up the hell taking place below. Doubtless there were more.

Ned was a roofer, and that was all the excuse he needed to buy new tools, all the excuse he needed to be on the roof, and even to commute to and fro on the rooftops. But as far as Dion's hypothesis about Ned being in the right place at the right time to stop crimes, well . . . Nancy was about to toss a variable into the experiment.

The variable was herself. She wondered how far she

could go with this new experiment, how much she could do, really, without Ned's disappearing powers, without her mother's weaving genius, without Granny Tina's gift for making things strong.

Ned had taught her climbing, after all, and he was the best climber. Rachel had taught her weaving, and wasn't she the best weaver? And Granny Tina had taught her—well, nothing about making any *thing* strong, but about making herself strong on the streets. She would keep her distance from Granny for now, and rely on the extra energy she'd already gotten from the stories. And on her vibrations.

The next morning Nancy got her experiment going. She began by being invisible. Visible people looked threatening, or vulnerable. You noticed them in your gut, because they worried you, one way or the other. Invisible people looked like they knew where they were, where they were going. *They* weren't scared or worried. They had their "street face" on.

Each morning Nancy filled her backpack to the brim, not just with schoolbooks and her knitting, but also some laundry, shirts she needed to wash, or sometimes already had washed. Sometimes they were even wet, which was more authentic, though heavier.

When she left for school she took a route that went across rooftops, acting as though she belonged there, playing the part of the guest of someone in the building, who didn't know her way around. If she saw anybody she marched right up to them and asked to borrow some clothespins. She picked different fire escapes each day by which to ascend to the roof or descend to the street, and the two times she was surprised by some nosy tenant, she said the same thing she and Ned had said the time they'd gotten caught on their own fire escape: "Oh, sorry, I'm your new neighbor, and my parents insist I learn to use the fire escape." The second time she'd really laid it on thick, saying, "They don't *have* fire escapes back home in Connecticut," rolling her eyes at the absurdity of New York.

Nancy also took care to blend in style-wise. She moussed her hair down so it didn't stick out as though electrified the way it usually did. She wore her black sweater if it was cool, and if it was warm she kept her uniform blouse tucked carefully into her skirt. She wore her Doc Martens; everybody wore those, so they didn't stand out. The only painful thing was leaving her "fun" tights at home, and wearing plain black ones. What with the attention her tights had been getting, it was probably just as well.

The result: nobody thought anything of her. Polite girl, kind of cute. Must be a weird family. Nothing remarkable. She walked around acting the way Granny Tina had taught her to act, no matter what New York neighborhood she was in, never lingering on the edges, but walking straight up the middle. "Walk like you know where you're going," Granny had said when Nancy started going out on her own at age eleven. "Someone who wants to bother you will have to break up your flow."

So Nancy flowed. She flowed across lonely roofs, leaped across alleys, went around the back ways of buildings. She got so she could do it without making much sound. She got so she could tell that someone she'd just walked by had already forgotten they'd seen her. She got so she knew that someone walking below in the alley did not know that she was above on the roof. And she got good at hitting marks on the ground with stones or roof tiles or clothespins, even once a bent knitting needle—although she decided that, as weapons went, knitting needles were expensive and too likely to mark her as a suspect.

26

The next week there were three newspaper articles about the so-called Angel of Brooklyn. A dealer menacing a kid on Nelson Street in Red Hook had been nailed in the eye by a pebble from a peashooter and had to have emergency surgery before he could appear in court. There had been an attempted knifing on John Street in DUMBO, that had been foiled by an unidentified yell from above. And a mugging in a Brooklyn Heights alley had been interrupted by a flying clothespin.

Nancy considered the details in the two cases she hadn't been involved in: Were they accidental interventions?

Intentional ones? Twice, in the night, she woke abruptly, thinking she still heard the rough, mean voice; the scared, protesting voice; the pushing and scuffling in that alley; the garbage bag bursting against the Dumpster, the clatter of scattering keys and credit cards.

She wondered if her father had seen the article. She clipped it herself, and saved it, just in case. She hid it in the back of her little red dresser at Mama's house, knowing Rachel would never guess what it meant that she treasured such a clipping.

And then Ned came while she was doing home-work in Mama's kitchen and placed all three clippings before her on the table. "Thought you'd be interested," he said. "I've noticed you reading these lately."

Nancy stared down at her own personal clipping, the words of which she knew by heart—as well as the byline, Nobody in Particular (it was a *Post* article)— and beyond it her history notebook. In the margin was an insult from the hand of Annette: a picture of a little ghost drawn in green marker. The green ghost was what Annette had decided would be the child of a marriage between Nancy and Ghost Boy. Nancy placed her hand over the ghost and touched the edge of the clipping with her fingertips.

She began carefully, "The thing about these stories—"

"Hmm?" Dad turned away and cut a piece of bread to put in the toaster, put the little copper kettle on to boil.

"He doesn't seem to think there's anything, you know, *special,* about the Angel of Brooklyn."

"Special?"

"You know. Other than knowing where to go, there are no special talents or abilities. Shouldn't it be more heroic?"

"You mean *superheroic.*"

"Yeah, like a comic book. Flying or teleporting or seeing through walls or something."

"Teleporting?" asked Ned.

"Like beaming up. Being gone from one place and appearing in another."

"Isn't that what you used to think I did?"

They grinned at each other, faces open. But their secrets weren't. Ned said, "Isn't conking criminals a superpower?"

"Why should it be?" asked Nancy. "Any fool can drop things off roofs."

"True." Ned tore the cover off a tea bag. "But how does the Angel know where he's needed?" He paused, then added, "Or she?"

"Pure chance?"

"You're playing the 'pure chance' card *again*?" asked Ned, shaking his head as if he were throwing off water. "Strange if there wasn't something else involved."

"Something else?" Nancy slid the clipping out of the way before she closed the book over the green ghost. The nervous feeling leaped up again. Despite all her experimentation, the desired result hadn't materialized: there had come no silk, no tiny transformation. Okay. She'd stalk the rooftops if that was what she had to do. But how different it would be if—if only—

Well. It hadn't. And that was that. If she tried anything further in that direction, it would be with the knowledge that her own Angel activities came from just her as she was, nothing more.

27

On Thursday when Nancy got out of school, Dion appeared, slipping out of a Joralemon Street doorway to walk beside her.

"Ghost Boy!" said Annette from the other side of Nancy.

"Learn much at school?" Dion asked. "I mean the one of you that's not an idiot, of course." He was holding his nose, shooing away bad energy waves from Annette. He looked even taller and gawkier than before, his long coat fluttering along, all raggedy behind him.

No one was going to show up out of nowhere and

make Nancy feel small. "She's my friend," she said. *My best friend who's crossing the street and turning the corner to get away from you, and I'm going with her.* But she didn't go with Annette. She stepped off the curb, glanced back at Dion to see if he saw that she was walking away from him and wished him not to follow. But he wasn't looking. He was scooping a left-behind Chinese jump rope off the sidewalk.

Against her better judgment, Nancy paused. The jump rope was busted, popped, pulled so hard that the bind between the ends had broken, no more elastic loop.

"I hate when that happens," she said before she could stop herself, and took a step toward Dion, unable to resist reaching for the springy jump rope.

Dion took the ends of the jump rope in his fingers and knotted the ends together deftly, making a knot so tiny and smooth and faultless it was hard to see it was there.

Nancy's hands were aching for the jump rope, to have it between them, bridging them, wrapping around and under and crisscrossing them in its boingy rubber band way.

Dion held out the rope in a neat striped bundle.

"Remember my name?" he asked.

It scared her how often she had said it to herself. She could have embroidered it on her pillow in her sleep, but to let him know that she remembered it . . . Not yet.

"I'm leaving, Nancy," yelled Annette from across Joralemon.

"I'll call you later!" To Dion, she said, "Danny?"

"It's an unusual name," he hinted. "It's Dion."

She folded the bundled jump rope into her palm. Now that it was there, her hands could just stop itching to move it around and make things out of it. She wondered if she could remember the Eiffel Tower, the cup and saucer, the cat's cradle. . . . No, cat's cradle took two people. You couldn't do it alone. "Dion?" Oh, he was gone.

He didn't stop when she came pelting up behind him, just continued his way to the Carroll Street park. "Mother's waiting for you, isn't she?"

She didn't answer, stunned at first—he had never mentioned her *mother* before—and then defiant. When they reached the dome he climbed up on it. "What about *your* mother?" Nancy asked.

He straightened his coat around him in sharp, angry

movements, his eyebrows—a five-o'clock-shadow of eyebrows, she saw—furled together. Good, she could make *him* mad, too. But then he turned his shoulders toward her and said, "Mina says Mom could die."

"You love her," she said.

"She's a pain in the ass," he lied gruffly.

"So are you. Do you get it from her or from your father?"

"What do you know about my father?" he retorted.

"What else do you get from your father?"

"What do you *think*?"

She wasn't about to tell him what she thought.

"Your mother wouldn't hurt herself," he said. He didn't say anything about his father.

"Could you hurt yourself?" she asked him, noting his shaved eyebrows, his head that needed hair.

He jumped down from the dome like a gymnast, hardly bending his knees to land perfectly. *Where'd he learn that?* she wanted to know. Wished he'd waver a little so she could steady him, wished he'd stay. He moved away quickly, stretching out his legs.

"DION!" It was the biggest yell that had ever come out of her mouth, and it stopped him half a block away.

"What?" She could see his mouth move to let out the word, though she couldn't hear his voice.

She said my name, thought Dion.

Her heart danced along inside her as she made herself walk to him at a normal pace. "Get back up there," she said, grabbing his arm, so thin and hard inside his clothes. He let her lead him back to the dome. Even below the level of the rooftops of the brownstones and the tall trees, she knew they were the highest things in the world. The sun beamed down and warmed their heads.

"My mother is afraid of the city," she told Dion. "She doesn't go out."

Even Annette didn't know this. Teachers at school didn't know. People who had known Nancy since kindergarten didn't know. Dion hadn't. He said, "I've never seen her even once."

"Yeah well, you'd scare her to death, Ghost Boy, that bald head, sitting up here like—"

He sat up, held himself proudly.

"Quasimodo," she finished.

He hunched his back a little, to make her laugh.

"But I wouldn't want to lose her," she said.

"My mother's not afraid of the city," said Dion, his eyes full. "She thinks she can save the whole world."

"How?" *Like my father?*

"She's a counselor. Rose Browning, M.S.W., that's her professional name. She helped people with their problems." He dropped his face into his palms.

Nancy trembled. She didn't want to crowd him, and she wanted to stay. She gave him her V8 juice out of her pack and waited while he cried. He stopped at last, and rubbed his nose on his coat sleeve, and sipped the V8. "Eight vegetables," he said.

"It's good for you," said Nancy.

"You know what I like?" Dion asked.

"Grape juice?"

He shook his head. "Cream soda."

They both laughed.

"You know," Nancy began. She curled the toes of her shoes under one of the bars of the dome. "I'm afraid of heights."

"That's just natural," he said.

"Well, *you're* not, if you walk on that rail by the BQE."

"Yes I am."

"You're like a spider," she said. Shivers ran up and down her spine at her own daring.

"A spider," Dion said, nodding.

"My mother says—" She stopped herself.

"Your mother likes heights?"

She shook her head. "She says that fear of heights is fear that you'll throw yourself off."

Dion's body jolted. "How do you know these things, Nancy?"

"My father," she said, practically stammering.

"Your father! What does he know about—"

"About heights? He's a roofer. I told you."

Dion studied her face a minute. "About my mother," he said.

She waited. He'd opened the door. Now she'd hear the story. Instead, he asked a question. "What do you mean, a 'roofer'?"

Duh is what Annette would say. "A guy who does roofs."

He nodded several times. "My mother was on the roof. And I don't think she was afraid she'd throw herself off. I think she was afraid it wasn't high enough to kill her." He said it casually, in a tone of voice that reminded her of those cute baggy-pants boys Annette and Shamiqua and the other homeroom girls liked, the ones Nancy hated, who could say any cold thing as if it didn't matter. "She'd hit the ground," Dion went on, "but it wouldn't kill her." His voice cracked at the end.

Nancy's fingers wrapped around the bars, gripping so hard her bones showed.

"No. Dad came up and found her and got her back from the edge." Dion stood up, right on top of the dome, and wavered there, more like Dracula than Quasimodo. Nancy grabbed his big, cold hand and said, "Sit down."

He sat, and didn't let go of her hand, looking at her with his beautiful sad eyes. "He told her she couldn't go back to work till she was rested. But Ma can't rest. Now she—" He drew a finger sharply across the inside of his arm, like a knife.

"Self-destructive," Nancy said, like some psychologist herself.

Dion's finger crossed one thigh, then the other.

Nancy nodded. "Then she's no better?"

"Not until your grandparents—"

"Then she'll be all right—"

"No worse," he said. "No more cuts. But they can't heal."

"What kind of cuts don't heal?"

"Come on, you're not *that* stupid," he said awfully.

Nancy pulled her hand away, pulled her knees up to her chest and hugged them. She remembered what Grandpa had said about his mother's problems. A Rose that pricked herself?

Dion threw off his cap, rubbed his head with both hands. "I'm sorry! Sorry!" he said. "She won't *let* them heal."

"And you had to cut yourself, too."

"My hair. It's not the same. I don't want to go home, not until I find an answer for my ma."

She lifted her hand to the back of his head, and let her fingers run lightly from the crown to the nape of his neck. *Velvet*. She'd been right. She didn't have to ask what kind of answer he wanted for his mother. He wanted to find the Angel of Brooklyn. And if it wasn't him, himself, then . . . "Last weekend the Angel of Brooklyn was in the paper three times," she said.

He didn't comment.

"Did you see the papers? Well, my father was on a job all week in Corona." Corona was in Queens.

"What were the weapons?"

"You mean what were the crimes?"

"No, I mean, what did the Angel of Brooklyn throw down?"

"A pebble, and a clothespin."

"A clothespin!" Dion grinned. "You said three."

"The other time he just yelled."

Dion, smiling, looked at her sidelong. "I shot the pebble," he said. "And my father went and reported it as the Angel."

She thought he'd laugh himself right off the dome. She couldn't let him see how incensed she was.

He laughed as hard as he'd cried. "I had this idea that maybe I'd attract the Angel. You know, *draw* him to me. He'd want to know who was stealing his thunder."

Nancy bet the Angel *did* want to know that, all right. She wondered if the Angel knew there were two thunder-stealers.

"He didn't show up, though," Dion said. "Maybe he was somewhere else, huh, not Brooklyn? *He wouldn't be the Angel of Brooklyn then, would he?* She thought it, but didn't say it. She asked, "What would you have done if he had shown up?" She thought she knew. He'd take him to his father, that's what, hold him for ransom until they got all the stories out of him. It would be the story of the century for New York—except that it would be all wrong, about angels, for pete's sake, not spiders!— and Niko Papadopolis, Nick Pappas, Nestor Paprika, and Nobody in Particular would win the Pulitzer Prize all together.

Dion said, "I want to talk to him, that's all. I want to know what it's like."

It was only what Nancy wanted herself, but she'd have been an idiot to believe him. Too much was at stake for her and her family. If word got out, everyone would want to know too much about them. Look how they were already being threatened, Grandpa Joke first of all. Wasn't Nancy in danger of exposing them to more trouble? And now she'd gone and told Dion about Mama.

A spider had to choose its shelter or get backed into a corner. Nancy pulled away from Dion, jumped from the dome. A train was rattling into the station, and she ran to get on it.

28

Grandpa Joke, wearing his nice jacket and his outdoor shoes, must have been waiting for Nancy to come through the front door. "Got an errand," he said, rushing past her on the stairs. "Granny's sleeping. Your mama's—" He waved his hand toward downstairs and shrugged.

"Still weaving like a nut?"

"It's all this light," Grandpa said. The longer the days grew, the longer Rachel worked. She was using every minute, working intently. Nancy thought it might be the money that Rachel was thinking of. Ned was working long hours, too. And there had to be a reason Grandpa went back to OTB.

In the doorway Grandpa paused, stood with his hand on the foot of the traveling saint, and called up the stairs: "Nancy!"

"What?" she said.

"Say 'yes,' not 'what,'" he said.

She said nothing.

He pressed the palm of his hand against the statue as though in exasperation. He said, "Don't pick up the phone."

"How—"

"Saints preserve us," he said, and closed the door between them.

When the phone rang, she picked it up.

"Dr. Greene, please," said the familiar, quiet, formal voice.

"Whom should I say is calling?" Her grandfather had taught her how to behave on the phone.

"Niko," the man said.

"Niko Papadopolis? The same as Nick Pappas? And Nestor Paprika?"

"So you think you know everything, girl?"

"Pretty much," she said.

He said nothing for a moment, then, "Tell him I called."

She went downstairs and told Mama to listen for Granny. Without waiting for an answer, with just a pat on the feet of the saint, she hit the sidewalk.

Nancy found Grandpa Joke in Curley's diner next to the OTB parlor, in the second to last booth. His eyes were closed, as though he were asleep or trying to calm himself. She slid across the blue vinyl seat. "Grandpa?"

"Shh, Nancy!" He sounded dark and tired.

"Come on, let's get out of here. It's beautiful out. We could go walk across the bridge."

"Shush, buggy. I can't go out today."

"Yeah, well, you're out."

He said nothing.

She leaned closer. "Grandpa Joke, Dad's been clipping all these newspaper articles, and they're all by the same person. Nick Papadopolis. And I happen to know that your patient the other night was his wife, Rose Papadopolis."

"How?" He opened his eyes and looked over her head at the door. "Oh, Nancy baby, don't you know we're all connected?"

The waitress said, "What'll you have, Nancy?"

"Just a V8, please, Annie." Annie went away again.

"Nancy, my love. This is information you don't need. It can't help you to know it."

Tears filled her eyes at how afraid her grandfather was. "I know you, Grandpa Joke. Don't you lie to me, no matter what your big secret is."

His eyes filled up, too. He rummaged in his pocket for his handkerchief. There was a shower of OTB stubs and lottery tickets, his cigarette lighter, and a folded index card that unfolded itself so that Nancy spotted Dad's handwriting. No handkerchief. As Nancy handed Grandpa her paper napkin, she palmed the card and pulled it toward her, hidden under her hand.

Grandpa Joke waved the napkin away. "You just excuse me, Nancy. I'll get a tissue from the front."

She thought she heard him coming back, but instead it was Annie with the V8. She smiled at Annie, made herself take a sip. And Grandpa Joke didn't come. When she turned, he was gone.

"Where'd he go?" Nancy asked, leaning over the register.

"Hush, Nancy. Go on home," said Annie. "Go home quick now."

The sides of the booths were so tall you couldn't see people if you didn't walk right up to their booth. Nancy had just walked past them all without looking into any of them. As she glanced back now, one little dark-haired girl with blue-gray eyes was peeking around the corner of a seat. It was Dion's sister. The person across from her was a broad-shouldered, dark-haired man. Niko Papadopolis.

Nancy took a step toward them, but Annie said, "You're all set, Nancy. Now go home." She took Nancy by the shoulder and turned her out the door.

"It's okay, Annie. You don't have to push."

"Your Grandpa's waiting for you. Now go."

Grandpa Joke was in the doorway of the OTB, watching for Nancy. "We're all connected, Grandpa Joke," she said fiercely. "Isn't that what you told me?"

"Yes. But what *kind* of connections are they, Nancy?"

"What do you mean by that?"

"There's some you want to stay separate from," he said.

"Why, if I can help?"

"How can you help?" He said it gently, but still it hurt.

"Grandpa, you're the one who said to show kindness."

"Stay away from that man," he told her.

"You don't." *What he doesn't know won't hurt him.* He hadn't said to stay away from the son or the mother or the daughter.

"Listen," he said. "Listen good. I'm a good doctor, but I don't have certain talents your grandmother has. The people that need her are very good at finding her."

"Is that a bad thing?"

"Some of them are bad. And it's not all they want, just a little medical help. They draw a different kind of strength from someone like your Granny."

"Is that what this Niko is doing?"

Grandpa sighed. "What I have observed is that over the last year he has followed some of the patients. Events coincide, and you notice a pattern. He was in the background. Then he was—"

"In the foreground?"

He frowned. "Mostly patients get better and go away. But some of them . . . I make a judgment. Sometimes it's best to pay them off. That's all some of them want. If I can get them to go away and leave us alone for a time, it's better. But sometimes—more often lately—they come back."

"Why?"

"We're easy money, see?"

The light dawned: Nancy saw the pattern in the horse-racing situation. Grandpa's winnings paid off the

Healer seekers. "But that's not why Niko Papadopolis keeps coming around, for the money."

Grandpa bowed his head. "They don't leave you alone so easy, not if the one that's sick isn't getting better."

"That's stupid!" Nancy burst out. "Why should it cost so much to go to the hospital?"

Grandpa Joke looked at her as though she were knee-high to a centipede. "It's not as simple as that," he said gently. "Don't you see, it's spiders that respond best to your Granny's kind of healing?"

The focus burst open and clear. It was as though Grandpa Joke had stepped on a treadle of Mama's loom and revealed to Nancy that a fabric she had thought to be striped was, quite suddenly, plaid. A network of random strings fell into place.

"Grandpa," she said, her voice deep and hoarse, "he's a reporter. He's not just looking for healing. He's looking for stories."

"Your Granny hasn't got very many stories left," Grandpa Joke said.

Nancy shook. She thought she knew the kind of stories Grandpa meant. "Why aren't there more healers?" she whispered.

"In these times? With malpractice and insurance and—Why do you think *we* keep it so quiet? Yes, there are others, and they've gone underground the way your Granny has. There are so few, they'd suck her dry otherwise."

"Then a *newspaper* story would be devastating."

He nodded. "Go on home, Nancy," he said. "Go now, before anything else can happen."

Nancy let herself into the basement apartment without a word to Mama or Granny. She was right about the card she'd stolen from Grandpa Joke. It was in Dad's handwriting:

ATT. RAPE MOTT ST. AL
WATCH FOR N.

That most terrifying of words jumped right out at her. And just below it, WATCH FOR N. Nancy thought about Grandpa today—the words he'd been saying, the way his eyes had looked. N. might stand for her, for Nancy, or for Ned. Or Niko.

She knew where Mott Street was: in Chinatown, on the

cobwebs

Manhattan side of the Brooklyn Bridge. Last fall Rachel had sent her there to buy paper lanterns for Granny's birthday. Talk about mazes! She tried to picture a Mott Street alley and could only come up with the narrowest, darkest place. There wasn't room for anything more.

Nancy went through all the day's papers, then yesterday's. She found a little story on an inside page of yesterday's *News*. "The criminal was apprehended by his would-be victim," it said.

How had the victim apprehended him? Some kind of martial arts? Or did she get his gun or knife off him? Nancy stopped reading and looked around, almost expecting to find someone watching her, though she didn't know who. There was no reason for her to be reading this story, not as she'd been reading news stories lately—for the Angel. Only there was this note. She returned to the article and read it closely. There was no mention of anything falling from above—no hammer, no pebble, no clothespin. If there was no Angelness, was there, maybe, some spiderness? Suddenly she could feel her stomach inside her body, a round cold gray thing that seemed empty, but not in a hungry way.

Calm down, she told herself. It's not as though there were any draglines or silk in the story, nothing obvious like that.

She went into the bedroom and studied her face in the mirror. Tight braids. Green eyes. Grim face. Spinnerets or not, there was spider in Nancy. Wings or not, there was Angel in Nancy. Climb or fly, she would rise in her own way. She would help her family, her city, the best way she knew how. First she had something, someone to check on in Chinatown. And she knew who she wanted to take with her.

3. The Web

Just as you feel when you look on the river
   and sky, so I felt;
Just as any of you is one of a living crowd, I
   was one of a crowd;
Just as you are refresh'd by the gladness of
   the river and the bright flow, I was refresh'd;
Just as you stand and lean on the rail, yet
   hurry with the swift current, I stood, yet was
   hurried . . .

—Walt Whitman, from "Crossing Brooklyn Ferry"

29

The sky over the river was blue-gold with western light when she rang Annette's buzzer. Nancy couldn't get out onto Annette's little balcony over Pierrepont Place fast enough. She had to approach this just right with Annette, who sat soaking up the sun. The trees over the Promenade were deep green now; the neighborhood rang with the sounds of kids playing in the playground and the Kustard King truck dingling its jingle on the corner and boats tooting on the river.

Nancy sat beside Annette and poked her feet through the railings. "Let's go get ice cream," she said. It was too hot for tights, too hot for tights! What next?

What would Annette say if she took them off? What would Annette say about the way she'd walked away with Dion, about anything she'd done lately?

"You can't stay long, Nancy," Annette said. "And I don't want to eat. I want to feel thin. I'm meeting Mom to shop for an outfit to wear to that dance. It's tomorrow night, you know."

"What sort of outfit?" Nancy asked casually, but inside her mind reeled and Annette's long response went in one ear and out the other. So much for Nancy's plans to entice Annette to Chinatown: green tea ice cream on Bayard Street, five-dollar embroidered shoes, and those scrumptious coconut drinks that came in coconut shells from buckets on Canal Street.

"You know," Annette was saying, "long and floaty, with points that fly out when I dance." That dance! Nancy tried to picture herself dancing somewhere beside Ned's roof. She didn't have any dancing clothes. Her mother did, flowing skirts and tank tops, and maybe—what with the magic of elastic and safety pins and needles and thread—Nancy could patch together an outfit. Nancy suddenly felt completely inhuman, too weird to live, and it made her frantic. She jumped up so fast she almost snapped her legs off at the knees, because she'd forgotten her feet were stuck through the balcony railings.

"What's with you?" Annette asked, startled.

"What's Shamiqua wearing?" *Steady there,* Nancy said to herself. What if Annette wouldn't come with her? She would have to be brave enough alone.

"Something slinky."

"You mean sleazy?"

"She's not, you know. She's nice."

Nancy was silent, and sullen.

"What do you know about it, Nancy? It's not like *you've* been around!" Here it came now. Annette's black eyes were pools of hurt. Quickly she snapped them shut, as if in concentration, as she twisted her hair up onto her head and jabbed at the knot to make it stay.

Peace, thought Nancy. *Peace first.* " 'Nette? Would you do an act of rebellion with me?"

Nancy and Annette conducted a science experiment on Nancy's legs. They coated one leg with shaving cream, and the other leg with Nair. Annette said, "Do you want to hear the poem I've been working on?"

"Errrr," said Nancy, pretending uncertainty. She wasn't pretending when it came to her legs; *they* sure felt rebellious. She had to concentrate hard to keep them still.

Annette recited,

> "My Mom's in love with General Tso,
> My father flew the coop,
> And I'm the little wonton
> That floats in chicken soup."

"Woe is me," said Nancy, like always, and thought it was strange—a Chinese food poem, today.

Annette made a little bow.

The shaving cream leg felt cold, and the Nair leg felt hot. It felt hotter still as Annette slowly and carefully (and expertly, Nancy noted) shaved the shaving cream off Nancy's leg. Only of course she shaved the hair, too, no stopping that, though Nancy was dying to stop her.

"Please," she said through her teeth, tears beginning to slip out of the corners of her eyes and down her cheeks.

"What? Does it sting?"

Nancy shook her head.

"Try to act normal," suggested Annette.

"This *is* normal for me."

"That's the trouble," Annette said. Nancy knew it was ridiculously weird to cry over shaved legs.

"Come on," Annette said, looking at her in sympathy, rinsing the razor. "It really doesn't hurt, does it?"

Nancy shook her head again. "It just feels numb," she said.

Annette said, "Your brain is numb."

Nancy felt like the fingertips had been sanded off her hands, and she could no longer touch what she was holding. "Maybe I'm allergic to the shaving cream," she said. Now she knew how truly weirdly unhuman she really was. She could hardly say that to Annette. "The hair on my right leg is disintegrating, right?"

"It might take a couple shots. You have really hairy legs."

"It's hereditary."

"How come you're doing this all of a sudden?" Annette asked. "Must be that Ghost Boy." She was smiling slyly.

Nancy's whole body felt hot and cold, split down the middle. "It's Jimmy Velcro, didn't I tell you?"

"Ooh," said Annette. "Now I wish we were doing that sugar-water thing. Then I could just *rip* you." Instead she turned on the water in the tub and started rinsing Nancy's leg with the shower massage attachment. And maybe it was the hair on Nancy's legs (the hair that had been on her legs) or maybe it was her Ghost Boy, but she was crying again.

"Does it hurt?" asked Annette again kindly.

"No," sobbed Nancy. "That's the trouble." Annette just stared. Well, how could Nancy explain how cutting off the hair on her legs made her feel cut off from the air around her?

"Anyway," Annette said. "I have these cute socks. I haven't even worn them, Nance, so they don't have cooties or anything. They'll be so cute with your Docs."

Nancy slipped the ankle socks on: green and white stripes.

"You have to admit they are fetching," Annette said, grinning over Nancy's shoulder into the mirror. Polka-dot Docs, green-striped socks, and her long brown, *smooth* legs.

Nancy felt breezy. Pretty. "Whatever turns you on," Nancy said, not wanting to admit how she felt.

But Annette could tell she liked the look. "Yipe!" she yelled, glancing at the clock. "The time!" *She's as relieved to be leaving as I am,* thought Nancy.

"Use your phone?" Nancy asked. She called Rachel. "I'm not coming home tonight," she told her. "I'm going to Dad's."

"Why?" Mama's voice on the phone sounded odd, bleak.

"Because I want to," she said, hanging up the phone.

"Yeah, well, what are you going to do, Nancy?" said Annette, her face anxious. She threw a jacket over her shoulder, headed for the door. "I'm meeting Mommy for dinner, remember?"

"I'll come with you."

Annette's eyes widened. "But Nance, we're going shopping for the dance. At Bloomingdale's."

Thank you, thought Nancy. *Thank you, universe!* She wouldn't have to go to Manhattan alone. Annette would be with her. "Don't worry, 'Nette. I'm not going to cramp your style."

"That isn't what I meant."

"I know, Annette honey. I'll ride the train with you, that's all. I'll get off somewhere"—quickly she decided where, and resolved not to change her mind—"different."

They ran for the train. Annette used the Clark Street station with the elevator, so naturally, Nancy couldn't guess whether a train was coming or not.

When they were under the river, the long stop-free stretch on the train, Annette finally asked, "Where are you going?"

"Chinatown," Nancy said. She got off at Canal.

30

There was no reason to visit Mott Street except to see what was there—and to maybe be seen, seeing it. That's why Nancy was in Chinatown on a crowded Friday evening, dodging the buckets of turtles and frogs, the mechanical windup toys, baskets of crabs and tables of fish on beds of ice, the Chinese ladies hauling shopping baskets. That was why she was peering into shop windows and buying a bright green fish kite on a long stick—to blend in, to be seen, to have an excuse to look up, to check out the alleys and rooftops at the same time.

At last she found the combination she was looking

for: a narrow alley between two buildings, one of which had the orange-red untarnished copper flashing of a brand-new roof.

Nancy sat on the doorstep that probably led to an apartment over the stores. She jammed the kite stick into the yarn inside her backpack. She pulled out Dion's jump rope. Some things you just never forgot, like tying your shoes or knitting or cat's cradle. Though it had been years since Rachel had first taught her, she made only two false starts before she succeeded in winding the rope into the cat's cradle.

The point was to have something to do with her hands while she pretended to be sitting there waiting for someone, while she gazed nonchalantly at the street near the alley, watching for Niko Papadopolis. Somehow she thought that he might be looking for the same thing she was.

There was no reason that he should have been there *then*, on a crowded Friday evening, at the precise moment *she* was there, looking for the precise clues she'd already searched out. But he was, and afterward, long afterward, she wondered if she or the kite or the jump rope acted as a lure. If it had been her, he didn't know it: though he'd heard her voice on the phone and in his own doorway, he'd never seen her face.

There in front of her, stood the girl, Mina.

"What happened to the angel tights?" she asked Nancy.

Behind her stood her father, his hair like dark clouds against the sky.

"Too warm for them today," said Nancy, as a normal girl would. "Like my socks?"

"Let's go, Meen," said her father.

"I *know* her!" Mina said, to clear that up.

Niko must have thought Mina was old enough to know people he didn't. He backed away a little, gazing up, listening.

"Where are your angel wings?" Nancy asked.

Mina said, "I was never an angel. Those are cardinal wings. It's my totem bird."

"What does that mean?"

Mina said, "It's the thing I like best," and patted her chest, over her heart. Niko, glancing at the two girls in a puzzled but accepting way (was Nancy a teacher's aide?), moved a pace or two away to talk to a lady selling ducks and crabs.

"What is it about cardinals? Because they're red?"

"People have animals in their spirit, my mother says. Cardinals are in mine."

Nancy wondered what was in hers. She glanced at Niko, who was talking to the duck woman. "How *is* your mother?" she asked in a low voice.

Mina shook her head pessimistically in a way she must have seen someone else do. "Not so good, but the Healer says—"

"Let's *go*, Mina." Niko was back, his eyes intent on Nancy in a way she didn't like. He certainly didn't like Mina mentioning the Healer. He reached for her hand.

"Wait!" the girl said. "What's that?" She touched the elastic jump rope Nancy was winding through her fingers.

"It's a Chinese jump rope," Nancy answered. He wouldn't—say anything, do anything, accuse anybody— in front of his little daughter, would he? "Do you like to jump rope?"

"I'm the best jumper in my class," said Mina.

"I'll bet you are," said Nancy sincerely.

But Niko Papadopolis said, as if she'd been sarcastic, "She *is* an incredible jumper." *Is he proud of Dion like that?* It made her wonder what this man would do if he thought his son was the Angel of Brooklyn. Was Dion trying to make him think that?

"Want to jump?" asked Mina.

"No." With an eye on Niko, Nancy wrapped the jump rope around her hands, flipping and popping it into the form of a cat's cradle. She held it up to Mina. "Know what to do?"

But Mina didn't know cat's cradle. "Show me?" she said.

"Another time," said Niko.

"Gotta go," said Nancy. She rose, stuffing the jump rope into her backpack. She tapped the pole of the fish kite along the sidewalk jauntily. *Have I made myself a target?* she asked herself. That was the point: now she would no longer be invisible to Niko. *Well, at least there are two angels now,* she reassured herself shakily. *Maybe three. Maybe a fourth, with red wings.* Why did it matter so much what Niko thought? It did.

Nancy leaned the pole of the fish kite over her shoulder, and let it ride the wind just over her head as she headed for the bridge back to Brooklyn. She ought to be a normal girl like Annette, thinking about the dance tomorrow night, shopping for a dress after dinner with her mother. *Imagine Rachel staying out long enough for dinner and a dress.* Nancy felt everything but normal. Normal girls thought of dancing at *dances*, that's when they felt like dancing, not when they turned the corner by City Hall and started walking up the ramp of the Brooklyn Bridge.

It was really spring now, no doubt about it. Practically summer. Nancy's green kite battled and blew, swimming against the warm current of wind.

Nancy blamed Annette that she couldn't get that dance out of her mind, blamed her pretty shaved legs, blamed the girls in homeroom, Shamiqua and the rest.

"James is gonna pick me up at eight," Annette had said to Shamiqua this morning. "Think he'll bring me a gardenia/a camelia/a lobelia?"

Sounds like Ophelia, thought Nancy. *A loony girl who trusts the wrong boy. It happens.*

"He's so sweet/real neat/complete."

Smelly feet. Try cornstarch.

"Jenny says she's going in a limo/a Lincoln/a Caddy."

She lies! Thinks so much of herself, that girl.

"A Boxster/a Roadster/a—"

"A monster," Nancy had said out loud. *Quasimodo.*

They'd all stopped and looked at her face, then resumed, slower.

"Yeah, we're just taking the train."

"The taxi."

"The bus."

"We're walking."

"How about Nancy?" they'd asked Annette, as if she were a deaf moron. "She coming?"

"Me?" Nancy spoke for herself. "Bet you wish you knew."

"Yeah? How you getting there?" asked Shamiqua.

Over the roofs, she said to herself. *I'm going to just drop myself down on a little woven string. . . .*

"She coming?"

"Are you?" Annette had asked, right in front of them all.

"Who you coming with?"

My Dion, thought Nancy, and nearly died of embarrassment right there in homeroom, though she hadn't said the words aloud.

"Oh, come on, 'Nette. You know Nancy'd never come." That was Shamiqua, of course.

"Whatsa matter, Nancy? You don't like to dance?"

Just because I've never danced doesn't mean I don't like to.

Out in the middle of the bridge she told herself she didn't care. Nancy couldn't be anything but joyful here, strung between Brooklyn and Manhattan, on a web her great-great-great-grandfather had spun.

I like to dance. I do like to dance. I would like to—

"Weird chick, what you doing with that Chinese kite?"

31

Nancy jumped about a foot. Dion, brown as dust, gray as air, blue as sky, sat on the rail at the foot of the Manhattan-side tower of the Brooklyn Bridge.

Act normal, she told herself. Not Nancy-normal, but human-normal. Annette-normal.

"I've been shopping," she said. She held the kite high. "And my name's not Weird Chick."

"No, it's Nancy Greene-Kara. You think I don't know?"

There couldn't be any place safer, really, than this bridge, this giant brown web in the big blue sky, the rose and gray and green city all around, people everywhere and airplanes and helicopters, all of New York City to hide in, and just her and Dion in the center of it. "You think I don't know you're Dion Papadopolis?"

The paleness went out of his eyes and some deepness came in, so that instead of the washed-out blue of April sky, his eyes became more like the East River reflecting it, a blue-gray with a mood or message beneath it. Nancy's knees wobbled along with the traffic on the bridge. She leaned hard on the rail.

"You finally remembered my name," he said.

"I've remembered your name since the first time you told me," she said, "but you never told me your last name. I figured that out myself."

"Congratulations."

She could see that she made him nervous. He wanted her to keep walking, she thought, just go away now. Maybe it was the setting, but she felt different around him today, closed off.

"And your father's Niko Papadopolis. And your sister's Wilhelmina Papadopolis. And your mother"— she'd saved her for last— "is Rose."

She knew too much. He hadn't counted on her hunting him the way he'd hunted her. She knew this in her head, but her body was telling her nothing. None of the usual shivers or vibrations, just the dull shuddering of the bridge as the cars thundered over it on the roadway below. Nancy cried out to him from inside, *What's wrong?* But he didn't seem to hear.

The silence stretched out between them like the cables between the bridge towers, going a long, long way. She wondered what she could ask that would make him go. The kite dragged at her hands, pulling with the wind. She wondered what she could ask, instead, that would make him stay. "Do you like to dance?" Nancy heard her mouth say to Dion.

"Do I like to *dance?*" He was as astonished as she was.

She danced there on the brown bridge, gray Wall Street people and multicolored biker dudes and fashion models and freaks walking by, a black barge and a red tugboat making their way shoulder to shoulder down the river underneath, white traffic helicopters buzzing overhead, and, over there in the harbor, the orange Staten Island Ferry crossing in front of the mint green Statue of Liberty. She felt dizzy from all the motion. "The twist? The monkey? The swim? The cha-cha?

Cotton-Eyed Joe? A little head-banging?"

"The mashed potato," said Dion quietly, and did a little hand dance, as if he remembered it vaguely. The water and sky were blue, and Dion was blue.

"There's a dance at my school tomorrow," she said. Seen that Nancy at the dance with that Ghost Boy? Seen how his eyebrows aren't there? Seen how still he is? Seen how she dances? *A slow dance,* thought Nancy. *His arms around me.* "But I'm not going," she said, retreating.

"Never? Ever?"

She shook her head. "I'm different from them. The girls—"

"What's so different about you?"

"You know," she told him. She hopped up to sit on the rail, testing her nerve. She caught his eyes with hers. The kite rippled in the wind above their heads. Frizz pulled out of Nancy's braids and blew over her cheeks, in her mouth, and everywhere. *What am I keeping it all tied up for?* She cupped his cheek in her hand, felt how he'd had to shave there as well as the rest of his head, felt him lean his cool cheek into her hand as if he didn't mind that her hand was sweaty from her long walk and the climb up the bridge and the dancing. At least her hands hadn't lost their way of sensing things.

Wait. Was it her *legs* that had felt things before? Yes. Yes. The vibrations she felt were just from the cars. Beneath that, or above that, or wherever she'd gotten used to gathering information, there was nothing.

Because I shaved? Nancy was alarmed. *I've lost my senses,* she said to herself, and made an effort to use what there was in her hands and eyes.

She zoomed in on Dion as if she were a lens, and she saw that he wasn't wearing his long coat today—too warm—only worn old jeans and his dusty shoes, and, under a faded jeans shirt (like the kind his father wore), his Alta, Utah, shirt. He calmed her. "Have you ever been to Alta, Utah?" she asked him.

He smiled, his cheek coming up under her hand.

"No," he said. "I stole the shirt off a clothesline."

"Criminal," she said.

She didn't know how she had the nerve to keep her hand on his cheek, how she found the nerve to put the other hand on his other cheek. "But—"

"But what?" His eyes on hers were so sweet, and the kite made luffing noises.

"What difference would growing your hair make?"

She wondered if it was like the difference her hair made.

All he heard was sympathy. "It makes a difference to *me!*" he said loudly, and threw off her hands. A lady pushing a stroller scuttled by, in a hurry to pass the scary teenagers.

Nancy thought to say, *It won't make a difference to your mother*, but didn't. The kite bounced off the netting around the tower.

Dion said, as he had that time on the dome, "Sorry." She nodded.

"I sort of like you," she said. "God knows why. You're weird as anything, and I hate the creepy way you lurk around following me. You could just ask me to go somewhere, you know, instead of spying on me."

"Like you'd go."

Smile. "Not if I didn't want to."

"Then I'd have to try—"

"What?" She looked him sharply in the eye.

"To make you want to."

"It's just—I *do* want to." She hurried on, *don't stop me now, I don't lose my mind that often and I don't know when it'll happen again.* He looked surprised, pleased. He turned away from the city to look up at the fish kite and the webbing and the tall bridge tower and the sky. Her glance swept over his shoulders, and she thought they seemed stronger, that again he seemed taller. She wanted to touch him again, but he'd turned away; she stared all the harder. "It's just, you're the most interesting person I've met so far. Even if it's only because you're so weird." Nancy jumped down from the rail. It was a big jump, but she landed as smooth as silk, her knees like shock absorbers. Or was it the suspension bridge that absorbed the shock of her jump?

"Come back," said Dion in a voice she hadn't heard. His voice was low and thrumming music like the cables that resonated, singing low chords along with the motors of the cars crossing the bridge.

Somehow she made herself turn for home, tossing her backpack over her shoulder.

"There are more things I have to do first," shouted Dion into the wind.

She whirled and called back, "Like what?"

He held his hands up to the air. "There are things I have to know."

"Like your father wants to know? Things like that?"

He looked stunned. Because she was right? *Oh, God,*

she thought. *All this spider stuff I've been saying, my version of flirting. All it's done is given us away to them, worse than walking right up to Niko and telling him I'm the Angel's daughter.*

She walked away from him as fast as she could, out over the barest widest openest part of the bridge where the cables dipped low. Was he following? She couldn't tell without turning back completely. She was almost to the center before she dared one swift glance around to see Dion still sitting on the rail, blue-gray against the rose-shadowed skyline.

Oh. Her stomach dipped. She had so wanted him to follow her. There had never been anything in the city—the world!—like him and never would be again.

She whirled to face him. "Hey! Spider!" And, reeling, she stepped into the bike lane and got pasted by a bike messenger going forty miles an hour.

32

When she came to, she was draped like a little kid over Dion's shoulders, riding him down the narrow steps that led off the bridge to Cadman Plaza. Cold. Hurt. Confused. Her leg hurt. There was hot liquid running down it.

"Stop!"

Dion turned and let her down onto the steps. It was dirty there, dark and smelly. Nancy thought she might throw up.

"Put your head down!" Dion said, and pushed her head between her knees. Orange spots whirled inside her eyelids, but she did not faint again.

"My backpack?" she asked, thinking, *Knitting. Sweater. Clothespins.* "My kite?"

"Kite's lost," Dion said. "I'll get you another one sometime. But your backpack's here."

Honestly. He'd been carrying her on his back and her pack on his arm. He must have been *some* strong for someone so thin.

He was on his knees, watching her face. When she looked down, big mistake: she saw her thigh. That biker must have plowed directly into her, his wheel smashing into her leg. Her skirt blew out of the way. One of Annette's striped socks was in tatters. Nancy's thigh bore an incredible gash, the skin around it pale and shaven, with goosebumps like a plucked chicken. She pushed her skirt down, mortified.

Dion saw. "Don't do that!" he said. "Keep the air on it." He stood up and looked around. People bustled past them on the stairway, annoyed at the obstruction.

Nancy tried to stand. It was rough, sore, hot, flaming—

"Will you let me—" He touched his shoulder. "I was carrying you. You passed out."

Nancy didn't want to be carried. She really, really didn't want to. She took a few steps, but it was hardly worth it, it hurt so much, and it made her bleed more.

He turned and lifted her onto his back.

"How can you—" Her voice was shaken apart by his steps and by the fainting feeling that came over her every time she thought of her leg, the skin, the cut, the shaved hair.

Somehow he got her to her house. She didn't ask how he knew where it was. "Mama!" she called as Dion banged on the door, and they practically fell into the basement apartment, collapsed into chairs in the kitchen.

"Oh, my Lord," Mama said when she saw what had been done to Nancy. She was out the door in two seconds, up the stairs in three. But it took a few whole minutes to bring Granny Tina down to the ground floor.

Granny ought to have been in the wheelchair, Nancy could see that right away. Dion could have carried her down, maybe but Mama had helped her. And, judging by the expression on Granny's face when she saw Dion, she wouldn't have gone anywhere with him.

"Here?" she said to him in a dark and thunderous voice like nothing Nancy had ever heard. "Does your father know?"

Dion shook his head as though he were dizzy. He had only seen the Wound Healer once, and didn't know she had glimpsed him in Rose's hallway. He said, "It's Nancy I'm here for."

"Nancy!"

Some kind of steel came into Granny Tina. She leaned hard on the counter.

"I need you up here, Nancy."

Dion helped her up, his hands on her waist, and for a moment she put her hands to his head. Granny elbowed him out of the way, and lifted Nancy's skirt to find the cut. "Oh, honey," she said. "What's this you've done?" She stroked Nancy's shaved calf.

"Dion brought me home," Nancy told her, not answering. "He carried me all the way."

"From where?"

"The Brooklyn Bridge," said Dion stubbornly, though Nancy was sure he knew she didn't want him to tell. "She got hit by a biker."

"Carried you?" Granny straightened and regarded both Dion and Nancy with her darkest eyes. "Rachel, you take care of her."

Rachel was already at the sink, readying cloths and

pads and liquids to clean the cut. Now she froze. "No!" she said ardently. She dropped the things onto the counter, leaned her hands on the edge, and glared at Granny. "No, Ma."

Granny stood stony as a statue and said: "Rachel."

It was as if the air stopped moving in the kitchen. Everyone held their breath, including Dion.

Grandpa appeared in the doorway. He caught his breath when he saw Dion, and Dion backed toward the garden door. "You?" Grandpa Joke said.

Nancy had had enough of this. "I'd never have made it here without Dion," she told them all. "It's not his fault some fool of a bike messenger mowed me down. Maybe he should have taken me to the emergency room?" Trickster Nancy, testing them all in front of an outsider.

"No," Mama said steadily. "No, he did the right thing." And she smiled at Dion and said, "I thank you."

Granny and Grandpa watched Rachel and decided somehow together, without even exchanging a glance, to give way to her.

"Well, is somebody going to take care of my leg or what?"

"Your mother is," said Grandpa. He handed Nancy

a clean sheet to drape over herself. Nancy tucked her shaved legs behind the ends of the sheet to hide them.

"It's too much for me," Rachel protested, seeming so concerned about what they were asking her to do that she didn't wonder what Nancy was being so modest about.

"Exactly," said Granny. She reached out and took Rachel's hands. "I'm asking you to do it, though. We're all asking."

"Is that best?" asked Dion. *How dare he?*

Grandpa touched Dion's shoulder. "It will be," he said. "It would take too much out of Tina to do it."

Rachel pulled her hands harshly from her mother's grasp and growled, "Everybody get out." She stood over the sink, examining her hands—for dirt, Nancy guessed. She kept her back to them, and Nancy saw a tremble in her mother.

"Yes, Rachel," said Granny in another voice Nancy had never heard, an accepting voice, a you're-the-boss voice. Dion went out with the grandparents, and shut the door.

"All right, Mamba," Nancy said. "What are you going to do that Granny couldn't do? Cast a spell?"

Rachel said, "Hush, Nancy. There's no magic involved here. It's just nature."

What kind of nature, Nancy was about to see.

33

With a needle, with thread so silver it was nearly clear, with gauze woven as carefully as any heirloom blanket, Rachel fixed Nancy up.

"What kind of thread is that?" Nancy could see it coming off the spool, but it didn't look so clear on it.

Rachel looked Nancy in the eye and said hoarsely, "It's silk." She threaded it through her hand before she fed it through the needle. Nancy, staring, saw the thread thicken as it passed through her mother's hand. Rachel, too, watched the thread closely and began to breathe more normally.

"Is this what Granny's doing for Dion's mother?"

"Is that his name? Your fly on the wall?"

Nancy nodded, wondering where he was. "Mama, answer me."

"This is all she *can* do," Rachel said.

"Meaning what?"

"I mean, if this doesn't work for his mother, well, there isn't anything more."

"There's nothing stronger?"

The question stilled Rachel's hands, but then she went on adjusting the thread, her eyes on her work. "So now that you know about your father, what do you think?"

Nancy wasn't expecting the question, not with her mother here doing natural magic, or whatever this was. Doing healing. "Dangerous," she whispered, mindful of Dion nearby. "It scares me. He's so vulnerable. He could be squashed! Thing is, Ma—" She stopped, feeling the needle poking through her skin. Through her skin!

Rachel paused. "Does this hurt, Nancy?"

Nancy shook her head. "Don't know why."

They said nothing for a moment, one feeling the strangeness of a needle penetrating, the other struggling to swallow the sensation of being the one to push it through.

Rachel shakily asked, "Thing is what?"

Nancy said, "He acts indestructible. Like he's James Bond. Double-oh-Ned."

Her mother laughed fondly.

"Ma, could I—"

"What?"

"Mama. Could I be transformed that way? The way Dad does?"

Mama swallowed, unwinding gauze carefully, not stretching it too far. "It seems unlikely," she said. The gauze came off a larger spool than the thread, clouding in a way that seemed more than a trick of light. Nancy took Rachel's lead and didn't mention it.

"Why? Because it hasn't happened yet?"

"It's not impossible, but—"

"But what?"

"Well, it has to be a very strong strain."

"You mean it's hard for him?"

"Yes. *No,* I mean a *genetic* strain," Rachel said. "Dad's a real throwback. It's unusual, even among spiders."

"Even among spider-humans, you mean. It's normal, among spiders."

"How can you joke?"

Nancy rolled her eyes. "How can you not?"

"Because the next one could be you."

"Couldn't it be *you*?"

"No," Rachel said most definitely. "To make a match with someone like me—a healer, down both sides of my family—"

"You are?"

"Yes," her mother said. "As much as Granny Tina is. I'm supposed to be. And you lose the use of it if you don't practice. But how can I have a practice when I can't go out?"

"Mamba, are you worried the strain will be lost in me?" *No wonder they watch me so closely.*

"It's what your grandpa says. You keep us all connected. It's an enormous responsibility."

Mama didn't know what she'd been up to lately, the responsibility she'd been trying to share with Ned. "And what if nothing develops?"

Rachel had finished wrapping Nancy's leg, first in the silvery gauze, then in a normal, store-bought hospital-white gauze. Now she pulled Nancy's skirt off over her head and took a pair of her own soft long johns from a drawer. Together, she and Nancy drew them up over Nancy's feet and began to lift them higher.

"Your legs!"

"I know. A disaster." Nancy pulled the long johns higher.

Rachel tugged them back. "You shaved."

The lump in her throat was back. "I'm sorry!"

"*Sorry?* Nancy, I thought you realized . . . Tell me again how you got hit by that bike." Rachel called out, "Mother!"

The door swung open and Granny Tina was there; she must have been just outside the door, in the living room, while Rachel had been working on Nancy. Dion was nowhere in sight.

"Mother, she shaved," said Rachel.

"And nearly got herself killed," said Granny Tina sarcastically. "See where it got you. Stupid sheep!"

And Nancy suddenly got what they were saying, what they'd *been* saying and she'd been resisting all along: that it was her hair that let her know when the subway was coming, when Dad or Dion was near, her hair that acted as a sort of extra sense or reflex. Rachel helped Nancy down from the counter, made her lean on the counter as she hopped toward the doorway to the greenhouse. "You think if I hadn't shaved, I wouldn't have had this accident?" Her mother and grandmother exchanged glances, their eyes glowing.

In the greenhouse Rachel sat Nancy on the loom bench to rest a moment. "Is that what *you* think?" Rachel asked her. She pulled the bands off Nancy's braids and began to fluff out her hair.

Nancy felt jolted, jangled, and nauseated again. "I want to lie down," she said. "Where's Dad? Where's Dion?"

"Not here," said Mama. "I called Ned. Grandpa's going to bring you over there later. But first, take a nap. Rest a while. You've had a shock." She laid one of her soft blankets beneath the loom.

Nancy wriggled onto the blanket and lay gingerly on her back. She thought, *The hair on my legs is already growing again.*

"This hair thing," she said. "Is it unusual?"

"Not among spiders," Rachel said, smiling.

What would happen if Dion grew back his hair?

Above her the threads snapped in place, grayish-white like a map being printed in a newspaper, the street lines crisscrossing, crosscrissing. What if they added on to each side of Manhattan, filled in the river with more and more streets all the way across to Brooklyn? *Think of the added humming, different without the river in between, think of the change in the rhythm of the city.* Nancy heard it now: *swoosh* went the shuttle through the shed. *Boom* went the beater, pressing the new street into the newsprint. *Bam* went the beater, thrown back out of the way. *Clunkety* went the foot on the treadle. *Clash* went the heddle frames switching position. *Swoosh. Boom. Bam. Clunkety. Clash. Swoosh boom bam clunkety clash.*

Rachel was back into her rhythm. Nancy dozed off. Tina made her slow, creaking way out to the greenhouse.

Words flew unheeded far over Nancy's head.

"You know, she might—"

"She could—"

"Oh, Ma, do you think so?"

"She's got to learn to ignore the world—"

"To focus on a feeling—"

"She can't do that if she doesn't feel—"

"She can't feel if she's just following—"

"I don't think she will anymore, Rachel."
"That boy's been following her—"
"She's been following that boy—"
"His mother's the one—"
"And his father—"
"What are we going to do about them?"
"How did she ever find that boy?"
That boy.

Nancy woke to the sound of weaving, her ears full of it. Started to hear the difference in the heddle positions. Started to hear the difference in the treadles.

Her eyes opened, waited to see, as well as hear, what would come next. Started to see how the street-threads were going to fall into place, in advance. The ground was solid and still and safe beneath her. She tested the pull on the wound on her thigh, slowly bending her leg at the hip, at the knee. She reached a hand toward her mother and felt Rachel's strong arms pull her up from the floor.

"How's it feel?"

"Okay," Nancy said. She put weight on her foot gingerly, moving toward the door. "I want to go to Dad's," she said.

Rachel nodded. That was odd: though Mama didn't believe she'd ever go out again, she must have believed in her healing.

Grandpa was waiting in the car. Nancy walked carefully up the stairs, the way a spider makes its way toward a new hole in its web. *Will it hold?* She had figured out a new idea while she half slept under the loom. Maybe a fly in a web *was* stuck, but it changed the way the day went for the spider. Without it, the pattern would be different: the web untorn, the spider still hungry. She herself, Nancy walking slowly up the stairs, was a difference. *The pattern will change,* she thought bravely, *because I am here.* "Amen," she said to that.

34

It wasn't that Nancy was slow. She just hadn't realized, before she shaved her legs and let her human side overpower her spider side for a few days. Now she saw what a human, even another spider person, would see in her father. If you could trap the Angel of Brooklyn, you might bend him to your use. Him or *her*.

"Can't you see?" Nancy asked Ned, tapping her finger on *The New York Times*. They were finishing a breakfast of eggs and brioche from the Uprising Bakery, a special treat to soothe Nancy's hurt leg—and psyche, said Ned.

"See what? Want another brioche?"

"Yes." She couldn't get enough to eat this morning. "You think you're following Niko Papadopolis's work. But he's following yours."

Dad didn't deny it. He ran his fingers through his hair, leaned his head against her arm, and sighed. "What's that you say, Nancy . . . 'small, but wiry'? That's me, too, you know."

"You're not exactly small, Dad."

"Well, I *can* be. That big oaf can't keep up with me."

"Dion says he plays basketball, Dad. Got a jump shot like you wouldn't believe."

Ned nodded. "So he's a *jumping* spider?"

"Yes."

"It doesn't matter," said Ned, after a beat.

How could it not matter?

Ned looked out his beloved window, over his beloved rooftops and his beloved city. Nancy, beside him, looked, too. "We can't let Granny go there again," she said.

"She may insist."

"Or Niko might."

"He doesn't know what we are made of," said Ned stoutly.

What am I made of?

Ned asked, "Which side has that young roof dweller of yours settled down on?"

"Dion?"

He nodded. He glanced out the window.

"He's not there," Nancy said.

"Sure?"

"Pretty much."

Ned cocked his head and looked at her. "Which side?"

"He loves his mother," she said, "He doesn't trust his father. I don't, either."

"Niko Papadopolis," said Ned. "What's his story?"

"He wants to be at the top of the food chain. If he could just tell everybody what to do . . . everybody in our family, that is."

"He can't tell us," said her father.

The sun beamed through the penthouse windows, throwing a net of shadows across the floor. It lit the V8 juice and Ned's Bloody Mary, and made the seeds of the raspberry jam shine. She asked, "How did you stop that rape?"

For a moment, Ned looked jolted, surprised. But then he began to tell her.

Ned had yelled—no, called, really. Yelling would have

been too loud. "Hey." Period, not exclamation point, but not question mark, either. And then, again, "Hey."

Two faces had looked up, faces scared in different ways, and saw nobody.

"So you leaped down, decked the man, put your arm around the girl and—"

"No," said Ned. "That isn't what happened. I scooped gravel from the roof and dashed it down into the attacker's face. The man's hands flew up to his eyes, and the girl—the smart, brave girl—snatched the gun. Stuck it in his ribs and cocked it and told him to march."

"Didn't he run when he got to Mott Street?" asked Nancy.

"He sure would have. But this girl got him in a hold with his arm behind his back, and when she cleared the alley she spoke to a woman selling ducks, and in an instant, ten guys grabbed the criminal and held on till the cops came."

Nancy grinned, nodding. "She was lucky."

"Lucky! She was brilliant. She kept her wits about her and took her opportunity, and she cleaned his clock! My part was throwing gravel." Ned's head dropped into his hands. "Some angel."

Nancy thought about how spiderwebs signified neg-lect. They made a place look unwatched, uncared for, invisible on the face of the earth, hidden inside the walls of the city. That was a spider's deception. Made it look safe for flies, then foiled them.

"And there's another thing, Dad." She sounded, to herself, as breathless and silly-urgent as the girls in homeroom. "Say you'd caught that guy, taken him off to the cops. Where would that girl be?"

"She'd be saved."

"Yeah, well, this way she saved herself. It's better."

"Better how?"

"Because now she knows she can! I mean, that's what I don't know. If I could grab the gun and hold it on him and make him march—"

"You?"

"Well, of course me. I could be that girl."

"That girl, little egg, got that gun on the guy because he had gravel in his eyes—"

"Oh, really?"

"Or else, she was—"

"You mean, *your* gravel? Ned Kara's?"

"She was maybe dead or worse back there."

"If not for you?"

Stalemate. They both wanted to believe the girl would have found another way out. They both understood that her way out came because Ned threw gravel. That was the way it had happened. But things could have gone another way entirely, if, say, one string had been woven from another harness, if it shot over instead of under, if it were blue instead of green.

The pattern of what he did—what he'd been doing since he was fourteen, from his rooftops and below—would not change, unless Niko Papadopolis got hold of it.

35

Nancy knitted on the chaise lounge on the roof out-side the little penthouse, watching the sun move from one side of the sky to the other, waiting for Ned to go to Rachel's and go to work and come home again. She knit about a zillion stripes along the sweater's front; when she held the sweater up, midafternoon, it reached from her hips to her breastbone. Before long she'd be starting on the sleeves. She laid it down, unwrapped the jump rope from her wrist, made a cat's cradle, looked through it at the city.

Someplace over there Annette was getting ready for the dance. Nancy wondered what her dress was like. She ran her hand up her leg—still smooth, though not as silky—and fooled with the edge of the bandage on her thigh. Already she felt steadier and stronger, but not much like dancing. She thought about dancing on the Brooklyn Bridge for Dion and felt her face get hot, and the hair on the back of her neck stand on end. She closed her eyes in embarrassment, though there was nobody there to see except some pigeons, and daydreamed instead that Dion was dancing *with* her on the bridge.

A shadow passed across her face. Nancy opened her eyes. Dion had his old jeans on, his scuffed boots, and a gray T-shirt. *Camouflage,* Nancy thought, and patted the chaise next to her good leg. He sat. He took the jump rope off her hand, and stretched it out, examining the knots he had made to connect the ends into a loop. The jump rope was a strong elastic woven strand of gold, green, and purple threads, not as bright and sharp as they were when it was new, before Nancy and Dion had found it and made it theirs. She grabbed it back, she pulled him toward her, and he came with the rope as it contracted.

She reached her arms around his back and leaned her head on his shoulder. He put his face into her hair.

They both sighed, and she felt—and she knew he felt—the opposite of how she felt when her hair stood on end. Her hair all stayed in its place. She felt that *she* was back in place, as if this place—Dion's arms—was a place she had known for a long time. It was as though she had been struggling to get back to this place and now she had finally gotten here.

"Can I kiss you?" Dion asked, in the deep chord of a voice he had used on the bridge.

He kissed her.

She kissed him back. She held him, her arms around his neck, and brought her legs carefully up into his lap. He picked her up very gently. He leaned on the parapet and slid to the rooftop with her in his arms.

For the longest time they stayed there, and Ned did not come home, or if he did, in his spider form, he went away again and left them on their own.

Nancy wasn't sure if she'd slept. When she opened her eyes, Dion's were closed. With her fingertip she touched him where his eyebrows were a line of tiny feather tips. He startled, then smiled. He said, "I know you."

She said, "I know you, too."

A cloud crossed his eyes, then, or so it seemed, because the deep blueness that had come into them on the bridge the day before suddenly gave way again to the familiar nervous paleness. "My mother's really bad," he said. "She's going to die unless I get her help. That's why—I wanted you to know that, whatever happens, it's nothing against you. Nothing against your family."

She pushed herself off his lap so that she was sitting on the roof beside him. "The whole thing is hurting my family. It's hurting my grandmother."

"Is it? Is she—"

"What is your father trying to do?" Now her hair stood up, as though it were trying to make up for the lost hair on her legs.

"Same thing *your* father is trying to do," he said. "What's best."

"What's best for who?" His father would say *whom*. His father would say a lot of things!

He closed his eyes. "Us, I guess."

"Not *me*. Not my family."

"I meant my family," Dion said.

"I know you did!"

"I'm sorry."

cobwebs

There was silence between them for a long moment.

"My father's trying to live a good life," she said. "He's trying to help people."

Dion got up and sat on the edge of the chaise, clasped his hands between his knees, as if to warm them, looking down.

Nancy struggled to form the question she wanted to ask. "What were you like, *before*?"

"Before my mother—"

"Before you started living on the roofs."

"You mean, before I ran away?"

"Well," she said, looking into his eyes. "You didn't run very far."

He could have argued that living on the roofs was symbolic of distance. He just said, "I was pretty normal before."

"*That's* hard to believe. You mean you, for instance, had hair?"

That was more symbolism he wouldn't address. "It's funny," he said. "Fewer people seem to notice me the way I am now."

"Who noticed you before?"

"Teachers. People in the neighborhood. People

seemed to—you know—have an eye on me."

"That's because they knew who you were," Nancy said. "They'd seen you around, or seen you with your parents or your sister—"

He cut her right off. "Now they look away," he said.

Yes. "They would, wouldn't they?"

"Or they look right through me."

"What do you mean by that, Ghost Boy? They don't recognize you? Or you're invisible?"

He only grinned. She backed off the subject, but had to ask, "What's it like? Living on the roofs, I mean." She had an idea what he might say, had imagined him enough to think she knew how it was: puddles, asphalt, cooking smells, mist and lights, and him in the shadows.

But he said, "There are a lot of pigeons. More than you'd believe. Even babies."

Nancy smiled. "People talk about how you never see baby pigeons," she said. "Really you never see any baby birds."

"Unless they fall out of the nest," Dion said.

Nancy nodded. She had once seen a scene she didn't want to remember precisely: a gawky pink bird form without enough feathers to fly. Dead. "Or get pushed," she said, shoving the image out of the front of her mind.

Dion shook his head. He said, "It's been good, the parts where it's just been me. Good enough. I'm warm enough, and it's quiet. I can think."

"What do you miss?"

"Nothing!" His voice filled up. "Lots of things."

"What about food?"

"Oreos," he said, almost sobbing the word. "Mina supplies me when she can."

She picked the most unemotional aspect of life. "What about school?"

"I seem to go right on learning things," he said after a moment. "What I miss is gym: games, and playing things. I liked it when you danced on the bridge. I thought I could go back to my school and go to a dance. School would be better if you went to my school. Or I could come to your school."

Nancy thought of her school and said, "Maybe we should start our own school." She wanted to plan something with Dion, to know he would be there, and yet there was this whole other mess between them, and only she could do anything about it. It wasn't so easy to find words that wouldn't send him flying off the handle, but she gripped his hand and made herself speak.

"Your father should back off," she said. "What does he have to keep covering all these stories for? Doesn't he want you to go to school?"

Dion, making excuses for his father, said, "He's got enough to think about. *He* can't save the whole world."

Nancy wondered, if it were between her and Mama, which one would Ned look out for? "What is he trying to do, catch my father?"

"Catch him?" Dion pulled his hands away and tucked them between his knees. "Your father is the Angel of Brooklyn."

"Your father made up the whole thing! There is no Angel. It's just a nice story to make people feel better." They were pushing each other away with words, but their eyes were locked together.

"But it's good news," Dion said. "Don't you see?"

"Stop him," she said. And again she said, "There is no Angel. No *one* Angel."

"Then what does your father do?"

"Same thing you do. And me."

"You?"

"Who else would throw a clothespin?"

He whistled. "Pretty good."

"Dad's just the same," she said. "He wants to beat up the bad stuff. So he throws rocks at it and jumps on it or gets its attention. It's bigger than he is. He's just higher."

"And smaller," said Dion.

She looked at him warily. "Wouldn't you like to be the Angel?" Her hands were gooey from sweating and tears.

"What?"

"It's stupid, I know. There's no such thing. I just wish it were true. *I* want to be the Angel."

"What for?"

"So I can't be seen. So I can't be hurt." He knelt in front of her. *Oh, his eyes.* "So they won't know who's helping."

"I'll know," he said.

She kissed him; he was strong, sweet. If they could get his mother fixed, maybe his father would look out for him.

"Help my mother," he said, staring into her with his ghost eyes. "Or there's no telling what my dad'll do."

"Are you threatening me?" she asked.

He might as well have been leaving, the way he seemed to recede from her. "Warning you," he said.

"Get away from me," she howled at him. She tore her eyes away, turned her back.

He was up and gone, over the wall and onto the next roof. She made it to the wall. They stared at each other across the space.

"Go now," she said. "And don't come back. I've forgotten your name again."

His fingers on the wall were the last thing she saw as he rounded a corner in a blur of gray. Nancy put all her energy into getting to that corner. When she did, he was already gone.

She collapsed back onto the chaise and imagined she felt him putting distance between them, felt it stretch out as he went away.

Then it was true. There was no real connection between her family and his, other than the one Niko had formed by blackmailing her grandfather and demanding the very lifesilk of her Granny. How could there be anything good about that, no matter how good her heart told her Dion was. What stories would Niko feel free to tell if his wife died? How easy it would be for him to let the whole entire city know who the

Greene-Karas were and what they were! And what would happen to them then?

What came to her mind most readily was home-room, and what they would say.

"Heard about that Nancy Greene-Kara? Heard how she's half insect?"

"Well, she always bugged me!"

"Knitting with those knitting needles like antennas."

"You know, she didn't even shave her legs."

"Ew. Nasty."

It figures, thought Nancy. *The first person I ever felt like I belonged with should drag me into this.* It occurred to her that she'd been in it before she ever met Dion. She'd have been in it one way or another, would have met him one way or another.

On his way to the next dusty rooftop, Dion caught the drift of Nancy's heavy thoughts. *It figures,* he thought. *The first person I ever felt like I belonged with should turn out to be someone who wouldn't take a chance on me. Scared. Well, who could blame her?*

36

Nancy passed Saturday night and most of Sunday on the roof, getting better at putting weight on her leg, feeling alone even when Ned was there, and worrying.

Someday soon the phone at Granny and Grandpa's was going to ring, and they would get up and go to the house on the curved street. Nancy, as usual, would ride along in the backseat, to keep Granny company during the time when Grandpa went inside to check the condition of the patient. If Granny used that time to tell Nancy one of her action-inspiring stories, would there be enough left for Granny herself?

No one else would be admitted to see Rose. Niko

Papadopolis would want no spectators. He wouldn't care if Granny sat in the car while the checking went on, and he wouldn't care if Nancy was left alone once the treatment began.

Nancy devised a plan around the only person there she thought she could wrap around her finger. The plan depended on the jump rope Dion had fixed. She packed it into her backpack on Sunday afternoon when Grandpa came in his car to take her back to Carroll Gardens. Ned and Grandpa, each holding one elbow, got her up the stairs, though she told them they didn't need to: already her thigh was pulling and hurting less than this morning, further testimony to Rachel's healing ability.

"Hey," she called, West Virginia–style.

Granny sat in the stuffed chair by the front window in the living room, as if she were waiting for something.

"I started knitting my first sleeve!" Nancy announced from the doorway.

No answer. She went and stood in front of Granny, holding up her hands with a jump rope cat's cradle in between. Granny Tina didn't think twice, reached in with both hands and turned it into the soldier's bed.

Nancy took it back and made candles, the one where Granny had to twist her pinkies around the strings while she pulled it into the manger form. Manger was the first move Nancy didn't know, and she watched closely to get it right.

But she wasn't holding it right, because Granny went *tch*, like a little girl, and said in a cranky voice, "I can't reach, Josie. Hold it closer."

Nancy glanced at her face, but Granny's eyes were on the strings as she twisted them into place. She held her hands up to Nancy again.

"I'm Nancy," Nancy told her. Granny blinked.

Nancy's turn to make the soldier's bed. Granny's for candles. Nancy's to try the candles-to-manger transformation. She tucked her pinkies under, the way Granny had done it, plunged her fingers into the right spaces. But the strings slid through her fingers and, once again, it was just a big loop of jump rope. "Oh," Nancy sighed, crestfallen.

Granny took the rope and Nancy thought she was going to show her, but instead Granny wrapped it around her own fingers. They spun and popped and plunged, and she let go with cat's whiskers. Held them up in front of her face and meowed with an expression worthy of entertaining Mina herself.

Then her fingers went dipping and diving again, and when they stopped there was a perfect bridge between them, looped and wound through every finger, exquisitely tense. She said words in Italian, words Nancy couldn't understand, except that they included her grandfather's name: *"La Scaletta di Giacomo."*

"Huh?"

"Oh, come on, honey, you've heard that old story. It's right in the Bible. Jacob's ladder, with the angels ascending and descending between heaven and earth." Granny turned her hands so that the ladder hung vertically.

"Show me how," Nancy said.

Granny showed her. It was just a few steps beyond cat's whiskers, and when it was done, the stretching tension between Nancy's fingers was perfect and divine, truly the most satisfying thing she'd yet made with her hands. She wanted more, and quickly wound her hands through it again. She wished there were more steps going onward from it, but where would they go? It was perfect as it was, a ladder, a connection, a bridge between heaven and earth.

It wasn't exactly a story, but it gave Nancy something new all the same.

By Monday Nancy's legs had a light stubble. "Is this what's supposed to happen?" she whispered to Annette in homeroom.

"Yeah. I shave mine every other day."

"I hadn't realized it would be a regular thing."

Annette rolled her eyes. "Where have you been hiding? Everybody knows the hair comes back thicker once you've shaved."

It was the first piece of good news Nancy had heard in a while. *Really?*

Annette scrutinized her face. "You *like* that idea?"

"How was the dance?" Nancy asked quickly. She pulled up her kneesocks and patted her skirt where the bandage was. She hadn't told Annette about her accident and didn't show her the bandage. Nancy didn't know a lot about medicine, especially spider medicine, but she knew that stitches shouldn't heal—and disappear—within forty-eight hours of a big gash in the skin.

Annette had had a good time with Jimmy Velcro. It made a lump come in Nancy's throat, hearing about

how they'd danced. Nancy pulled her knitting out of
her backpack and sat working her way past the elbow
of her sleeve. *Let them talk if they want to.* She hadn't
seen Dion. Not on the roof, not on the train, not in the
grocery store.

"Hey, Nancy, whatcha knitting/crocheting/doing?"

"My Grandma/Nana/Nona does that. She made me
the best socks/scarf/sweater."

"Nancy, can you knit socks?"

"I never tried," she said.

"You could, I bet, if you could make a sweater
with stripes/colors/ribs like that. You could go into
business."

"We *all* oughta knit socks. Then we could quit worrying about our hairy legs."

Everybody cracked up, Nancy included, all of them
laughing together. Who'd have thought it? Annette
came and leaned on her shoulder and asked, teasing, "Is
that knitting or purling?"

"I'll make you a baby bonnet, Annette," Nancy
threatened.

"Listen," Annette whispered. "When I went to the
dance? My mommy had a *date.*"

"Really?"

"Wouldn't that be great if she got married again? Then I could go out all I want."

Nancy was astonished.

"Is that what you want?" she asked.

"I do *now*," said Annette. She kissed Nancy's cheek and whispered. "That Jimmy Velcro . . . "

"Ooh la la?" asked Nancy. It was what they used to say about watching smooching in movies.

"Oh, very ooh la la!" said Annette. She turned back to the other girls, giggling. That was all right, Nancy thought, and considered the idea of Annette kissing Jimmy Velcro. She would have liked to tell Annette about Dion. But she wondered if Annette would understand any more than she'd understand if Nancy told her she was never ever shaving her legs again.

37

"How do you heal her?" Nancy asked Granny. She was forking up spaghetti out of the pot and serving Granny for once, instead of the other way around. Granny was feeble, but at the moment her eyes (and head) seemed clear.

"It's like giving her energy." Granny pulled the pitcher across the table, poured beautiful red sauce over the noodles.

"Granny, you haven't got any energy to spare."

"Why haven't I?"

"You're old," she said flatly. "You're sick. I was trying to show you my sleeves this afternoon and it was like you weren't here."

"Maybe I wasn't!" Granny said carelessly. "Are you worried I'll die?"

Nancy stuck a knot of noodles into her mouth to fill it, and didn't say a word.

"What do you think happens when you die?" Granny asked.

"How do I know?" Nancy said with her mouth full.

"Listen, girl, there's only so much energy in the world."

"Right! So you'd better *conserve* it while you can."

"While I can! Honey, you know there's always the *same* energy in the world. When something dies, its energy goes into something else to make it live, or make it stronger."

"Or to transform into something else," Nancy said.

Granny pointed her fork in a way Grandpa Joke would have disapproved of. "What do you mean, *transform*?"

"Change into something else, the way heat changes water." She remembered this from science classes, but had never seen how it applied to anyone she knew.

"Answer me this: does the heat *want* to change the water?"

"No."

"Well, what if it did?"

"That's like saying a ray of sun can direct its energy into a specific drop of water. It doesn't work that way."

"How do you know it doesn't?"

Nancy put spaghetti in her mouth and studied Granny's dark eyes, the thinness of her hair over her scalp, the shakiness in her hands. She hoped her own hands would never shake like that. Her hands that had made Jacob's ladder and cat's cradle just yesterday . . . "Can *you?*" she asked Granny.

"I can choose where to direct my energy."

Nancy didn't say anything, not yet.

"Most parents direct it to their children."

"But not you?"

"Who says I'm not? There's some left for my grandchild, too."

"Haven't I got enough energy?" Nancy asked cautiously.

"Haven't you been feeling different lately?"

In more ways than one. "Yes. But I thought that was because of me."

"Of course. You've got plenty of your own energy, Nancy."

"Then—"

"Nothing else?" Granny's eyes held her steady, but a wisp of cloud had begun to come into them. She was tired.

"Those stories you've been telling me," Nancy said. "They seem so moving. Real. Like I'm *in* them."

"You've heard them before."

"Afterward I try things I wouldn't try before."

"Or is it just that you understand better?"

"Or am I changing?"

"Nancy. Don't you want to grow up?"

What a stupefying question. Nancy put down her fork, sat there with her hands to her cheeks, then nodded slowly.

"Don't you want to grow stronger?" Again, Granny pointed the fork at Nancy, her eyes intense, though cloudier, her hand trembling.

"Maybe." Nancy was afraid to say more.

"So?"

"What will I have to do, if I get stronger?"

"What will you *have* to do?" Granny hit the table so hard that she lost hold of her fork, which flew across the table and landed in Nancy's lap. "Ask what you'll be *able* to do!"

"But, Granny—"

Granny was still speaking, saying over and over, under her breath, "Just like your mother. Just like your mother."

"I am *not!*"

Granny looked up at her, muttering, "Don't you *dare* be."

Nancy banged the door of the greenhouse open. Rachel was on the floor, inside the loom, warping up yet again, as though there were some great rush on gray silk shawls. "Mama!"

Rachel practically clobbered herself, jumping. "What?"

"Pay attention." Nancy climbed into the loom beside her mother, crouched holding her skirt around her feet, knees to her chin. "There's a woman—"

"What woman!"

"She lives in Cobble Hill."

Rachel's face closed up. "Yes . . . "

"She's got a little girl, just ten, did you know that? And she's sick, Mama. She's so sick, she can't heal. And Granny's helping her. She's trying to heal her."

Rachel nodded. "It's not going well," she said.

"It's taking her *away*."

"The woman?" asked Rachel.

"She's taking Granny with her."

Rachel's eyes reflected the color of the grass outside.

"Her name is Rose Browning. Mama, you can help her, and she can help you. You've got to."

Rachel ran her strong, graceful, hardworking hand across her silver-gray warp strings. "What help do I need?"

"She's a counselor, Mama. A therapist. She could help you get out of here."

"Can't you see I don't want to get out?" Mama's voice was as languid as the green afternoon.

"Mama, I love you. Dad loves you. What are you going to do, stay inside forever?"

"It's not in me, Nancy," Rachel said.

"Oh, *nonsense*," said Nancy. The word was stronger than the worst swear, and said exactly what she meant. *Nonsense*, like not listening to the universe, fate or destiny or whatever Grandpa said. "It's what people choose that matters!" she hollered.

"Or what chooses them?" her mother yelled back.

"Like my sweater stripes?" asked Nancy. "I don't

know which is true, Mama. Only this—what you always tell me to look at—the pattern. But *you're* not looking." She strode out of the greenhouse and down the steps to Rachel's apartment, and there she spun around and stood nose-level with the grass, like Thumbelina, stuck in the hole with the mole.

"You ought to, for Dad and me," she said to her mother, loud in the shady courtyard.

Rachel rose and came to the door of the greenhouse, the fingertips of one hand fussing with the fingers of the other. "How can I?" she said in a hoarse whisper.

"Not even for Granny?" Nancy said.

In a daze the Greene Mamba went back to her loom, picked up her shuttle, sat, and trod on the treadle, resumed sliding the shuttle back and forth.

Nancy dashed back to the greenhouse. She sank to the floor beside her mother, leaned her head on Rachel's knee. Rachel couldn't press the treadles that way. "Oh, Ma," Nancy moaned. "My granny. She's losing power, Grandpa says."

"She's also giving it up," said Mama. "And that's a different situation."

Nancy, turning quickly, saw the corners of her

mother's mouth forcing their way down. "Why? I don't want her to!"

"But she's giving it to you, my pet."

"You're the one who needs it."

"Me? I'm not weak at all," Mama said.

"And I am? I need power?" Nancy drew herself up angrily.

"Not the way you used to," Mama said.

"Who says? I'm the one who goes out. None of this 'I can't live up high.' 'I can't live down low.' You two! You and Dad! *I* live in *both* places. I go to school. I do the shopping. I ride the subway." She was yelling into Mama's face.

Rachel didn't flinch. She placed her hand on Nancy's head, tangled her fingers in the hair that wouldn't behave.

"Help Rose," Nancy told her mother, "and you'll save Granny. And yourself, too."

38

The phone rang. Granny looked vaguely toward it as though trying to remember the purpose of this odd invention. Nancy knew she didn't remember Grandpa saying not to answer it.

"Should I?" Nancy asked. Granny nodded. "Hello?"

"Tell the doctor to come tonight," said the man's voice. His voice was flat, plain, but around the edges there was a ripple of emotion. He was afraid.

"Come where?" But she knew who it was. Didn't *he* recognize her voice?

"Just tell him to come, girl." He hung up.

• • •

the web

This house call was not like the other house calls.

To begin with, Grandpa Joke insisted on going alone, only to be shouted down by Granny, who out-insisted him. Once Granny was going, Nancy refused to be left behind.

"I'm going in to check on the situation," Grandpa told them. "There will not be anything that can be done."

Nancy horned in. "Granny won't stay in the car."

Granny refused to vitiate her energy by even arguing. She simply got her jacket on, and her shoes, and grasped her canes in her gnarled hands. She stood in the doorway, Nancy just behind her, daring Joke to go down the stairs without her.

He tried. He tried to get past them both, hiding his face behind the hat he pretended to be putting on as he went through the door. But Granny's grip, strong from years of doing everything that mattered with her hands, landed on his elbow. "Giacomo," she said, and the moment would be frozen forever in Nancy's mind: Granny looking up intently into Grandpa's face, her eyes smoldering hot on him, Grandpa's face under the hat, riveted on his wife. He was unable to refuse her.

No, there was never any question in Nancy's mind, afterward, that this was what her Granny wanted to do.

But Grandpa said, "I'm going to tell him you're too ill to come. He won't know you're here. You're not even in the car. I'll do what I can for the woman, and then we'll go."

"To Häagen-Dazs," suggested Granny, in a weird moment.

"Right," said Grandpa Joke, exchanging a glance with Nancy. "And eat ice cream."

"And that'll be the end with Niko Papadopolis," Granny continued.

And Rose Browning, Nancy thought.

Grandpa put his hand on Saint Christopher's foot before opening the door to the street. "Saints preserve us," he said.

"Forevermore," said Granny.

And Nancy said, because it was a prayer, "Amen."

When Grandpa Joke parked in front of the house that was in the middle of the block of maybe the only curved street in Brooklyn, things looked different. The house was not gray and faceless and dark, not trying to go unnoticed, not tonight. All the lights were on, bold and bright and blazing into the street, and opera music played though the open window.

Niko came charging out the front door. Nancy slouched below the seat, pulling Granny down with her. (Grandpa had been right to put her in the back with Nancy). Niko took Grandpa's arm as if he were his long lost best friend, and ushered him as quickly as he could across the sidewalk, a muscled arm across his back.

Nancy's arm was around Granny, keeping her down low. Niko wasn't looking back at the car anyway, too anxious, Nancy supposed, to get back inside with Grandpa. But what would he do when he heard that Granny Tina wasn't here?

Suddenly Nancy snapped to attention, never sure what came over her (was it Dion's presence inside the house?). She jumped out of the car and yelled, "Grandpa? You won't be long, will you?"

Everything froze. Niko halted as he was dragging Grandpa along. They each stared back at Nancy with a different kind of dismay.

"Nancy!" called Grandpa, reaching for the post at the bottom of the stoop as if he needed support.

"In," Niko ordered Grandpa. The door shut.

Grandpa, Nancy thought, did not want Granny to worry about what was going on in Niko's house. Nancy would worry for her, then, worry how she could possibly help fix things for Dion's family and for hers. "Just what am I supposed to do?" she asked Granny in desperation.

Granny's hand reached toward Nancy through the open window. "Nancy," she said. "I want to ask you—"

"What?" Nancy bent to look through the window.

"Whether I ever told you how Giacomo and I decided to get married?"

"Gran," she said, "what kind of ice cream are you going to get?"

"He didn't propose. He didn't ask my permission. Like your grandpa."

Like Grandpa? She's gone from me, thought Nancy. *Next she'll be calling me Josie or Rachel or Joke.*

"You need to know this, if you're going to be going around with boys," said Granny.

"Boys?" *What boys? Where?*

"It's so romantic," said Granny. "I'm going to go tell Giacomo."

Nancy stood back from the car to field her. But

Granny didn't move. "Listen," she said.

All right, it didn't matter, as long as Granny continued to stay out of sight and safe in the car. If listening to a story would keep her there, Nancy would do it.

She didn't get in the car, though. She plopped down on the sidewalk, which was still warm from the day's sun, though the sky was already dark. She didn't want to hide in the car. She wanted to be present, here on the sidewalk like a gift from Grandpa's real life (the one he had outside this house).

"He never came and found me," Granny said.

"Who?" Nancy wanted to wash her cobwebby mind out until things seemed clearer.

"Grandpa. Instead he was always there, when I arrived somewhere. He'd make sure he got there first, make it look like I was doing the finding." The Brooklyn evening stilled. Had Grandpa made Niko turn down the music? Niko had shut the windows, that was what had changed. It was too warm, almost muggy, sticky, to have all the windows closed. Nancy didn't see any air conditioner.

"You should have seen his face, how he'd grin when I'd turn up at some party." Granny threw back her head and laughed. "Oh, you should have seen him!"

Nancy would have liked to see him now. Nancy and Grandpa, getting Granny home to a nice cup of tea and her soft bed. She could feel the house behind her, unyielding, guarded.

Granny went on with her tale. "Well, I asked around, you know, and all the doctors seemed to think he was a good prospect. The nurses, well, they were just gleeful about him."

"Gleeful?" Gawky Joke couldn't have been a ladies' man.

"We used to sit and knit at the nurses' station, passing the time. Yes, everyone was a knitter back then. When they showed off their knitting, they all had rows he'd done. Good with his hands, and smart to boot. One day I walked into the coat room and of course he was already in there, though he'd never admit he knew I was coming. And he said to me, 'All right. You want to get married? We'll get married. Come on.'"

Granny had skipped over a lot, Nancy thought, then realized that she'd heard the missing bits, or somehow knew them. It was as if she were inside young Tina back in the Bronx as she bustled down the hall behind young Giacomo. Nancy could see out of Tina's eyes. As she slipped her arms into the sleeves of the coat Joke held for her, she felt the satiny lining. As she hurried to keep up with long strides, she felt the tension in her calf muscles. As he led her down the ward steps and out onto the sidewalk along the Grand Concourse, not pausing till a red light held them back, she felt her excitement.

"Giacomo, where are we going?"

He spoke gently then. "To the church."

"What church?"

"We'll walk to the first church we come to, and that's where we'll get married."

"Today?" His eyes stayed ahead, ignoring the people waiting for the bus, the roller skaters, the ladies with strollers full of babies.

All right. Why not marry him today?

There appeared a church of gray stone and stained glass.

"Do you know what it was?" Granny asked.

Nancy shook her head.

"Presbyterian. *Scots* Presbyterian."

Catholic Joke had known all along that the first

church they would come to was the kind Tina had gone to back home in West Virginia.

It was the end of the story. Granny Tina leaned back in her seat, closed her eyes, still in the story, in whatever they said and did after finding that church. She didn't have to tell Nancy. Nancy knew. She could feel the arms around her, feel the warmth—

Where am I? Who am I? Nancy. Here on this street on this sidewalk.

Granny was resting too deeply, her dreams too heavy. Nancy held her breath, listened to Granny breathe, to the rustling sycamore leaves, to the distant subway rumble, felt the movement of the city through her bottom, through the sidewalk, through the dirt beneath.

"Nancy?" Granny sounded weary. "I'm thirsty."

How unlike her it was to ask for anything. "Thirsty?" Nancy sat straight up and looked around. No thermos, no water bottle. *Oh Lord,* thought Nancy. *Why did I let her tell me another story?*

"I'll run up to the corner," she said. "It won't take a moment. Don't move."

"Nancy, where would I move to?"

At least she knows it's me. At least she's that clear.

"Okay," Nancy said. She went charging down the street through the shadows.

A screech of metal stopped her in her tracks at the corner. A clothesline overhead? No, it was the gate of the grocery store being cranked down. Through the diamond webbing she saw the lady working the crank.

"Wait!" she shouted. She sighed and waved through the grocery store gate. "Please!"

The lady tried to wave her away. She came near the window and told Nancy, clearly and slowly, "I am closed."

Nancy pressed her face through the diamonds of the gate so the lady could see how sweet and innocent she was. "Please?"

Again the squeaking sound came. The lady wasn't making it. She opened the glass door without opening the gate and said, *"Cerrado."* Just in case Nancy spoke Spanish. But the lady was Korean, and Nancy didn't speak Spanish, so it made her smile.

"I need a water for my grandmother. Please?" She poked her money through the gate. The lady bustled off, shaking her head, and brought the water.

"*Komapsumnida*," Nancy said, the way Granny had got Mrs. Kim to teach her to say thank you, years ago at the grocery near their house. A safety net of kindness, extended to this neighborhood, too.

The lady locked the door again and walked away. As Nancy headed back to the car, again came the squeaking sound, so familiar. It was a funny time of night to do laundry.

A moment later she thought it might have been the car door squeaking. It had been opened, all right. Granny was gone.

39

She ran up the steps of the house. For some reason she didn't knock. She stood there and listened and tried to feel. A wrong mood, a weird mood, a mood about this place made her not knock. Then a noise in the hallway inside sent her leaping off the stoop to crouch behind it in the dark on the ground. The water bottle fell splat behind her and sent a silent puddle of water out around it. Nancy's foot was getting wet and her thigh throbbed, but she stayed still, still as Ned on any rooftop.

The hinge creaked, the door opened, and Niko's voice barked, "Go on out!"

Oh, thank God. Let it be my grandparents.

But the figure coming toward her was Mina.

How could her father shove her out alone? was Nancy's first thought. *What was going on inside that they'd put her out?* was the second. And if she hadn't been so busy wondering where Dion was (her third thought), she'd have paid attention to the fact that Mina was standing watching the stream of water bubbling across the stoop.

"I *thought* you were out here," Mina said.

"You thought—*what*?"

"You're always here, aren't you?"

"How do you know?"

"How do *you* know that *I'm* here?" the girl asked. Nancy kept her face straight, but inside she thought: *I like this kid, the way I like her brother.* For the first time she wondered what their parents were really like.

"I'll show you what else I know," she told Mina, and unwrapped the jump rope from around her wrist. She taught Mina cat's cradle. The soldier's bed sprang up. Candles lit beneath it, folded their light into a manger. The manger's straw turned to diamonds, like a miracle out of "Rumpelstiltskin." The diamonds blinked and glimmered, became cat's eyes. And the cat's eyes looked for a kitten and wove the cat's cradle again.

Then Nancy took the rope from Mina and twirled her hands through Jacob's ladder, so fast and sure that Mina was dazzled.

"Show me that!" she begged.

"Inside," Nancy said.

"They don't want me inside," Mina said.

"Who doesn't?"

"My daddy. And that doctor. And the old spider lady."

"What about your mother?" Nancy asked gently.

Mina wound the jump rope tightly around one hand in a way that didn't form any figure, and twisted it even tighter.

"What about Dion?"

"Dion who?" the girl said angrily, with a look of her father about her.

"Your brother?"

"He should have been here before."

"He's here now?"

"That's why *I'm* out here." Mina mimicked an adult voice. " 'Too many kids in here!' "

"Dion sent you out?"

"I'm supposed to be getting—"

"Getting what?"

"Ice cream." It was the snack of the evening. Mina stopped. "You want to go in, don't you?" she asked.

"If you let me in, Mina, I'll teach you Jacob's ladder."

"Pinkie swear?" They linked pinkies, and Mina took a ribbon from around her neck and used the key on it to open the door without a sound. "You have to be silent," she whispered. She slipped off her shoes, crept barefoot down the hallway, and stopped just before a door that was ajar. Nancy followed. Inside, a pale dark woman wrapped in silk of silver-gray, in so many lay-ers it was as though she'd never be warm. Granny, slim as a ghost in the chair beside the bed. And Grandpa Joke, hovering above them both and looking breakable as a bubble.

"You're here, then, Nancy," said Grandpa. Granny held out her hands impatiently, reaching palms-down for Nancy's. Nancy lifted up her hands to Granny's. Her hands were still smaller than Granny's and maybe always would be. Granny's knuckles shone, the bones pressed up beneath her skin, and the gold of her wed-ding ring gleamed in the light from the rose-shaded lamp.

"Nancy, this is Ms. Browning," Grandpa said. Nancy

turned toward the bed, turned her body away from Granny, thought she'd reach for Dion's mother's hand, but Granny held on tight.

"Call me Rose, cherub." Her eyes were the color of Dion's, but the pupils were large and black, with darkness or love or kindness.

"Hi, Rose," Nancy said over her shoulder, trying to pull her hands away. Granny would not let go. Nancy wanted to turn, to pull harder, but instead felt her palms rise up to meet Granny's as though to squeeze out whatever gap remained between their hands. But she wanted to talk to Rose—

"Well, kiddo," Rose said faintly. "You're the one my two are both in love with, huh?" It was almost more than she could say, but still there was a strength in her voice that reminded Nancy of a gym teacher she used to have, back in middle school, who made her laugh so that she didn't mind not being able to do one single intelligent thing in gym class.

"Mina says you've got magical hands. She says you made the Eiffel Tower? And my Dion—"

"Stop!" Granny said to Rose. Rose fell against the pillow as though the two sentences she'd spoken had exhausted her. Granny, exhausted herself, sent a different energy into Nancy's hands, an *asking* energy. She seemed to fade before Nancy's eyes.

"Gran?"

Rose, from her pillow, said to Nancy, "Then you're the next Healer."

40

The next Healer? Nancy yanked back her hands.

"Wait!" Granny growled. She gripped Nancy's hands so tightly it hurt. Again Nancy felt hot pressure in her own palms.

"Are you?" Hoping, Rose lifted herself onto one elbow and reached toward the bond of the locked hands. She was asking whether Nancy could help, whether Nancy could heal her. "Nancy?" She touched Nancy's wrist with two shaky fingers. Though Granny lunged forward with her upper body, her hold on Nancy's hands did not change with Rose's touch.

"What's happening?" Niko barreled into the room, pressing through the doorway with Mina, pushing Grandpa out of the way.

"Are you?" Rose asked Nancy in a voice that made it sound like Nancy shouldn't worry if she wasn't. Nancy was frantic not to disappoint her, but what was required?

"Is she?" asked Niko in his hard voice.

"Is she what?" asked Mina in her soft one.

"The Healer," said Grandpa.

The room seemed to ring with the echo of his words.

Nancy wanted her hands out of Granny's hands.

Granny wouldn't let go. She held on as though she were desperate not to release Nancy. She shook Nancy's hands in hers, pressed against them and drew Nancy's eyes to hers. There were no two possibilities in Granny's eyes, only one.

"Nancy!" Granny called out in a voice that stilled the murmuring echoes. "Nancy, are you?"

Nancy wanted to be.

She held tight to her grandmother's hands and in a dazzled instant she saw a view of Rose, up on her feet, her cheeks pink and healthy, up and about in her house, doing things. She thought of herself, Healer Nancy, making it happen, thought how it would feel, how Dion and Mina and even Niko would love her then. She gripped Granny's hands and felt the energy flow between them and out of them and into them.

Once again Granny demanded, "Are you?"

Wanting it wasn't enough. Nancy suddenly felt the city around her, gray and plain and dusty, and in this view of it everyone, including her, was the same size, paying the same subway fare, with the same troubles, the same fights, the same lousy chance of getting by, getting through, getting along, getting over it. Everyone had the same overwhelming sadness, and for this moment Nancy felt how Rose must have felt—powerless. And knew that it was true.

She felt a huge, drowning wave of disappointment. When she looked around the room, released from Granny's eyes, she sensed that this same disappointment had washed through all of them, that they all knew the instant she did.

"No, I'm not," she said in the tiniest possible voice.

There was a rumble and a slam from the hallway as

the only person who hadn't squeezed into the little bedroom got himself out of the tight spot his heart was in. *Oh, Dion, come back.* He was gone.

"Good God, girl!" roared Niko, crazy with fear. "Have you been wasting our time here?"

Granny's grip lightened. She didn't exactly drop Nancy's hands, but she took her hands away, pulled her eyes away, away from them all. Nancy didn't want to see her grandmother's face, or Rose's, or Niko's, or any of them. She wanted to see Dion, but he was gone.

She had never felt so hurt.

She never afterward wanted anything so much.

She wanted to be—

And she wasn't.

She never wanted so much to fade away, disappear, and hide.

She never understood her mother so well as at that moment, or wanted her so much.

But no! Mama had what Nancy didn't, what Granny hadn't been able to suck out of Nancy's palms with her powerful ones. Mama Rachel had what Rose needed. Nancy didn't.

Yet Nancy was here and Rachel wasn't.

Well, Nancy would do something about that.

She would get Mama here somehow.

But first to get out, to get free, to go. But first—

Grandpa left the room in despair. There was no ground under her feet and Nancy felt gigantic, and ungainly. She reached out for the support of the door-knob.

Niko leaned over Rose in a gesture that forever shifted Nancy's ugly image of him, cradling her somehow without putting his weight on the bed or on her.

It was Nancy who caught her pale, spent Granny as she fell. For a moment Granny seemed gone. She opened her eyes six inches from Nancy's. "I'm perfectly fine, Josie," she said. Nothing moved but her mouth and the slowly turning light in her dark, dark eyes. "I've been happy every minute. Never a bit of pain until now."

Pain?

"Don't be sad, Granny," Nancy said, not thinking of what she was saying or where or how loud, only hurrying to say it.

Pain!

Grandpa and Nancy lifted Granny onto a narrow

couch in the hallway. Grandpa felt expertly for Granny's pulse.

Niko Papadopolis burst out the bedroom door. "What's going on?" His face was pale, his eyes colorless like Dion's, his lids puffy and red. Was his Rose, then, dead? Dying? Where, oh where, had Dion gone?

"Now you're here you'll stay here," Niko said to Nancy abruptly. "I'm not having you going off to the police. You can watch Mina while we look after my wife."

The expression on Grandpa's face showed Nancy all she needed to know about Granny's condition. His hands in fists at his sides, he said, "My granddaughter is not part of our agreement."

Was it threat or sadness in Niko's face? "Inside," he barked at Mina and Nancy. Nancy wanted to run for the front door, take Mina with her.

Where was Dion? Had his father thrown him out, too? Or had he just left again? *He* wouldn't go for the police, would he, not for his own father?

Where was *her* dad? On some rooftop, safe and calm? Well, wasn't this a crime? *Be drawn to this one, Dad!* And Mama, who could help if Nancy could only get to her and make her come . . .

Niko and Grandpa growled unintelligible words at each other. *Get out,* Nancy begged Grandpa silently. She walked along the hallway that led to the back of the house. There was a dresser there, painted a soft pink, and on it was a photograph of a family. Younger, sweeter, rosier, and the mother a female version of Dion, except for her bright eyes (and she had hair). Seeing it, Nancy understood Dion's ghostly gray look, his father's drained face. A formal, posed, studio portrait, an item the Greene Mamba wouldn't let in the house, but to Nancy it was an advertisement for family bliss. A mother and father, together under one roof. A boy and a girl. Normal. Perfect. And now Rose was dying. Was Granny?

Nancy bolted for the front door, unthinking. But Niko got her by the arm, held on hard.

"Niko!" Grandpa thundered. "There are other things! Other people! My wife!"

Niko let go of Nancy and grabbed Grandpa by the shoulders. "There is nobody else!"

"There's nothing more to be done for your Rose!"

"Never say that," Niko pleaded, wilting.

Grandpa's hands came up to take Niko's shoulders, but he was not shaking him back or pushing him; he was just holding him, making him be still.

And then a sound came that sent them all running back into the living room, forgetting the front door. It was Mina, screaming as though she were strangling.

41

"Rose?" Sad, bewildered Niko leaned a hand on each side of the doorjamb. "Rose?" he asked more quietly.

But the scream came again from the living room.

Nancy got there first. Mina crouched in the corner of a chair, tears flowing, pointing.

Niko went to her, took her forearms gently, looked into her eyes. Then he saw what she was screaming at: a spider, furry and black, dangling from a dragline beside Mina. "Little Miss Muffet," he said gruffly, and swung his arm toward the dragline.

"DON'T!" Nancy yelled. "It's bad luck to kill a spider."

"Spiders are vermin," he said. He rolled a magazine into a pipe.

"Bad luck," Nancy warned boldly.

He whacked at the spider with the magazine. He missed and hit the silk, and the spider fell near the baseboard.

On the couch in the hallway, Granny mumbled, "Ned?" Her hands shuddered where they lay on her stomach.

Grandpa laughed a phony, desperate-sounding laugh. "Why don't you leave it alone, Niko?"

"I'll leave nothing!"

"Papa," said Mina. "You're scaring me."

"I'm getting the spider for you, Rosebud."

Mina said, "No. You'll hurt it."

"Don't you want me to? You were screaming two seconds ago."

"It's bad luck," she said. Niko threw Nancy a disgusted look.

"Let me get rid of it for you." Nancy picked up a water glass from the table, drained it into a dried-out plant. "I'll show you how to make a bug ambulance," she told Mina.

An ambulance. Nancy put the glass down over the

spider, slipped an envelope from the coffee table under the glass, and lifted the spider in its glass dome toward Mina. Mina stepped forward, fascinated, wary.

"See all his legs?" Nancy asked. She was relying on Mina. How could she rely on this kid?

"Eight," Mina said. She looked at Niko for praise, but he just looked appalled. "*You're* not afraid, are you?" she asked Nancy. "Not afraid of spiders?"

Nancy gave the spider a closer look. He was blackish-brown, with awfully long legs and a familiar look in his eye. "Heights. Falling. Razors." She listed her fears. "But never spiders."

She carried the spider-under-glass toward the front door, opened it, wondered if it was going to be an easy escape.

There was a firm hand on her back, a strong grip that pulled her hair. "Let the kid do it," Niko said.

Yes, she would have to rely on Mina.

"Let Dion come with me," Mina said.

"Him?" said Niko with a short laugh. "*He* didn't stay long."

"He's gone?" Nancy asked, to get information. Had he ever really been here?

"What do you know about my son?" Niko whirled toward her.

"Nothing," Nancy said. She felt all of their eyes.

"Nothing is what he's good for," Niko said.

Nancy turned away from him and handed the spider ambulance to Mina, and turned back and said to Niko, "That is *so* untrue," so softly that only he could hear. The way he stared at her! The venom! Maybe he *was* the type to hurt his own. "You know I'm right," she whispered, and thought she saw pain to the depths of his eyes.

Mina said, "I'll be careful."

"You're a brave girl, Wilhemina Rose," her father said.

"Don't let him out too near the house," Nancy told Mina. "He'll just come back in. Take him down to that tree by the curb. Let him out in the ivy. Spiders like that."

"When you're done," Niko said, "go up to the corner and pick out some ice cream the way I told you before."

Nancy began, "But the store's—"

"Enough from you!" Niko said to her, and Grandpa's eyes behind him stopped her further. Granny lay staring on the couch.

There went Mina. If Nancy had done her job right,

Mina wouldn't get freaked out and squish the spider under her foot.

In the doorway Nancy closed her eyes and sent a strand of wishes across the space. *Be there,* she asked. *Be here.*

She should have wished for herself, too. When she turned back to the hall the spider fear was gone from Niko's face. "We need to get you out of the way, too," he said to her, as if he were planning to squish her in place of the spider.

"So I'll go," Nancy said obstinately.

"She'll stay with me, if I have to be here," said Grandpa.

Suddenly Nancy knew what she wanted. She headed for the bedroom, for the figure in the lacy cover of silk. Just a glance through the door, that was all she got, and it was all she needed to get Niko away from Grandpa and Granny.

He grabbed her arm and pulled her back. Nancy realized what she hadn't understood a short time before: he was out of power. Niko's power was his writing, his research, his digging. He was like a burrowing spider who needed a surprise place from which to jump out at you. Now he'd lost the surprise advantage; he would have to rely on his jumping. She could guess how wildly he might jump, if he feared everything was slipping. If she could just get away, get Mama . . .

In the meantime dealing with him was a matter of making him think he was in charge. She could pull what she wanted out of Niko. She tugged her arm away, to make him grip tighter. He nudged her ahead of him out of the bedroom, into the hall, toward the living room again. Each time he took her in a new direction she let out a whine, an angry hiss, a yowl.

"Let her be, Niko," said Grandpa. "She can't—"

"You're holding out on me," Niko said, shaking a finger at Grandpa Joke. He didn't know about Rachel, Nancy saw.

"You ought to go to jail," Nancy said. The redness in Niko's face deepened.

"Be what you are, Niko," Grandpa said wearily. "And leave the rest of us be."

"I'm not what you say!" Niko moved toward Grandpa.

"Stop!" Nancy covered her face with her hands. "I won't bother your wife," she said. "Put me anywhere. Out the door. I'll sit in the bathroom on the toilet if you want me to."

Niko actually listened, his face exhausted, exasperated.

A sudden mind picture of Dion on the geodesic dome sailed into Nancy's thoughts, the pale blue Brooklyn sky behind his head. *Where are you now, Spider?* "But, please," Nancy said. "Not high up. Nowhere high."

"Good idea," Niko said. God knew what he thought of her. The point was to make him worry about what she might do if he didn't keep her under his thumb. Sure enough, he took her elbow again, pulled her into the hall, placed his hand on the small of her back and guided her up the stairs.

She protested, "Down, not up!"

He humphed and kept climbing.

"Down!" Nancy resisted, made him push her along. He didn't stop when he reached the roof door, just threw it open. They struggled in the doorway. "I told you! I'm afraid of heights. No place high!"

"So don't look down," he retorted. "Stay away from the edge. See if *he* shows up." She fought him, pretending with every dramatic bone in her body. "And if he does, tell him—"

But just as it occurred to Nancy that Grandpa might be getting away right now with Granny, the same thought must have occurred to Niko. He sped her through the doorway so fast that she tripped over the threshold and fell on her knees.

He scooped her up and set her on her feet. "You okay?" As if he cared! Without waiting for an answer, he went. The door slammed and clicked locked. Nancy was by herself on the roof of Dion's house with nothing over her head but the night, never sure, then or after, which angel Niko thought would come for her.

42

Nancy spun around the rooftop. The healed-over place where she'd cut her thigh ached. Her knees were scraped raw but not bleeding. She brushed the grit off them and rushed along the edges of the roof.

The sycamore trees led her to the front of the building. Mina must be down there, walking under the trees, going for ice cream. Did she know she'd have to go all the way to Atlantic Avenue to find it? Surely the store lady was long gone by now. The leaves hid Mina, and the car, if it was still there. Were Granny and Grandpa down there, heading for the hospital? Or were they still trapped in Niko's hallway?

The two sides of the roof led onto the other rooftops, and they stopped at the end of the block. The only way out was to go down the fire escape at the back of the buildings. But first, there was the climb to the parapet and the drop four stories to the courtyard below.

Come on, she told herself. It was only what she'd been practicing, those nights outside the penthouse, for real. Fear of heights was nothing more than fear of throwing yourself off.

Nancy stood looking at where she had to go, and spots bloomed before her eyes. Her thigh hurt. She felt steaming hot with emotion and with the need to do something fast, and frantic with her inability to make herself move.

The spots cleared and she saw an edge, and space beyond. But not Brooklyn below. Not Granny. But somehow Granny was there, showing Nancy how not to be afraid, for the sake of saving her.

A barn floor, hay, and a boy's face looking up. He was holding a ladder by the rungs, tipping it away from the edge.

"George Webb!" screeched Josie beside her. "You bring that ladder back here, boy!"

"Ha!" George sneered over his shoulder. "Come and make me."

"That stinker," said Josie. "That smelly old cow turd. That stinking skunk."

"Stinking skunk cabbage," she said.

Nancy had only vaguely heard that there was such a thing as skunk cabbage. What did it mean: a story without its teller?

Josie crossed her eyes and laughed.

Where am I? thought Nancy, knowing, the same way she knew Josie was Granny Tina's sister, and George was Tina's brother. Did that make her . . . Tina?

"Now what do we do?" she asked Josie and the air. "How do we get out of here?"

She and Josie stepped closer to the edge and looked down. There was only one way down. A long rope hung limp and straight from a pulley above the high loft window. Grab the knotted end, the air seemed to tell her. Shinny down the hanging end. Keep the two ends of the rope balanced and you won't go plummeting to the ground.

"Don't you dare!" said Josie. "Dad will—"

Nancy jumped to her feet. If she was in Granny

Tina's body, then where was Granny Tina herself? Why was it then, and not now? Faint and spotty-eyed again, Nancy bent at the waist, hung her head down to stop the spinning feeling.

Nancy looked up to find herself on Niko's rooftop. She felt a funny little thrill. It was hardly the place for that, but suddenly she was not afraid, just calm, her shudders stilled. She descended the ladder that led down the back of the house to the fire escape, and she felt light, soft, part of the wind, not a leaf or kite to be blown by it.

Nancy jumped to the first landing of the fire escape. Unlike the wind, the iron resisted her. She landed in a heap of hurting thigh and knees, and kept herself from falling over the rail by throwing herself against the scratching, scraping brick wall of the house.

She got up and dashed for the alley. At first she thought she'd forgotten its location. When she realized that the alley had been gated off, blocked and locked, she felt a chill ripple over the sweat she was already in. She was caught in a tangle of swingsets and clotheslines, trees and garden fences, and the brick walls of the backs of the houses.

Stupid, stupid, stupid!

"Nancy! Don't go!" Her mind spun. Where a second ago Josie's voice had seemed to be, now she heard Dion. It wasn't that she was confused, that she thought he was her sister. Something deep inside her turned and trusted and went toward him across the courtyard.

Later Nancy would learn that Niko had spotted her through the window near Rose's bed. Later she'd learn that Niko thought she was going to get away, sic the cops on him because he held Grandpa and Granny against their wills, because he hoped Granny would come to and rise to the occasion and do more for Rose. If he left to catch Nancy, the old man would escape—fair enough—with his own sick wife. Who could know Niko's craziness in stopping Grandpa Joke from going? Torn, he bolted for the hallway, then back to the window, glimpsed his son's bristly head inside the flapping gap that a towel on the clothesline made as it billowed.

Grandpa Joke caught Niko's eye away from Dion, reached long strong graceful hands, and pulled him back. Niko saw in Grandpa Joke's face a waiting, a wishing, a wanting to say—

"Rose?" He looked at his wife's face (Grandpa would tell Nancy later) and saw no more struggle, but stillness, goneness.

Later she would hear that Niko thought his wife was dead.

"Rose?"

He touched her thin face so tenderly, holding her like flowers between his hands.

Grandpa Joke put a sympathetic hand on Niko's shoulder. He would not tell the police about Niko and give him away. He only wanted to get away himself. But what about Nancy—his granddaughter? A connection broke in Grandpa Joke's mind, he told Nancy later. He left her to her own devices. He thought only of Granny Tina.

Niko flew roaring out of the bedroom, through the kitchen, out the back door to the courtyard awash in washing. "Don't go!" he bellowed after Nancy.

Behind him, Mina was back. "Look, Daddy! Look!"

Nancy looked back in time to see two things, all

she could see in her glimpse through the courtyard door: legs in bright green clogs.

Niko didn't look, though if he had it might have changed things for Nancy and Dion. He shouldn't have frightened Mina like that about the spider. But there was no going back now, no going back to his little girl to tell her about her mother. Instead he went after the big girl he thought had taken away his attention at the crucial moment.

He was too angry to go back and see what—or who—Mina had brought in with her. Angry about healers. Angry about angels. You shouldn't have to go after them, Niko thought, shouldn't have to bring them to you, tie them down, pen them up to get them to help you. Weren't angels supposed to seek out the presence of evil? Wasn't that what the Angel of Brooklyn was always doing? So why hadn't it sensed the evilness of Rose's wounds, her approaching death?

Poor Niko. He didn't know the difference, Nancy saw later, between having a gift given and grabbing it. He didn't recognize the Angel when it came to his house in its many forms. He didn't see the green shoes. He didn't glance back through the window. He didn't know the true, new Healer came, because he was climbing to the roof to chase after Nancy.

Later on he'd get a chance to ask Mina what happened when the Healer came. "Nothing spectacular," Mina would say. "She just said, 'Hi, I'm Rachel.'"

43

Nancy chased Dion across the wet blanket of grass, scampered away from Niko, in and out the squares of yellow light that fell from apartment windows into the courtyard, Dion blending in with the fluttering shadows that fell from sheets and shirts that hung above them in the night air, the hair on Nancy's legs raising the alarm as she raced through the tangled damp maze.

"There's a way out," said Dion, and led her to another gate, the kind of garbage-can alley that only nosy kids knew about, not their busy, worried parents—even those who had taken the trouble to gate up their own alleys.

They had a block's head start on Niko. Nancy ran

pell-mell down the street. She was in time to see Grandpa slam the back door of the car, leap into the driver's seat, and peel out.

"Grandpa!" she yelled. She and Dion were abandoned and pursued, all at once.

"If he's leaving, my mom must be—" Dion stood still on the sidewalk, stunned, ruined, empty. His mother, dead.

Nancy reached out for him. *If only Mama . . . If only I . . .*

Dion went red-hot furious, threw her hand and her sympathy right off him. If this was how he felt, what was his dad going to do? He turned back to Nancy. "He'll kill me for not being there. Run!"

Nancy didn't have the energy to run, but she didn't dare stop and face Niko. If she could get to where Grandpa was going, she might be able to help, to somehow send the energy and memories and knitting and weaving back into her Granny Tina. *There has to be enough for both of us!*

She raced behind Dion down an alley to the courtyard behind another block of apartments. The buildings rose around them. The bottoms of these fire escapes were the overhead kind that extended to the ground if you were coming down, and sprang up too high for anyone to get up. "I'll give you a boost," said Dion.

"But my leg—"

"Can you jump?"

"Hardly!" she said.

"All right," he said, and stood, hands on his hips, looking up at the clotheslines. Laundry, just hung and heavy with dampness, weighed the line low. Dion leaped up in an unearthly basketball leap and pulled the tail of a shirt toward the ground. "Grab the clothesline," he told Nancy.

"What?"

"Grab it. Hold on."

"And do what?" Heaving and terrified, they stood snarling at each other among the clotheslines.

"Follow me."

"You think I'm an idiot." Niko was coming.

"I think you could do it."

"Based on what? Your desire to kill me?"

"My desire to— Nancy, you're a spider, aren't you?"

She felt her eyes flare open the way she had that time on the roof when the mugger was below. It was a gut reaction of fear. It was a gut call to act.

"What would you know about that?" Niko was *coming*. Could Dion jump like that?

He reached toward her, and she recoiled. "I just want to—" He reached again, and cupped his hand around her cheek. "Trust me," he said.

She knew she wasn't the first girl in the history of the world to be persuaded by such a request. But again rose up the something deep that told her to go with him. "What do you know about being a spider?" she asked.

"I know," he said. Niko was coming. "Nothing bad," Dion said. "Hold the rope and jump."

She grasped the rope in her two hands. "Your father—"

"Hold on tight!"

He gripped the other rope in his hand, and was pulling hard toward his chest with muscles he must have gotten from his father. Thanking the universe for making her small and wiry, Nancy sailed up toward the fire escape as if she were a shirt clothespinned on. When she reached the iron railing of the fire escape, she held the line steady. Along came Dion hand over hand, quick as a spider monkey on hands that were callused now.

"Go!" he whispered up to her, the sound welling up against the brownstone walls.

He landed on the fire escape beside her. She grabbed his hand and pulled him up the flights, as fast as Ned had ever climbed, her thigh complaining. She crawled over the parapet, reached down to help Dion up.

Niko came leaping, like a basketball player, like a wolf spider, every jump an enormous pounce. He was behind them now, but they were younger, lighter. Across the rooftops they went. Nancy's legs began to wobble beneath her as she ran and climbed and leaped the gaps, her knees like rubber, bending with no answering spring, her thigh screaming now.

And then the walls stopped, the roof fell away.

Below there was nothing but fire escapes and clotheslines,

fire escapes and clotheslines,

fire escapes and clotheslines.

Their straight lines and angles spun out of a center so deep it disappeared. With it Nancy's gut spun, and she felt herself turning inside out, or wanting to, wanting to throw up and cry and fall or throw herself off. Too many instincts fought against one another, her mother's urge to be on the ground, her father's yearning for the air.

"Down the fire escape!" she said.

No time for terror, just drop, descend. The second descent in one night, but there was no time to think of that. It had been bad enough to be in a hurry, but to be chased!

This was that rusty, awful kind of fire escape that needed a paint job, needed replacing, and the grit of corrosion flaked away under her hands, scraping them. She was taking too long. Her hands were so sticky with sweat and fear that the rust stayed with them and rubbed harder as she picked up more rust on the skin of her palms.

"Only as far as the clothesline," said Dion. He grabbed the pulley rope at the top windows of this brownstone. It sloped away and up again to a window on the other side, but in the dip it nearly reached the line hung between the next set of floors down.

"Do this," Dion said. He grasped the rope and stepped off the fire escape, dangling five stories up. Then gravity took over and his weight dragged the pulley rope into the dip, where he let go and caught the next line, then slid back to the other wall. Then down to the next and the next, as easily as if he were dangling from cell to cell of his geodesic dome. Far below her, Nancy felt, as well as heard, his soft-soled boots land lightly on the wet pavement.

"Nancy, come on!"

Niko was only two rooftops away, headed straight for them.

"Nancy!" Dion's voice sounded hoarse, desperate.

And she trusted him. She wrapped her fists around the rope, made her shaking legs pull her over the fire escape railing, stuck her heels through it backward to perch there quavering.

"Do it," said Dion.

"Don't!" yelled his father from above.

Nancy stepped into thin air.

Should she have trusted him?

Her body dropped sheer. She held onto the rope so hard it burned. Oh, it hurt, that jolt of her weight on her hands, her hands on the rope.

She rocketed down the rope slope to its center. Her right hand found the target. Her left hand fell shy, short and shy.

Her body slammed sideways. The clothesline snapped, broke like a thread. Nancy closed her eyes, an

instinct against the murderous ground beneath her.
Oh, wrong, wrong! Nancy expected the concrete, the
asphalt, the ground-in glass, the hard-packed dirt, the
blades of grass.

It didn't come. Instead there came a fragrance of
flowers, of soap, of wind. The touch of fabric against
her face: T-shirts, towels, baby diapers, all slowly rising.
Nancy was as light as wind. The city was enormous
around her. She opened her eyes to see someone's boxer
shorts, should-be-small polka dots like gigantic spots
before her eyes. Gigantic? Or was she small? For the
moment she was all darkness, part of the darkness, dark
in the dark, wind in the wind.

Her left hand flailed, her right hand up above her
head still held the rope. No, not a rope, no harsh burn-
ing clothesline this, but a soft thick cord that fit her
hand and didn't slide through it.

Look, Dad!

Look, Dion! And, thinking of him, came back to the
form he knew. The toes of her Doc Martens touched
the ground and Dion's arms wrapped around her.

"Nancy. How did you do that?" A whisper like her
heart.

"How?" It was too dark to do anything but feel that soft rope. She shook it off, shook Dion off.

"You stupid kids!" roared Niko from the roof. He stood staring down in horrified amazement.

"God," said Dion. "God! I thought you were dead. *You.*"

Niko came leaping down the steps of the fire escape, all those stories up and getting nearer. "Girl!" he yelled. "Now I know what you're all about."

Some old bat stuck her head out a window and squealed when she saw him. "I'll have the law after you all!"

"Nancy! Come on!" Dion said.

"I have to get to the hospital," she told him, knowing it in her knees. She left him there on the ground, left his father on the steps, left his mother God-knew-where. She went after Grandpa, after Granny.

She knew, in the moment of turning the corner, that Dion had taken her by the hand and brought her the way he knew she wanted to go, the way Grandpa Joke had once led Granny Tina to the church.

EMERGENCY ENTRANCE, said the nearest lit-up sign.

44

It was his hands she fell for: large, with Italian olive skin, fine black hair feathering the backs.

And it was his eyes behind his glasses, large, intelligent, cinnamon brown as the back of one of her father's horses, with now and then a little sparkle around the edges that made her wonder what he'd be like if he laughed. He didn't laugh, not in that OR, with a mask over his mouth, not in this emergency room, in this curtained cubicle.

Push back the cobwebs, Nancy. Those weren't *her* memories, they weren't real for her. But what she felt was real. Niko on the roof, telling her he knew what she was about: did he mean he knew another spider when he met one? Dion on the ground, telling her to come down. Herself, dropping, while her heart rose up to the sky.

Had it been real, spinning silk, falling into the shape of a spider, coming down on eight legs instead of just two, up to the very last moment? Now that the chase was over, and Nancy's body could move gently, her mind swung into motion. She pushed the memory across the space between her and her grandmother, reaching from deep within her.

Now was real, now in the emergency room waiting room, waiting forever, and finally, after four in the morning, looking up into Grandpa's big brown eyes. They weren't laughing. Nancy slid her arm through Grandpa's elbow, noted the gray among the black hairs of his hand and arm. "Grandpa?" she began.

"Come see her, Nancy," Grandpa Joke said. It was a long walk through a maze with no magic string to lead the way back out again. She passed little scary curtained cubicles and night-light doorways, wishing only to stop and plant herself on the floor and refuse to move forward with time. But her body kept going, and her mind did.

The only way Rachel could have come to Niko's apartment was for Ned to have called her, which meant he had somehow heard Nancy's calls, that he really had been the spider Nancy had saved.

And then the thought she had held off, the way she—or was it Granny Tina?—savored the idea of ice-cream after dinner, the fact that she had survived the fall from the high clothesline. At the time her thoughts had been end-of-life thoughts. She had accepted the thud of her body against the ground and merely waited for it to happen. Now, free of that ending, she relived the fall. A strand of silk from her own spinneret had cushioned her fall. The giant boxers on the line didn't just mean big butts in the house (as Annette would have said, though there wasn't much funny here and now), but a small Nancy falling—a small human Nancy, or a small spider Nancy. *Take it, Granny. It's good news! It has to be!*

What had made it happen? Needing it to happen? Wanting it to happen? Finally growing? Or Granny dying?

There was no stopping this walk down the hall. There was no stopping that fall from the roof. No stopping the spiderness. She wanted to tell her dad, but maybe he already knew. She wanted to tell Dion, and maybe he knew, too. He'd been there.

She didn't want to tell Grandpa Joke, who pressed his elbow against his side, caressing her arm. "Honey," he said, "this night is going to just get longer."

"Oh, Grandpa," Nancy said. "If only Niko hadn't kept us."

Grandpa shook his head. "Niko didn't realize you can't change what's going to happen. We can't any of us change what's going to happen."

"Niko—" Her voice rose angrily, tears falling at last.

Grandpa touched his finger to her lips. "Niko wanted miracles," he said.

An image of Grandpa's hands came to her. An image of a church. Dion's hands. The Emergency Entrance sign. A bridge, a web, a connection. The strand connecting Granny and her was stronger than most. "He wanted to trade Granny's life for hers!"

"Granny did what she desired," Grandpa Joke said.

"Maybe Granny could have been saved—"

"You can't put up that wall, Nancy. Niko—he's one of the family. He and Rose and those kids."

"What family?" She stopped again, leaned on the cold concrete wall. "We don't have any Greek cousins!"

Grandpa said, "They're from a distant branch of the family." He picked up her hand, saw the bright scrapes on her knees from Niko's roof. He ran fingernails across her palm, and laid the silken tendrils he raked up gently over her scrapes.

"The boy knew we were the same kind," he said. "He's a connector, like you. You knew, too, in your way."

"Knew what?" She rubbed her knees. There was a smooth substance there, drying up.

"About being a spider," said Grandpa.

"All of us? Even you?"

"Who do you think got us all into this mess?"

"You're the original connector," she said.

Smiles in the midst of tears.

"What will happen to Dion and Mina now?"

"What do you think?" he asked.

"We'll help them. Their father's kind of crazy, Grandpa."

"Not really, Nancy. We'll forgive him. And they'll help us, too." He turned his head away, tried to hide his tears.

"How can they help us?"

"Nancy," he said, looking at her closely. "When we left, Rose wasn't dead. Maybe she'll live. She's young, strong—"

"Mama was there," she told him, clasping his hand.

"Rachel?" Oh, the hope and gladness in his eyes.

"Yes!" She didn't have to tell him how Rachel had known they needed her, or why she'd come: because it finally became evident that Nancy wasn't going to be able to take her mother's place in the healing world. Grandpa clutched her hand five times harder, hauled her full-speed down the hallway.

"Tina!" he called. "I'm right here!" He pushed through a curtain into a tiny cubicle. "Can you hear me?" he said, louder.

Nancy stood back. Granny was like a shadow in the dimness of the nighttime hospital, a shadow becoming part of the darkness itself. "Joke?" her weak voice said.

"I'm here!" Grandpa Joke was holding her hand, and crying.

Like the day Rachel was born and every day since. He's always been here for me.

What did it mean that she had Granny's memories? Her life was passing before her eyes. Before Nancy's eyes. *Don't forget a single thing, she told herself.* Or so Granny told her. It would all seem different tomorrow, in the light. All the cobwebs would be covered in morning dew, every drop reflecting the ground and sky. Nancy pushed through the curtain and went all the way in. The cubicle was barely wider than the bed. Grandpa backed out to give them room.

"Listen, Granny! Mama went to help Rose. She was there! I saw her shoes. All the way to Cobble Hill, Granny. Isn't that impressive? Granny, *listen*." **Green shoes,** she thought at Granny. **Green eyes. Mama's hands on the loom, on the silk, on a hurt place.**

Granny said, "Your Grandpa Joke was adorable when he was younger. Absolutely adorable like that boy Dion." It was hard to imagine pigeon-toed old knock-kneed baldy-headed Grandpa Joke being adorable. Like Dion.

Nancy thought, *It's more than trusting him or feeling sorry for him.* She realized: *I love him.*

"I love him," said Granny. "Josie, will you tell them for me?"

Nancy took Granny's hand, held on hard. "Josie's not

here right now, Gran. But *soon*. I'm Nancy." *Know me. Know me!*

Granny Tina's voice grew soft and tired. "I know, Nancy." And then, "Do you know, sweet lamb, my whole life has been one great long beautiful time?"

Nancy laid her head down near Granny's knee. Granny's hand moved gently to her head. "Such curls, like Ned's head. My beautiful girl. Such curls." Her hand rested on Nancy's head and Nancy stayed there, unmoving, not daring to cry, thinking: the stores in their neighborhood, the birds in the backyard, the slides in the playground, Granny teaching her to climb them.

At last Grandpa put his hand on Nancy's shoulder, raised her up, walked her away.

"I'm leaving," she told him, and, distracted, he nodded, slipped inside the curtain.

Down the tiled hallway. *Ned's head. Beautiful girl. Such curls. Such curls.* They were the last words she would hear her Granny Tina say.

45

The subway was still the fastest way to go, if it was going directly where you wanted to go. The F train was worth the five-block dash Nancy had to make to get there. She tore down the steps, feeling the rumbling that told her the train had come to her as though called. She rushed through the cars, violently hauling the heavy doors open until she reached the car that she figured would stop in front of the exit at Seventh Avenue.

It was so early, so empty. It might have been dangerous, but Nancy thought only about where she was going. Even Dion wouldn't have been able to keep up with her now.

the web

The sky was light when the train pulled out of the tunnel to cross the canal. The city lights had stopped twinkling and now merely glowed. When the train reached her station she sprang through the doors, bounded through the turnstiles and up the steps. She charged along the hard hill of the subway station.

The buildings of Park Slope were shades of brown like an old-fashioned photograph, colorless because it was still so dark. There was a light in the window of the Uprising Bakery.

She split the street with speed. Nothing seemed fast enough. She wondered if she was going her very fastest, after all. She rubbed her fingers together as she walked, felt a stickiness that was more than it was yesterday. The way a sticky chew of bubble gum went slick and smooth in her mouth—that was how her silk felt now. Trust it enough to take to the roofs? Not yet. There was more she needed to know first.

At last her feet found Ned's building, his gate and stoop and lock and the stairway inside. She wanted to collapse on the top step, but somehow turned her key and burst through the door.

Mama's green clogs were there on the mat. She

was here where Nancy had prayed she'd be. She was here, in Dad's arms, in his lap, in his chair.

They each freed an arm for her. Face first into her mother's soft skirt, four arms around her, four legs beneath her, silken hair and braids of dreadlocks against her cheeks.

And if Mama was here . . .

"Were you—did you—?"

"Rose will be all right, Nancy," Ned said.

A wave of feeling nearly made Nancy float with its power, from Dion, from Mina, from their mother. From her mother. Pride. Relief. Joy. But a different feeling mixed fast with it, jolted her to the ground.

"Granny's dying," she gasped.

Gently, oh, so gently, Ned said, "It's over, little egg."

And sadly, so sadly, Rachel said, "Nancy, she died."

Nancy jumped up and stood with her hands clenched in fists. "I wanted to—but I didn't—I tried! But I couldn't—"

Rachel took her hand, uncurled it. "You couldn't," she said. "It was too late."

"I was too late!"

"No," said Ned. "You couldn't save her any more

than Niko or Dion could save Rose."

"Or Grandpa," she whispered.

"I couldn't have, either, Nancy," her mother said. "This was what Granny wanted."

"Granny wanted you to save Rose." Nancy drew her hand away.

"And she did," Ned said. "Mama did. Your granny was there first. But she couldn't do enough. It was your mama who saved Rose. She *did*."

Rachel got up, came and took Nancy's hand again. "It was time for Granny to go," she said. "So she let go of her energy. To Rose and you and me."

"Rachel, tell her what the man said."

"What man?"

"Rose's husband."

"Niko?" Nancy yanked her hand away again.

Ned reached for it instead of Rachel. "He was on the rooftop, wasn't he, coming after you?"

Nancy nodded, swallowed.

"What do you think stopped him?"

Ned's eyes held hers, and the corners of his mouth turned up. "He watched how you got to the ground."

Nancy let out her breath in a nervous laugh.

"Well, that was almost a disaster."

"Almost," Ned agreed. "But what happened, what he saw, is what made him go to Dion."

Nancy's heart thudded. "You mean he'll have more stories to write?" That man! Was there anything he *wouldn't* jump on?

Ned's shoulders rose to his ears. "He's not going to write about his own son," he said.

"About you, then?"

He cut his eyes sideways at her, and wiggled his eyebrows. "Or us?"

"He'll be confused then. Nick Paprika, or whoever Nobody he is."

"One of us, I'm afraid," said Rachel.

"Like hell," said Ned. "Him and his Angel stories."

"Do you think he'll stop writing them?" Nancy asked.

"What do you think? Better, what do you *feel*?"

"That there are a lot of ways he could go," she said.

"Then you are wise," said her mother.

Nancy pulled away, went to the window. Or, rather, the window seemed to pull her. She itched to be outside in the air, up high again, wanted the city huge around her. Across the blue-gray-brown rooftops, the sky lifted like a shade to show the faintest edge of sun. The city glowed, and Dion was backlit where he sat on a wall several rooftops away.

"I'm going out," she said.

"Where?" Rachel asked. "Now?"

"Are you staying here?" Nancy asked her mother. Dad still sat, his arm hung around Rachel's waist like an old belt that knew by habit just where to rest. He looked up at Rachel's face.

Rachel said, "For now." She would go back to Grandpa.

"Grandpa could come here—"

"It isn't that," Rachel said. "Nancy, I love you. And Dad knows I love him. But I wouldn't ask him to live lower than a sidewalk. And I can't stay here. I have our work to do."

"Ours?"

"Mine and my mother's. Yours, one day, maybe."

"I can go both places. Why do *you* have to choose?" She was asking both of them, fed up with her fate. She didn't want to be a bridge between them.

"You're a—" from Rachel.

"You're different," interrupted Ned.

They gave each other a cautious look, and Rachel

said, "You're a different kind of—"

"Spider?" She faced them, her back to Dion.

They laughed at her. Her mama laced her white fingers through her dad's dark ones. "Human," they said together.

"I'm going," Nancy said, feeling the brightest sort of joy beginning inside, a tiny growing glow. Human and spider, both!

"Grandpa's all right on his own," Rachel said, then added, "Where are you going?"

Can't they see Dion? Is he so blue against the sky?

"Grandpa's not alone," Nancy said. "He's with Niko."

"However you know that," said Rachel.

"However I know." Grandpa was there, Nancy knew it in her legs, in her knees and anklebones, doing normal medicine to help Rose get better, watching out for Niko, forgiving him in this human and inhuman city the way Ned had watched out for Nancy last night from the rooftop, the way he had dropped in to help. The way Dion had. Now, in her legs, the hair on them and the skin of them, she knew that Dion had moved from the roof behind her and was heading down the lines.

She was faster—small but wiry—and Dion could not keep up. Warm updrafts from the earth lifted

Nancy and bore her toward the rooftops; when she dropped they cushioned her fall.

It was the saddest morning of her life so far, and it was the happiest. She had already done her crying; now she sailed along almost invisibly, giggling with joy.

46

In Nancy's head she held one last conversation with Granny Tina. Real or imagined? She wasn't sure.

"My sweater's done, Granny."

"Good," Granny Tina said. "Get rid of that black one now. No more hiding in the dark. A pretty face like yours needs color next to it."

"I still like the black one. It's New York chic."

"Like a funeral!" Granny shook her old gray head.

Nancy didn't have much time. *Hurry up and say it.* "Granny Tina," she whispered, "did saving Rose kill you?"

"It brought your mother back to life," Granny said. "It's her time now. And yours."

"Tell me the truth," Nancy said.

"The truth? You know there's only so much energy in the world. Time to pass it on." And she added words Nancy knew she'd heard somewhere before: "One blooms when the other fades."

It made Nancy cry one more time, knowing just what her Granny had done, what she'd given up. Was Granny crying, too? A little. But already she had that busy sound in her voice, that elsewhere sound. Going behind her cloud—as if that ever took any energy away from the sun!

"I'm going now," Granny said. "You wear that none-such sweater with its nonpattern. Stay warm."

"Don't go!"

"Stand out, Nancy. Don't be afraid. Wear it—"

"In the fall I'll wear it. It's eighty degrees out now."

Granny Tina shook her head again. "There'll never be another fall," she said, fading away.

"Not for you," Nancy said as Granny's colors went.

"Not for you, either!" Granny snapped back, just barely there. And as she went, Nancy heard her faint words: "Silly girl! The other kind of fall."

How had Granny known this would be when Nancy

fell, that very morning, fell for good, fell for real, fell down, down for Dion?

"I fell for you the first time I saw you," said Dion.

"Boy, you think you know so much," Nancy told him. "You were just looking for a mate."

"Yeah? That's all?"

"There just aren't that many spiders in New York."

"You're the only one," Dion said. She could see in his eyes that he meant it in more than one way.

She said truthfully, "It wasn't so instantaneous for me."

Maybe not the falling. But the connection, strong as silk, strong as steel. That had been immediate from the first time she had seen him, the skyline behind him.

Ever after that, every time she saw him, she fell, fell with her eyes wide open, knowing falling for him didn't mean being down, but both of them being up, up on the rooftops and sometimes strung between. Being angels. Being spiders. Blue sky above, gray-sidewalk-streets below, New York, and them in it. Him with his hair growing in so pretty on his head, her with hers on her legs.

"You could bleach it, at least," said Annette. Same as ever, she was always up-and-coming with bright suggestions.

"Maybe I'll bleach, maybe I won't."

Annette had broken up with Jimmy Velcro. "Guess he didn't have what it took to *stick with you*," Nancy said, hooking her arm through Annette's, leaning her cheek on Annette's shoulder, and checking out the pretty city lights.

"Guess I need a Ghost Boy," said Annette.

"Maybe next time try Twinkie Boy."

"But I dreamed him! I don't remember who he is!" They looked out at the city and wondered what was going on behind the windows that were lit so they could see, and the others dark so they couldn't, or up on the rooftops or down in the streets. It was peaceful now, but you never knew . . .

"The Angel's watching," said Annette, and Nancy didn't inform her otherwise. Look at the person beside you now. Do you know where she's been all day? Every minute? Saving lives? Listening from rooftops? Investigating rumors? Do you know—*can* you know?—everything she's been or will be? You can't know, any more than you can know what a spider's day is like.

Dion, though, was still on the roofs. He wouldn't go

home permanently, only when Rose needed him. They all kept their distance, but they had an arrangement now. Rose helped the Mamba, and the Mamba helped the Rose. Niko was still chasing after—and writing about—the Angel of Brooklyn, mixing in even more mystery, so as not to blow anyone's cover. The Greenes and Karas didn't hate Niko for what had happened to Granny.

Nancy didn't know what made her what she was, made Annette and Dion and Ned and all of them. Nancy hadn't asked to be a spider. It was simply the way things were. Maybe everyone had powers that other people didn't know about, the same way everyone had secrets.

Nancy danced across the roof, up and over the parapet, tossed her dragline to the air, and ran away on her thin striped legs. She felt where she needed to go. She got her message from the wind: to the bridge.

Across the long rooftops, the houses and churches and train trestle, over the canal to Carroll Gardens, through Cobble Hill and Brooklyn Heights, under trees in the sunrise, along sidewalks. Saints and flowers

and cats in windows, stoops and sidewalk chalk draw-
ings, the brown bricks of houses reddening in the
angled morning light, people snoring and dreaming
inside.

Meet me there, she said to Dion in her mind. *Meet
me there if you hear me. Meet me there if you possibly can.*

Blue river light and gray dawn mist met in a swirl at
Cadman Plaza. Nancy found the dark entrance, sprang
up the smelly stairway two steps at a time, stood still
for a moment on the pathway up the arc of the bridge,
O wonderful web.

The bridge soared above her, brown towers like
church windows, and the city grew enormous around
her as she walked. She grew small, so small she couldn't
be noticed, nearly invisible she was so small, so safe.
She could have been anywhere. She was here.

Tendrils of steam rose from the pink-gray-blue city
in the sunrise. At the far side of the East River she
stopped, wouldn't enter Manhattan, let the breeze
blow her back toward Brooklyn. Waiting. Watching.

His eyes were blue like the river in this even light.
His shirt was blue like the sky that wasn't full of blue
color yet. His face was sunlit like the faces of the

buildings in Manhattan, rose-gray-blue. Now Nancy knew that some people didn't see him, through looking away or ignoring or just not being aware. Now she knew that she had never missed him, not once, or, anyway, not since the first time she'd seen him on that ribbon of rail above the expressway and river. How could she miss him? Dion, laughing, drew Nancy toward him on the bridge.

Can he see me, my new size?

In the absence of danger, there was no need to be tiny or invisible. But it was good to know what they could do if they needed to. And they would.

Does he know why he's here?

She slipped into his arms; he fit.

Does he know why we are here?

She saw into his eyes: he knew.